FAT WHITE

VAMPIRE

OTAKU

ANDREW FOX

MonstraCity Press   Manassas, Virginia

MonstraCity Press

Manassas, Virginia

www.monstracitypress.com

Books by Andrew Fox

F AT W HITE V AMPIRE S ERIES

Fat White Vampire Blues (Del Rey Books)

Bride of the Fat White Vampire (Del Rey Books)

The Bad Luck Spirits' Social Aid and Pleasure Club (tie-in)

Fat White Vampire Otaku

Hunt the Fat White Vampire (available June 2021)

The Good Humor Man, or, Calorie 3501 (Tachyon Publications)

T HE A UGUST M ICHOLSON C HRONICLES

Fire on Iron

Hellfire and Damnation (available August 2021)

C OLLECTIONS

Hazardous Imaginings: The Mondo Book of Politically Incorrect Science Fiction

E DITED BY A NDREW F OX

Again, Hazardous Imaginings: More Politically Incorrect Science Fiction for Dara, my wife and partner

(I'm your biggest otaku)

One

JULES and Maureen Duchon were watching *What's Up, Tiger Lily?* on Turner Classic Movies when the Japanese gangsters abruptly halted, mid-pounce, and the drowsy couple's TV screen momentarily went black.

Jules sat up; the sudden shifting of his Orca-like bulk caused a tsunami in the mattress of their jumbo-king waterbed. "Ding-damned Cox Cable," he grumbled to his wife. "Give 'em a monopoly, and *this* is the kinda service you get. And we were just about to find out who stole the secret formula for the ultimate egg salad sandwich."

"Jules Duchon," Maureen said, "how many times have you already watched this movie?"

"Maybe five, six times. But I like it. It's the only Woody Allen movie I can stand watchin'. 'Cause it's the only one he ain't acting in."

Then something happened that neither vampire could remember ever happening before. To the accompaniment of the harsh electronic monotone which announced an interruption by the Emergency Broadcasting System, a Doppler radar weather image appeared on their screen. The image showed the entire Gulf of Mexico. In the middle of the image, a distorted green mass swirled clockwise like an angry emerald poltergeist. Its outer bands reached ominously towards New Orleans.

"Jules, stop your complaining," Maureen admonished him. "I think this is important..."

Together, they silently read the ribbon of text which spooled across the bottom of their TV screen. *Hurricane Antonia... first named storm of the season... presently Category Three, with maximum sustained winds of 125 miles per hour... projected to strengthen to a Category Four or Category Five storm before landfall... Hurricane Warning stretches from Port Arthur, Texas to Pensacola, Florida... Projected cone of impact predicts likeliest landfall between Morgan City, Louisiana and Mobile, Alabama... New Orleans Mayor Roy Rio has issued a voluntary evacuation order for the City of New Orleans and declared a mandatory evacuation order for low-lying areas... Mandatory evacuation orders issued for Grand Isle in Jefferson Parish and lower Plaquemines Parish...*

"Oh, *golly*," Maureen said, clapping her hands together with childlike glee. "A *hurricane...* how *wonderful!*"

Jules grinned. "You remember Betsy, back in '65?"

"How could I forget? That was one of the best weeks of our undead lives! Six days straight of blackouts! Downtown crawling with looters! It was like an all-you-can-eat buffet!"

"Yeah, back when neither of us gave a shit about our figures," Jules said wistfully. "When we could chug down as much blood as our bellies could hold, not carin' what kinda fried crap our victims been eatin'. Hell, by then I'd been buying my pants with elastic waists for years, anyway."

"Not being able to see yourself in the mirror sure helped," Maureen admitted.

"How about Hurricane Audrey?" Jules asked. "The great big one that wiped out the Mississippi Gulf Coast? What year was that — '71?"

"No, it was '68, and it was Camille."

"You sure it wasn't Audrey?"

"It was *Camille*, Jules. How could you forget? There was that hurricane party we crashed—"

"You mean the one on Frenchman Street?"

"Frenchman Street, oh, *yeah...*" She licked her lips at the memory. Jules remembered with sweet nostalgia them stumbling along the streets of Faubourg Marigny after their orgy of overeating, drunk with satiation, lyrics from the Turtles' "Happy Together" playing in an endless loop through his head.

The doorbell rang. "Now who the heck could that be at two o'clock in the morning?" Maureen asked.

"You want me to get it?"

Maureen shook her head. "*I'll* get it. Takes you five minutes to pull yourself outta this waterbed. By the time you'd get downstairs, they'd have given up and left."

She pulled on a lightweight silk robe, one of her new kimonos. She'd always favored kimonos for loungewear. Just a few years ago, Jules recalled with misty-eyed longing, her kimonos had billowed out over grand curves, like a set of king-size sheets set out on a clothesline on a windy day. But that had been before she'd been killed, then resurrected by Doc Landrieu with the assembled body parts of three much younger, much skinnier girl vampires. Now she had the body of a ballet dancer... a ballet dancer created by Dr. Frankenstein. The only portion of her that was original was her head. And even her formerly full face had gotten trimmed down by liposuction, a wedding gift from Doc Landrieu.

Jules listened to her answer the door downstairs. "Oh, hi, Doc!" she said. "What brings you over here this time of the night?"

Huh — here I am thinkin' about his wedding gift, and he pops up at my front door, Jules thought.

"I'm so sorry to disturb you on Jules' night off, Maureen," Jules heard his father-in-law say. "It's about the storm. Have you and Jules seen the news?"

"You mean the hurricane heading our way?"

Jules figured he needed to join the conversation. He clutched the wrought iron grab-handle bolted onto the wall studs on his side of the bed (otherwise the waterbed would trap him like a pool of quicksand), swung his legs out over the boundary of packed dirt, harvested from Maureen's tiny back courtyard, which allowed the bed to serve as a shared coffin, and stuck his feet into a waiting pair of slippers. Then he slipped on a robe, turned off the TV (who knew when TCM would play the rest of *What's Up Tiger Lily?*), and headed down the stairs.

"Hiya, Doc," he said when he saw his tall, gaunt, rather severe-faced father-in-law, his former boss at the city morgue. Doc Landrieu wore a nicely tailored (if somewhat old-fashioned) plaid sport coat and held an olive fedora in his hand. "Is everything okay with Mom? She's not climbin' the walls over this hurricane, is she? I remember Betsy gave her nightmares. She didn't get a good night's sleep for months..."

Amos Landrieu smiled ruefully, allowing Jules a peek at his carefully brushed fangs. "Honestly, Jules, I'd love to be able to prescribe your mother a tranquilizer," he admitted. "Ever since the mayor issued his voluntary evacuation order, she's been working my last nerve, much as I love her. But Edna's not the one I'm most concerned about. Should her worries get completely out of hand, I can hypnotize her into a soothing trance, even place her in hibernation, if that becomes necessary. No, the ones I'm mainly concerned about are you two."

"Us?" Jules said, surprised. "How come?"

"Yeah, how come?" Maureen said. "We made out real fine during past storms. When the electricity stops working, so does the air-conditioning inside people's homes. So folks go wandering outside, even after dark, trying to find a breeze. Plus, looters swarm like mosquitoes. You ask either one of us — some of our fondest memories are of hurricanes."

"This storm looks to be a killer, though," Doc Landrieu said. "Meteorologists give Antonia a twenty-five percent chance of heading straight up the Mississippi River to New Orleans. On a track like that, a Category Four or Five storm would overtop the levees and flood the entire city."

"Yeah, but Doc," Jules said, "we live on some of the highest ground in town. The Quarter won't go underwater. Neither will Bywater, where you and Mom are. Besides, vampires can't drown."

"Well, humans certainly can. How much blood do you and Maureen have stocked in your refrigerator?"

"I dunno... maybe four or five days' worth. But it'll be easy to go out and get more during a blackout—"

"Do you have a back-up generator here to keep your refrigerator running when the power grid goes down?"

Maureen scowled, then punched Jules in the shoulder. "Ever since the start of spring, I've been *begging* him to go out and buy a generator! And what does he say?" She lowered her voice an octave to imitate Jules' rumbly retort. "'Hon,' he says, 'we gotta wait for a good sale at Home Depot. I don't wanna throw away hard-earned money.' Now, *why* would Home Depot have a sale on *generators* just before the start of *hurricane season*? That would be like having a clearance sale on snow-blowers in the middle of the winter's biggest blizzard! So, Doc, the answer is *no* — we do not possess a back-up generator."

"Edna and I have one at our place," Doc Landrieu said. "As soon as the power goes out, Jules, you should bring your stored blood over to our refrigerator. To be on the safe side, do it *before* the power goes out — the police will start enforcing a curfew as soon as the storm draws close."

"You sure that's wise, me bringin' blood to your place?" Jules asked. "I thought you had a strict policy about no drinkable blood in your house. Haven't you told me that ever since you dug her up outta her grave, you been havin' to watchdog Mom every wakin' minute, so as to make sure she doesn't drink so much as a teaspoon's worth of the red stuff? I'm amazed you been able to keep her on the wagon this long."

"I agree it's a danger," Doc Landrieu admitted. "I'd be condemning her to an eternity of irresistible bloodlust if I ever permitted her to imbibe even a single swallow. But I have your and Maureen's welfare to

consider. Maureen's, especially — the unique circumstances of her resurrection preclude her from utilizing any of her former vampiric trans-
formational powers. So it would be impossible for her to become a wolf
and subsist on ordinary foods, as you could in a situation of dire emergency."

"Yeah, sure, okay," Jules said, gulping hard. He remembered all too
well those terrible nights in Baton Rouge when he'd needed to subsist on
dog food while in wolf form, after his vampire rival, Malice X, had temporarily driven him away from his traditional New Orleans hunting
grounds. "I'll bring over what we've got, and make sure I do it before the
cops shoo everybody off the streets. Thanks for thinkin' of us."

"Of course," Doc Landrieu said, fondly squeezing Jules' shoulder.
"You're family, after all. Should the situation turn dire, I intend to raid
some of the area hospitals, taking advantage of the expected chaos to
confiscate some of their blood supplies." His expression turned serious
once more. "I strongly suggest you two should plan to do the same."

Two

RAIN fell in a steady, warm drizzle on St. Charles Avenue, just uptown of Canal Street. Jules liked the rain; it gave his normally rank-smelling city a fresh, clean scent. He peered up at the sky. Power in downtown New Orleans had fizzled barely an hour ago. With the city's normally brilliant skyline now cloaked in darkness, the moon appeared especially bright. The yellowish orb, the color of a faded Easter egg, flickered in and out of visibility as banks of thick clouds, swirling bands of Hurricane Antonia, raced between it and the increasingly soggy Crescent City. Now and then, Jules could just make out the white, neo-classical top of the old Hibernia Bank Building, once the tallest sky-scraper in the city.

Just as swift and ephemeral as the bands of clouds were the bands of looters who had begun fanning out along the otherwise deserted streets and sidewalks of the Central Business District. Jules heard one plate glass display window after another shatter under the impact of baseball bats or rifle butts. No alarms sounded, however; the power failure had disabled all of them. The looters knew they could count on a temporary absence of the New Orleans Police Department from down-town's streets. The cops were all busy policing the tens of thousands of low-income residents who had opted to seek shelter inside the New Orleans Superdome, or they were attempting to ease the monumental traffic snarls of fleeing vehicles along the I-10 interstate and all major roads that led to it.

Jules waited in the dark alcove of the Pearl Restaurant, one of the few post-war-era dinettes left in downtown (and a sentimental favorite of his for that reason). He waited for a suitable patsy to appear. Someone possessing a handy combination of viciousness and marginal intelligence. He didn't have to wait long. Along came Mr. Droopy Pants in flip-flops, wearing no shirt, his tattooed belly gyrating like a bowl of grape jelly set atop a washing machine. The man pulled a Winn-Dixie cart heaped high with two flat screen TVs, a microwave oven, a brace of chrome plated pistols, a few portable DVD players, wads of gold chains indistinguishable from Mardi Gras throws, and, oddly enough, a four-foot-tall stuffed white bear.

Jules slung a hefty man-purse over his shoulder, making sure that a dollar protruded from its flap. He picked up a cup full of pencils, coins, and wadded up currency. Then he unfolded a long, thin tapping cane and stuck a pair of dark glasses on his nose. *Ain't had a good opportunity to pull this gag in years*, he told himself. *Good ol' 'Blind Man's Bluff'... it sure beats drivin' a hack night after night, canister of knock-out gas loaded in the trunk, tryin' to trap that one unlucky fare who asks you to drive them to an out-of-the-way neighborhood with bad street lightin'...*

He stepped out onto the sidewalk, tapping his cane frantically in all directions. "Can somebody help me?" he called out in a quavering voice. "I got lost somehow... it's all this wind and rain... I gotta get back to my apartment, but I got no idea where I am... help me! Somebody help a blind man!"

Sure enough, Droopy Pants parked his Winn-Dixie cart and crept toward Jules, who pretended, of course, to not know he was there. Jules kept on tapping his cane. From behind his dark glasses, he watched his would-be mugger check out the cup stuffed with dollar bills, then greedily eye the satchel.

He reached for the cup first. As soon as his fingers touched it, Jules' free hand pounced like a striking cobra and seized the man's wrist.

"*Whaaaat?*" the man squeaked. "But you's a *blind* dude—!"

Before his assailant could recover from his shock, Jules pulled him into a fleshy embrace, then leaned on him with the majority of his roughly five hundred pounds of undead adipose. The man helplessly toppled against one of the Pearl Restaurant's doors. Jules used his forearm to ensure that the looter's head thwacked solidly against the wooden frame of the door. The man crumpled. Jules let his overpowering weight press his victim into the rain-spattered, time-weathered floor tiles.

When you're as big as I am, Jules thought, his mouth searching blindly for the unconscious man's neck, *and your knees don't work as well as they used to, you ain't no cheetah no more. You gotta learn to think like a Venus Fly Trap. Let prey come to you.*

His victim spasmed beneath Jules' bulk, his body in shock, both from rapid loss of blood and from several bruised or broken ribs. Jules didn't bother looking down at him as he wiped his mouth with the back of his hand, then grabbed the diner's door handles to pull himself up. He reached into his satchel for his snub-nosed pistol, the old police-style revolver he used to destroy his victims' brain stems and ensure they wouldn't rise again as rival vampires.

This had been a good kill, one of his better recent ones. Pretty darned tasty. Better still, his conscience was clear. Any dude who'd stoop so low as to rob a blind man was a dude who'd deserved being taken off the street. Nobody could argue with that.

* * * * *

Maureen felt her conscience nagging her, buzzing around her nose like a pesky mosquito. As soon as the Central Business District's power grid had crashed, she'd headed immediately for the Superdome, figuring a blacked-out sports stadium packed with thirty thousand panicky, suddenly sightless refugees would provide rich pickings. And it had.

It'd been like shooting ducks in a barrel, in fact. Absolutely no sport to it. Worse than that — she'd actually felt *sorry* for the miserable women she'd found while they'd been searching for a private spot to go pee. The stadium's bathrooms had become hellish, stinking swamps, toilets choked with paper towels and human waste, overflowing like toxic gey-sers as the flooding of surrounding streets caused water pressure to spike. So the women trapped in the Superdome had staked out several of the stadium's stairwells as impromptu ladies' rooms. The stairwells' lower levels were just as flooded as the nauseating bathrooms, but at least the women didn't have to descend into the filthy bogs to relieve themselves; they could squat on the stairs above.

Even without the benefit of full vampiric powers, Maureen could still see better in the darkness than any normal human could. Plucking a blind groper out of a stairwell was easy; even the men hardly gave her any trouble. But her conscience — *that* gave her trouble *aplenty*.

Yeah, these folks were her food... but they were also her fellow New Orleanians. With every minute she'd spent in the Superdome, she'd found herself feeling sorrier and sorrier for the atrocious situation they'd been forced into. She felt indignant at how unprepared the city had been. Why hadn't evacuation plans been made for folks without their own cars? The storm hadn't hit the city directly; it hadn't been even all that close. So why had the flood protection levees started crumbling like sheets of soggy cardboard?

At last, mortification at her own actions made her lose her appetite. She slunk out of the Superdome and headed for home. Jules wasn't around; she figured he was out on the streets somewhere, picking off looters. That gave her an idea — why couldn't *she* kill some rotten bas-tards who were taking advantage of the disaster and pulling despicable crap?

This would be different from what she'd been used to; most of her kills during the forty or fifty years prior to her recent resurrection had involved her luring horny chubby-chasers, customers of her strip club, back to her house after her dancing shift had been over. Then, after she'd done her business, she'd stuffed their bodies down the incinerator chute. Usually Jules had been kind enough to dispose of the scorched leftover bones on one of his frequent trips out to Manchac Swamp.

This would be different; more challenging. Also more socially useful, and probably more fun.

She switched on her battery-operated shortwave radio, hoping to hear news of some miscreants she could hunt (she'd bought it a decade ago in a pawn shop on North Rampart Street, after an advice column in one of her home and garden decoration magazines had told her a shortwave radio was an essential appliance for every home in a hurricane zone). After a bit of fiddling with the dial, she found an all-news station. The news out of New Orleans was all bad. A big section of the Seventeenth Street Canal had collapsed near the Orleans Parish–Jefferson Parish line. Storm surge from Lake Pontchartrain was pouring through the breach, filling up the western portions of the city. In the east, parts of the London Avenue Canal and Industrial Canal had given way, too. So the big bowl of the Crescent City was being inundated with flood waters from multiple directions, from the Mississippi River–Gulf Outlet Canal as well as from Lake Pontchartrain.

As Maureen listened to accounts of hundreds of people in Gentilly, Lakeview, Broadmoor, New Orleans East, and the Ninth Ward taking refuge on the roofs of their houses or apartments, she struggled to overcome a sense of numb disbelief. Could this really be happening in her city, not more than a few miles from where she sat in her French Quarter home, high and dry (and in the dark, but that was a minor inconvenience compared with what so many of her not-so-distant neighbors were suffering)? Things had never gotten this bad before. Not even during Betsy — sure, the low-lying Lower Ninth Ward had flooded, with water covering the roofs of all those little working-class clapboard bungalows, but that had been before the Army Corps of Engineers had built the modern flood protection levee system. And even during Betsy, it hadn't been *the whole damned city* filling up with water.

How could she help? Where was she needed? Could she do *anything*? Then she heard a news story that nearly made her throw her radio across her living room. Some idiot vandals had decided that merely looting an old mansion on South Carrollton Avenue hadn't been good enough —

they'd set the venerable old house, a neighborhood landmark, already severely damaged by flooding on its ground floor, on fire. Strong wind gusts had spread the fire to three other nearby, partially deluged homes. So now four beautiful old houses were burning down to their waterlines, fire and water acting like tag-team destroyers, with the New Orleans Fire Department helpless to do a thing about it.

Maureen had never paid those four houses much mind until now. Until this moment, they'd just been part of the landscape to her, a quartet of down-at-the-heels mansions that she'd sometimes passed by in Jules' cab when he'd been heading out to pick up a fare at the Camellia Grill and she'd joined him for the ride (and subsequent meal). If she'd given them any thought at all, it would've been to curl her lip with distaste for the Uptown snobs, old-money, inbred, who'd hoarded their inherited antebellum antiques while sipping mint juleps on those broad, shady porches (she held a longtime grudge against old money snobs, dating back to her years unpleasantly ensconced among the transplanted European vampires of the High Krewe of Vlad Tepes). But now that those houses had been so outrageously vandalized, and in a time of existential crisis for her home town, Maureen felt like ripping somebody's throat out. With her fangs or her nails, it didn't matter.

Righteous anger granted her a sense of mission. Jules could take care of the petty looters stealing TV sets and smart phones from discount electronics joints on Canal Street. *She* would exterminate the vandals, those human vermin who dared act out their anarchic lusts on her city during its time of most abject misery and need.

Maureen the Avenger!

* * * * *

The next night, she set out on foot along Esplanade Avenue, heading for City Park. Esplanade Avenue had been built more than a hundred and fifty years earlier along the Esplanade Ridge, a natural pathway of high ground which ran from the Mississippi River, in back of the French Quarter, northwest to the terminus of Bayou St. John. So, along much of her route, the floodwaters hadn't risen to a depth of more than a foot or two. Unpleasant, but certainly passable.

Matters became a bit more marshy when she reached City Park, but she figured she'd have her choice of boats soon enough. She waded out to the City Park boathouse, storage facility for dozens of paddle boats, canoes, and small fishing boats which, in ordinary times, could be rented for a modest hourly fee. Storm winds had blown the big doors off their hinges, saving her the exertion of having to bust the chain which formerly had kept them locked.

In normal times, the rented boats could only be utilized within the park's network of interlocking lagoons. Now, however, three quarters of the city formed a giant lagoon. Maureen figured she'd have no trouble navigating north through the drowned park all the way to Lakeview, then east into Gentilly along the flood-erased banks of Lake Pontchartrain. She shone her flashlight's beam on a row of docked fishing skiffs, looking for one with a nearly topped-off fuel tank. She ignored the paddle boats and canoes; sure, she'd get a month's worth of exercise if she selected one of those, helping to ensure her retention of her purloined dancer's physique, but they were too slow for her purposes tonight. After all, she had to locate her vermin, do her avenging, and get herself back into her sealed coffin of a bedroom before sunrise. Or she'd be kaput.

She found a satisfactory skiff, started its motor, and backed it out of the boathouse. She quickly discovered that navigating through the flooded park was much more of a headache than she'd anticipated. A goodly portion of the thousands of trees which adorned the park had been toppled during the storm. Their branches protruded from the night-black water like ebony spears, threatening to tear the bottom out of her aluminum skiff or, at minimum, seriously muss up her hair. After twenty minutes of attempting to maneuver around this tangle of obstacles, she gave up and dragged her boat across the puddled road fronting the park, then plopping the skiff into the less obstructed waters of Bayou St. John.

Once she was in the bayou, her progress speeded up considerably. As soon as she began passing neighborhoods of darkened houses, she listened intently for any sounds stirred up by troublemakers or vandals. The moneyed clusters of homes perched on the bayou's various islands were all deathly quiet, however.

Matters changed quickly once she reached the far less affluent district of Gentilly. Houses there had suffered severe flooding, with water reaching the eaves of the single-story homes. Here, the sound of Maureen's motor approaching in the darkness aroused cries for rescue.

"I'm here! *Here*! Come get me!"

"Us first! I got two little children with me! They can't swim! And the water's full of snakes!"

"Don't leave me! Please! I got high blood sugar, and I ain't eaten or drunk *nothin'* in almost two days! I'll die up here on this roof!"

The pleas for help came from all around her. *I — I didn't imagine this*, Maureen thought. She berated herself for not having anticipated that dozens of trapped people would expect her to rescue them. How many passengers could she realistically fit in this boat with her? Two? Three, if they were small (and a cursory look-see at the trapped residents with her flashlight beam revealed that most were anything *but* small)?

She also had to face the fact that she would be putting any resident she "rescued" in mortal danger. Anticipating a surfeit of miscreants on which to slake her hunger and thirst, she had purposefully skipped all solid foods since the middle of the previous night. The long walk to City Park and her exertions extricating her boat from the forest of drowned trees had only intensified her hunger. If she gave in to her sense of pity and tried rescuing a handful of trapped residents, she couldn't assure herself that she'd be able to abstain from launching herself at their necks the moment they set foot on her boat.

"Where are you *going*?" the mother of two shouted from somewhere behind Maureen.

"You *can't* be *leavin' me*!" the diabetic woman cried. "I'll *die* here!"

"My boat's full!" she yelled back at them, hating the lie. "Someone else will come!" She hoped that this latter assertion, at least, wouldn't also turn out to be a lie.

She nearly turned back then for home. The night seemed to be turning into a fiasco. Yet a sense of responsibility for her trapped fellow New Orleanians continued to nag her. *Could* she control her bloodlust long enough to ferry a few of them back to dry land? Or would her essential predator nature assert its control and force her to snuff out the lives she'd intended to save?

She heard another plaintive voice ahead of her. "Please come get me! I'm so scared!" A woman's voice? No; the frightened voice of a young girl, a teenager at the oldest. "I'm afraid of the dark! My mama went swimmin' for help before night fell, and she never came back! Are you with the Coast Guard?"

"I'm not with the Coast Guard," Maureen growled. She'd given up on the notion of keeping her bloodlust at bay long enough to bring a passenger to dry land. She could smell the girl from a dozen yards away, smell her sweat, her fear. The moment that girl would set foot on Maureen's boat, she would become nothing more than an ambulatory bag of blood. "You don't want to get in this boat with me. You *really* don't."

"But I *do*! I've *gotta* find my mama! You've *got* to help me!"

The only way I'd help you, sweetie, Maureen thought darkly, *is help you into an early grave...*

Then she heard something else. A paddle striking the water? The approach of another boat?

"*I'll* help you, miss," a male voice boomed out. "I got me a boat here. Don't you worry yourself none. I'm comin'."

"There you go," Maureen, greatly relieved, shouted back into the darkness. "Good luck finding your mama." That was one little girl, at least, who wouldn't be pestering Maureen's conscience throughout the remainder of the night.

But after she'd glided past another block of drowned houses, Maureen heard a scream from behind her. The girl's scream.

"Get *off* me!" the girl shouted. "Don't you *touch* me!"

Maureen felt her hunger surge in her guts like a coiled parasite, a thousand-toothed lamprey eager to drain something dry. She turned her boat around. Maybe tonight wouldn't be a total loss, after all.

The girl's screams grew more frantic. The bow of Maureen's skiff bumped against the waterlogged eaves of the house. She cut off her motor and stepped onto the roof. The pressure of her hunger nearly made her blind. She clicked on her flashlight and directed its beam at the sounds of the girl's shrieking and the man's sub-vocal lust. She saw his face, dirty, covered in beard stubble, contorted with surprise. She saw the girl. Eleven or twelve. Experiencing emotions no girl that age should. That nobody of any age should... unless they'd earned it.

The man had earned it. Maureen would make sure he got what was coming to him. She'd seen enough. She clicked off her flashlight, but not before briefly illuminating her own legs, her long, delicately muscled, bone white legs. She didn't let him see her face. She didn't want him to see her eyes. She didn't want him to see her mouth.

"You like girls?" she asked. It was hard to keep the hunger out of her voice. Terribly hard. "You want some lovin', Mr. Tough Guy? I got all the lovin' you could want. Right here. Waiting for you."

Maureen the Avenger.

A moment later, the night granted her the reward she'd been craving. She was glad that clouds covered the moon. There were some things on this cruel earth a little girl had no business seeing.

Three

NOT *a bad night for a swim*, Amos Landrieu told himself. *Although it's probably best that I can't see the mire and trash I'm swimming through.* In his earlier life, he never would've dreamed of swimming down Napoleon Avenue. Nor could he have imagined the ultimate goal of his preposterous swim would be a supply of blood.

Nearly two decades had passed since Amos Landrieu had had reason to officially visit Baptist Hospital, the large medical facility on Napoleon Avenue. He recalled coming here during his final months as the city's elected coroner, when he'd needed to supervise the collection of a body whose owner had perished under questionable circumstances during an operation, necessitating a court-ordered autopsy.

Since his induction into the ranks of the undead, an unfortunate consequence of Malice X's campaign of intimidation and revenge against Jules, Amos had visited Baptist Hospital on other occasions, for less official, more personal reasons. He'd also visited Touro Infirmary, Mercy Hospital, University Hospital, Methodist Hospital, LSU Clinic, and Charity Hospital, in each facility relying upon his medical credentials and network of old contacts to grant him access to their hematology units. On each visit, his purpose was the same — to determine the location of the institutions' blood storage facilities and learn what sorts of security checks were in place to guard the supplies. And to plan how to circumvent those security procedures, should it become necessary.

He had been exceedingly careful since his resurrection to avoid drinking even a sip of blood; and he'd been even more obsessive about preventing Edna from ever beginning a blood-drinking habit. Yet he'd realized that his vigilance might fail some night. No one was perfect, not even Amos Landrieu. Either he or, deity forbid, Edna might succumb to his or her vampiric nature at some point. With that eventuality in mind, he'd decided to have fallback plans in place. He didn't expect himself to drive a cab and murder his fares, like Jules did, or for Edna to perform at a strip club (*now there was a notion!*) and lure victims back to her house, like Maureen had once done. Planning for non-violent thefts of blood seemed a much more palatable notion.

Baptist Hospital's blood storage coolers were down in the building's basement, in a room adjacent to the machinery spaces and the emergency power generators. Amos paused from his vigorous breaststroke (one of the few consolations of being a vampire — he could replicate the athletic feats of his youth, and then some) long enough to gauge the depth of the flood water in this portion of Napoleon Avenue. He clicked on his waterproof, heavy duty flashlight and directed its beam at nearby structures. Staring at the medical offices across the street from the hospital, he judged the water to be approximately fourteen feet deep. That meant the hospital's basement, its first floor, and perhaps even a portion of its second floor were underwater.

For an ordinary thief, at least a thief lacking scuba equipment, this would prove an insurmountable obstacle. Amos realized that for him, however, the flooding was a help, not a hindrance. Vampires didn't need to breathe (if they chose not to), and swimming beneath fourteen feet of murky, unlit water would ensure he wouldn't run into any hospital employees or security guards who might take it into their head to ask what he was doing absconding with a crate full of bags of blood products. Also, the coolers would've stopped operating the moment the flooding disabled the emergency generators. But being immersed in flood water would have maintained the unrefrigerated blood at a lower temperature than if it had sweltered inside a crippled refrigerator, surrounded by warm, humid air.

He swam to a corner of the main hospital building where he recalled utility doors provided outside access to the basement and its machinery spaces. He inhaled a deep breath before submerging. Then he stopped, smiled, and let the air escape his lips. *Old habits die hard*, he thought. He turned his flashlight back on and plunged beneath the water's oily surface.

His flashlight's beam did not project very far in the murky water, polluted as it was with every form of litter, residues, toxic chemicals, and miscellaneous filth that had coated the streets or lain inside homes and businesses prior to the flood. Amos couldn't see anything beyond ten feet out from the lens of his light. *Wouldn't it be fascinating to perform a chemical analysis of these flood waters?* he asked himself. *How many deadly substances could one isolate? Mercury, arsenic, the whole range of petrochemicals... even the humble cigarette butt, which must be present in these waters in the hundreds of thousands, contains a witches' brew of chemicals hazardous to children and other living things. I'll have to take a long shower at some point, whenever water service is restored; although being processed through an industrial decontamination facility would be more apropos...*

He found the utility door he was searching for. The pressure of the rising flood waters had bent the door inward and distorted its surrounding frame, making it a relatively simple matter for Amos to force his way inside. Buoyant due to air pockets trapped inside them, labeled plastic boxes that held medical supplies had floated to the ceiling. *Good*, Amos thought; *I'll be able to use a few of them to carry the plasma bags in.*

He tried to remember where the blood cooler room was in relation to the outside utility door. Was it to the left along this hallway, or to the right? At least he didn't need to worry about his air tank running low while he puzzled it out.

Five minutes later, he found the room containing the three coolers. Two of the three were closed but unlocked. Ominously, the third cooler's door hung open, swaying slightly as his approach stirred the water that filled the room. Amos experienced a few seconds of distress. Had the coolers already been emptied? Had staff managed to evacuate the blood products to a higher floor before the basement had flooded?

He shone his flashlight beam into the open cooler. Its shelves were still stocked with bags of plasma and blood products. He opened the other two units. They also remained stocked, plastic bags of "human juice" sitting on their shelves like rows of dead jellyfish.

I won't know until I get this material home if it remains ingestible or not. No recourse but to take it all, or at least as much as I can carry. I'll have to find some way to get Edna out of the house while I'm testing it. She mustn't smell it. I dare not tempt her.

He preferred that his intimate companion for the remainder of eternity *not* become a blood-lusting murderess. Not even as sweet, affable, and companionable a murderess as Dorothy Edna Duchon Landrieu would undoubtedly be.

* * * * *

Darn it, I wish Amos would get home already!

Edna paced the hardwood floor of her second story bedroom, pausing to smooth wrinkles from the satin coverlet which covered her bed (*why, even after a good neatening, did things always end up mussed again?*). For the eighth time since Amos had left on his errand, she opened the storm shutters which normally blocked all sunlight from her bedroom and peered out over Royal Street and surrounding streets in Bywater, watching for the return of her husband's forty-year-old Mercedes Benz sedan.

At least all that terrible wind and rain had passed. During the height of the storm, it had sounded as though a steam locomotive had been roaring across a trestle suspended a dozen feet above their house. Earlier that evening, Amos had climbed up on the roof and surveyed the shingles that had gone missing, most likely blown into the Mississippi River, just a couple of blocks distant. He'd said they'd have to get a roofer to come out and make repairs, whenever the National Guard and the police would lift the quarantine on the flooded city. Whenever that day would come.

What meal should she fix next from the storm supplies she and Amos had squirreled away? At least they had a generator; so as long as their fuel held out, they could store things in a working refrigerator, and she could use her electric stove. But all she'd been doing since the wind had died down had been cook and cook and cook. Their refrigerator was already jammed full of tuna noodle casseroles and pans of meat loaf and green bean casserole with French fried onions on top. By itself, the lime fruit Jell-O mold took up most of a shelf, and she couldn't very well stack anything on top of it. She hardly had room for anything more.

The worst part of this darned storm was being without her shows. The cable was out, of course, and when she'd asked Amos to consider hooking up the old-fashioned roof antenna they'd stored in their basement, he said it wouldn't do her any good — all the stations in local broadcasting range were down. She had her shortwave radio, but it was boring, hardly worth listening to. What had happened to all the wonderful radio dramas she and Jules used to listen to together — *Lights Out*? *The Shadow*? *Westinghouse Theater of the Air*? Or had it been *Mercury Theater of the Air*?

This whole situation reminded her of those dreadful decades she'd spent trapped in her coffin in the paupers' cemetery out back of City Park. Then it had been all Jules' fault. Oh, she'd forgiven him since, but *boy, howdy*! had she spent some years underground raging on that son of hers! Since Amos had dug her up a few years ago, she'd come to accept that she might've borne just a bit of the blame for her ordeal. Just a tiny bit. When she'd been on her death bed in her old house on Montegut Street, not more than ten blocks from where she stood now, she'd told Jules she'd wanted to provide him with one last hot meal. She'd insisted, over his objections, that he drain her of all her blood before she went completely cold. But she'd also said to do it *after* she was *dead*!

Well, that Jules of hers had always had difficulties with following instructions. And, true to form, the oversized dunce had bitten her neck when she'd still had an itsy-bitsy spark of life left in her. So, next thing she knew, she woke up inside a cheap pine wood coffin six feet under the top dirt of the paupers' cemetery out back of City Park. But even though it was a paupers' cemetery, it was still hallowed ground, blessed by a priest. And she'd quickly discovered to her dismay that a vampire planted in hallowed ground might as well be a stick of wood. She couldn't so much as wiggle her pinky finger. So she'd spent forty-plus years recycling fading memories of *I Love Lucy* episodes through her miserable head. If it hadn't been for Amos, she'd *still* be stomping grapes with Lucy and Ethel, or eating chocolates at the candy factory, or pregnant with Little Ricky, waiting for Big Ricky to get home from the club...

She shivered at the memory. Then she closed the storm shutters again, mindful of Amos' admonition that she shouldn't let anybody wandering the streets know the house was occupied. They didn't want some authority barging in and insisting they evacuate. Actually, this storm aftermath wasn't nearly so bad as her decades in the paupers' cemetery had been. The biggest difference was that she had Amos with her now. What a comfort in her old age! After her sour experiences with Jules' father, the sailor who had fallen in love with the sea (*good riddance to bad rubbish sucked out with the outgoing tide!*), Edna had severely doubted she would ever meet a man worth even the tip of her left pinky finger. But then she'd met Amos, a man worth her whole body, from the soles of her feet to the peak of her purple bouffant hairdo, and then some.

Now, if that wonderful man of hers would just get his wonderful behind *home*!

She heard a crash from downstairs. Had a stray cat gotten inside somehow and knocked over a vase? Had Amos suffered an accident?

Then she heard someone talking. "Oh *shit*... look what I've done to myself..."

A man's voice... Amos's? She hadn't heard it very well. But Amos wouldn't curse. Or at least he wouldn't use such a vulgar word to berate himself with.

A prowler, then? A burglar? What if he made off with the jewelry she'd inherited from her Great Aunt Beatrice? *Darn it! I* knew *I should've left those baubles in the safe deposit box downtown!* What if he stole her radio? Sure, there was nothing good on it — but right now, it was all she had.

What would Amos want her to do? Hide in the closet? Probably. But the more she thought about it, the more the notion of hiding herself away while some ruffian off the streets tore through her things and made a colossal mess of her parlor forced her to a boil. Like *heck* she was gonna let him have his way with her house and her things!

Before she had fully thought matters through, she stormed out onto the second story landing and was marching down the stairs, determined to give the invader a hefty piece of her mind.

She saw him. A white man in his late twenties or early thirties, T-shirt with sweat stains the size of waffle irons under the arms, frayed shorts that did nothing to conceal a pair of exceedingly hairy legs, like an orangutan's. He clutched his right forearm with his left hand and stared up at her with dumb surprise.

"Young man, *what* are you doing in my *house?*"

"I — uh..."

"Come on, out with it, speak up!"

"I — y'know, I'm hungry, and I need stuff..."

She noticed the broken glass all over the floor of her front parlor. He'd busted one of the French doors to get inside. "A nice young white man like you, you couldn't have just *rung the bell?*"

"Hell, ma'am, I didn't know anybody was home..."

Then she noticed something else. She saw it, and she *smelled* it. He clutched his right forearm because he'd cut himself smashing in the glass. His lower right arm was dripping with *blood...*

Edna realized how terribly hungry she was. And not hungry for green bean casserole...

"Young man, I'm warning you right now, you've got ten seconds to turn yourself around and get out of my house. Or you'll be *sorry*."

The man laughed in her face. "Wait a minute — *you're* threatening *me*? You? A ninety-pound old biddy?"

"That's right. You say you're hungry? Tell you what. I'll make you up a go-plate of meatloaf and fruit Jell-O. Got plenty of it in the refrigerator. I'll even cover it with some plastic wrap, make it nice and convenient for you. But then you're out of here. Or else."

"Or else *what*? You'll *scold* me? I'll tell *you* what. You go get me a towel or an Ace bandage or something for me to wrap my arm with. Then you give me all the cash you've got in this house, and all your batteries, and some canned food — none of that crap you've got in your refrigerator. You do all that, and you do it *fast*, and I won't hurt you."

Oh, Amos, she thought, staring with growing hunger at the man's bleeding arm, *I know you've told me to be good. I'm tryin', hon. I'm trying hard.*

"Mister," she said, jabbing him in the chest with a fingernail painted a pastel shade of mauve, "you need to learn yourself some *manners*. I made you a real charitable, Christian offer of a home-cooked meal, and you spat on my shoes. So I'll tell you again. You got ten seconds to turn your lazy butt around and get the heck out of my parlor. Or something's gonna happen that you ain't gonna like."

He slapped her forefinger away contemptuously. "I'm tired of arguing with you, you old bitch. I'm gonna take what I want, and if you get in my way, something's gonna happen that *you* ain't gonna like."

Well, Amos, darlin', I done the best I could.

She jumped on the burglar with the alacrity of a bloodthirsty tick jumping on a big hound dog.

Nobody's perfect, and in Adam's fall, we sinned all... and, anyway, a gal deserves a snort of the sauce now and then...

Four

J ULES was just finishing another looter, the seventh he'd drained since the power had gone out in the city two nights before, when he heard a familiar greeting ring out down Carondolet Street in the Central Business District:

"Hey, Jules! Fancy meetin' *you* here! The way my sinuses was buzzin' to beat the band, I figured there *must* be another bloodsuckah 'round here someplace!"

Jules, his vision and thinking still slightly fogged from his recent gluttony, looked up to see his former enemy and one-time partner, still dressed in his customary black buckskin jacket, festooned with fringes, and the big black cowboy hat that never left his head. "Oh, hiya, Preston," he said.

His head muzzy, he briefly marveled at how mundane their greeting was. A few years back, when he'd first met Preston, the black vampire had been one of his fiercest enemies, the leader of Malice X's posse. Later, circumstances had forced them to work as partners, jointly investigating both a series of blood-draining murders of black preachers and a cluster of mutilation attacks against the young women vampires of the High Krewe of Vlad Tepes. They'd gotten to be buddy-buddy enough that Jules had invited Preston to come to his and Maureen's wedding at the Trolley Stop Café, and Preston had attended (and enjoyed himself, from what Jules remembered).

"There sure is some bad shit goin' down in this town," Preston said, glancing quickly at Jules' drained victim, now crumbled on the sidewalk with Jules still squatting beside him. "And I don't mean *us*. Are you and yours plannin' on gettin' out of Dodge?"

Jules belched. "No. Why? Should we be?"

"Hell, *yes*. It may be Happy Huntin' Season right now, but this town is startin' to empty out like an elevator you just blew a big fart in. The Army, the Coast Guard, they been pullin' people out by the *thousands*. You ain't seen it, 'cause it happens in the daytime, but a whole fleet of buses been evacuatin' folks from the Superdome. Our den underneath the casino flooded out the day the levees broke. We all woke up that night to find our coffins bobbin' up against the ceiling."

"No shit — really? You guys all got flooded out?"

"No shit, man. Truth. Elisha's made arrangements with a black vampire family in St. Louis to have us shipped out there to their place, least till New Orleans gets pumped dry and the residents are allowed back in. Elisha's got connections with some bus drivers and their bosses, thanks to the Horse X trade. All us black bloodsuckahs gonna have our coffins loaded into the cargo holds of them buses that're evacuatin' people outta the Superdome. Then we'll be shipped to our buddies in St. Louis."

Jules licked blood off the sides of his mouth. A vampire evacuation? He'd never heard of such a thing before. "You guys are *leavin'*? Leavin' *New Orleans*?"

"Well, yeah... I mean, we don't plan for it to be forever, like. We figure New Orleans'll get put back together the way it was, sooner or later. But in the meantime, we got to keep keepin' on. Y'know what I mean?"

"Hang on just a minute," Jules said, feeling the pressure of unfinished business. "I wanna hear everything you got to say, but I gotta clean my plate."

"Oh, sure, you go right ahead. Hate to interrupt a man's meal."

Jules folded up his tapping cane and dark glasses, his "blind man" costume, and shoved them into his satchel. Then he took his revolver and a potato out of the bag. He screwed the potato, his customary, workaday silencer, onto the short barrel of the revolver. Then he fired a bullet into the base of the bloodless looter's skull. *Pluufff*. Basic vampire hygiene. He tossed the now burnt, holed potato into the damp street. "Okay, done. Now, you was sayin'—?"

"We're gettin' out, later tonight." Preston's eyes narrowed. "Hey. Here's a proposition for ya. Elisha's still on the grateful side for that time you saved my life, and for other stuff — your help solvin' the preacher murders and the deal you parlayed for the St. Thomas Project residents. I bet if I sweet-talk her just right, she'd be willin' to arrange for extra spaces on them buses for your coffin, Maureen's, and ones for your other kin. How about it? You up for seein' what undead life is like in St. Louis?"

Go to St. Louis? The only place farther out from New Orleans than Slidell, Louisiana that Jules had ever considered visiting was Doodle-bug's institute in Northern California; and Doodlebug was like a son to him (or a daughter). Yeah, there'd been that time he'd hauled himself out to Baton Rouge for nearly a week, but that had been under extreme duress... and it had also been one of the most miserable weeks of his undead existence.

Not only that, but he couldn't picture his coffin (roughly the size of a piano case) fitting inside the cargo hold of a Greyhound bus. On the back of a flatbed truck, yeah, maybe... but in the guts of a bus?

"Uh, that's real generous of you to offer, Preston, real neighborly... but I'd have to take this up with Maureen, Doc Landrieu, and my mother. How quick do you need our answer back?"

"It'd have to be tonight, man. Like I said, we's gettin' loaded onto buses before sunrise. You wouldn't have to be on the same group of buses with us, I guess... there'll be more at the Superdome tomorrow night. But you'd hafta give Elisha enough time tonight to make arrangements for y'all."

"Got it," Jules said. "I'll have a powwow with my family soon as I can get back to the house. Where can I find you later tonight?"

"The gang and me have our coffins over at Little People's Place, in Tremé"

"The jazz bar?"

"That's the place. The owner's a longtime customer of ours."

"Okay. I'll get you an answer by midnight tonight. Thanks, pal. Much obliged."

* * * * *

"Absolutely *not*, Jules," Amos Landrieu said sternly. "And that's my final word."

Jules clutched Maureen's hand tightly as they both sat on one of the sofas in Amos' parlor. So intent had he been on presenting Preston's offer, Jules hadn't yet asked about the piece of plywood which covered one of the parlor's glass French doors. "You *sure* about that, Doc? Preston thinks this town's gonna go completely empty. This might be our one chance to get out. My car's almost outta gas. Yours has to be runnin' low by now. There's not a workin' gas station within eighty miles of here, minimum. Preston's offer — this could be our only ticket out of New Orleans."

Amos' expression remained harsh. "There's no way I would trust myself and Edna to... those people. In fact, Jules, I'm shocked you would trust your own existence and Maureen's to their 'tender mercies.'"

"But Doc, this is *Preston* — me and him, we worked together as private investigators—"

"And he's one vampire out of, how many? Fourteen? Need I remind you, old friend, that they were the pack who *killed me*? Who broke into my old house, viciously struck me down, and then punctured me in a dozen places with sharp-edged glass straws, so they could share in the pleasure of draining me dry? And, as a side benefit, leave me looking like a human pin cushion for you to find? Do you think those are the kind of people to whom I could, in clear conscience, deliver myself and my spouse over to, completely helpless and in their power? A bunch who resemble nothing more than a sadistic pack of little boys who shared an ice cream soda while setting a cat on fire and watching it burn?"

Jules felt his face redden. "Well... if you put it *that* way, I guess I could see you bein' a little *nervous* and all, but still—"

"And that's not the only reason I have for saying no. Lord help me, I wish it were." All the starch drained out of Amos' stance; his shoulders sagged, and he suddenly looked like a hundred-year-old man. "Jules, do you know where your mother is, right now? Why she isn't down here sharing this discussion with us?"

If the blood in Jules' room-temperature veins could grow any colder, it would've, just then. "What're you sayin', Doc? What *about* Mom? Is — is there something *wrong* with her?"

Amos' face twitched. He stared down at the floor. "I — I had to put her in a trance, Jules. I came home early this morning, an hour before sunrise, to find..."

"To find *what*, Doc?"

"She — a burglar broke into the house, while I was away, looking for blood at Baptist Hospital. He cut his arm when he smashed in one of our French doors. Edna confronted him. She tried to get him to go away, she said. But the blood, dripping from his arm... it... it proved too *tempting* for her..."

The enormity of what his father-in-law was telling him hit Jules like one of those falling anvils from a Road Runner cartoon. "So what you're sayin' is... Mom fell off the wagon, right? She's a full-fledged bloodsucker now... cursed to drink blood for the rest of eternity or longer, like me..."

Amos' face turned ashen as he slowly nodded his head. "I'm so sorry, Jules. So very, very sorry. I never should've left her alone as long as I did..."

Jules put his cold hand on his father-in-law's shoulder, in a futile attempt at a warm gesture. "Don't eat yourself up, Doc. It was probably meant to happen, no matter how careful you were with her. I been knowin' my mother a whole lot longer than you have. She's had her issues, on again and off again over the years, with the booze. It got really bad for a while after my father up and left her, then even worse after Maureen turned me into a vampire. I can't *count* the times she got herself kicked outta some Canal Street movie theater for gettin' into a loud, drunken argument with a character up on the screen. Sidney Greenstreet seemed to set her off the worst, for some reason, with Joan Crawford runnin' a close second. My mother, a bloodsucker, like me…? I mean, that *sucks*, it really does. But, y'know, Doc, I can't say I'm all that surprised."

Amos raised his face to look at his son-in-law and friend. "That's… very decent of you to say, Jules."

"Don't mention it. You say you put her into a trance? Can I talk with her?"

"She's in a very delicate state. When I found her, she was delirious with bloodlust. I placed her into a trance in hopes I might be able to keep her in stasis long enough that her cravings would fade…"

"Kinda like detox for an alkie, or cold turkey for a heroin addict?"

"Exactly. But she is fighting against the trance. The best thing for me to do would be to enter the trance-state alongside her. That way, my own concentration on maintaining her stasis could not be broken; we would essentially hibernate together. But I hope you understand now why she cannot be moved to another location, especially not a strange new city like St. Louis. The emotional upsets and psychological disruption of waking in an alien environment would inevitably grant free rein to her bloodlust. I would have no hope of being able to control her under such conditions."

"If you wake her long enough to talk with me, would you be able to put her under again?"

Amos frowned. "I — I can't be sure of that, Jules. As I said, she's fighting me, even now. Just by sitting down here and having this conversation with you, I'm risking losing my sway over her consciousness. Really, I need to be upstairs with her, lying next to her, sharing her hibernation. It's the safest thing for her. I would've done it already, but I had her victim's body to dispose of."

Jules grunted. "So Doc, you and my mother are stayin' put." He turned to Maureen. "How about you and me, babe? You want we should take Preston up on his offer, just the two of us? We never really had us a honeymoon. Not that I'd pick St. Louis as a vacation paradise, but still...?"

Maureen furrowed her delicate blonde brows. "Jules... I know you just want the best for me, honey, and that you trust Preston... but there's history between me and Elisha. *Bad* history. I know how much you hate it when I even mention that time when Malik and I — uh, Malice X and I — y'know, when we were kind of, well, a *couple*, during those years when you and I were on the outs. Well, after he turned his sister, Elisha, they sort of had this weird *thing* for each other. You should have seen the *devil eyes* she would shoot at me whenever she saw us together! We had some nasty words between us on a few occasions. Once, Malik, uh, Malice, he had to break the two of us up before we transformed into vicious animals and started tearing each other to shreds. So, the long and the short of it is... I don't trust that bitch to not give our bus driver a post-hypnotic suggestion to drag my coffin out of the bus's cargo hold somewhere in the boondocks and leave it with the lid off, so I roast when the sun comes up. I sure wouldn't put it past her."

Jules felt his guts churn. "So what're you sayin', Mo? You're stickin' around, too?"

"I agree with Doc. No St. Louis for me."

"But Mo — what if all the people leave, and the blood runs out?"

"Didn't Doc say he went to Baptist Hospital to steal a bunch of blood for us?" Maureen said, glancing hopefully at her father-in-law.

Amos frowned again. "It's all bad, I'm afraid. I didn't even need to test it. As soon as I opened up a few of the plastic packets, the decay was immediately obvious. I'm sorry. I tried."

"I know you did the best you could, Doc," Jules said. "So, how about it, Maureen? You don't have a big stash of stored blood to fall back on. You can't change into a wolf, like I can, and scarf down as much regular food as your belly can hold. Doc's already explained he can't put you in a hibernation trance, like he did Mom, 'cause of the fact that your body's made up of the parts of four different vampires. You still gonna let your old feud with Elisha keep you here?"

Maureen got that stubborn-as-iron look on her face that Jules knew all too well. "Jules Duchon, my mind is made up. I am not boarding any bus that that incestuous whore has anything to do with. And that is *final*." Her expression softened somewhat. "Look, I know Preston is one of your buddies. But if you want help, why not ask Doodlebug? Doodle has always come through for us."

Before he could control himself, Jules rolled his eyes to the ceiling (then realized, from her angry scowl, that Maureen had caught him doing it). "You don't think I thought of Doodlebug already? We can't reach him, and he can't reach us. I don't know a damn thing about these new-fangled cell phones, but Doc said every cell tower along the Gulf Coast's been knocked out. Ain't no cell towers, ain't no cell phone calls, and there ain't no land lines, neither. Besides, there's not a workin' airport within two hundred miles of us. So even if we could somehow get through to Doodlebug, let him know he needs to ship us some blood from his institute, Fed Ex ain't on the job. It's like we're on a desert island, babe. You're Ginger, and I'm Skipper, and we're both stuck on Gilligan's Island. And this ain't no three-hour tour."

Maureen rubbed her husband's tense shoulders. "Well... we'll make out somehow, won't we? Haven't we always? Didn't you find a way to bring me back when I was just a pile of dust?"

Just then, a shrill, maniacal laugh echoed from an upstairs bedroom. "Send me more burglars! They're *delicious*! I'm *starving* again... I want my *ham-burglars*! I need my snackie, Amos, honey..."

Amos looked as though a stake had been thrust through his heart. "I need to go upstairs and see to your mother..."

"You go right ahead, Doc," Jules said, feeling utterly defeated.

Everything was turning to shit.

* * * * *

Jules hated using any of the pitiful reserve of gas, less than an eighth of a tank, remaining in the fuel tank of his trusty old Cadillac Sedan de Ville. But he knew he'd feel like a lout if he didn't see Preston before the black vampire left town.

He drove slowly through the half a foot of water which covered the lower-lying streets in the Quarter. Then he turned west into Tremé, the historic neighborhood founded by free men of color before the Civil War. Tremé sat squarely on the boundary between the sort-of high-and-dry sliver of the city that clung to the Mississippi River levee and its downslope, and the flooded wastelands of the Seventh Ward, Mid-City, Broadmoor, the Ninth Ward, and all the parts of town which had once been swamps along the shores of Lake Pontchartrain. Little People's Place, a tiny jazz bar, was situated only blocks away from Claiborne Avenue, where the flooding got deep enough to preclude any vehicular traffic — unless the vehicle in question was a fishing boat or a submarine.

He found Preston smoking a cigarette outside the darkened bar. "Hey, Captain Jules," Preston said. "What's the word?"

"We ain't going," Jules said.

Preston, sensing an unsettling sub-current in Jules' terse statement, didn't press for details. Jules didn't provide any.

"So when you leavin'?" Jules asked.

"'Bout five hours from now. Got us some trucks lined up to haul our coffins out to the buses parked by the Superdome. If you need some gas, feel free to siphon whatever's left in the tanks of them trucks after we're gone."

"Thanks."

Preston snubbed out his cigarette against the heel of his boot and flicked the butt into the street. He looked at Jules. "You gonna be all right?"

"Sure, we'll be all right," Jules said. He had a sinking feeling he'd just told a big whopper. "Say hello to that St. Louis Arch for me, okay?"

"Sure thing. Good luck, Jules."

"Same to ya, Preston."

They shook hands. Then Jules climbed back into his Cadillac.

He and Maureen were on their own.

Five

CROUCHING in the bushes beneath a half moon, Jules felt his guts churn. His semi-digested solid food (all scavenged from a looted Winn-Dixie: three cans of Heinz pork and beans, a tray of semi-stale strudel pastries, and about a third of a twenty-pound bag of Purina Dog Chow) thrashed about in his wolf intestinal tract like half a dozen pairs of sneakers in the spin cycle of a worn-out drying machine. He wasn't sure how much of his discomfort was due to the trots that he typically suffered anytime he scarfed down mass quantities of solid foods while in his wolf form, and how much was due to his level of anxiety. The latter was on the elevated side, due to the fact that he was about to pounce on a National Guard soldier. A soldier armed with an M-16 carbine.

Oh, I know them bullets can't kill me, Jules reassured himself (or tried to). *But they'll sure tear me up something awful if enough of them hit. I might get hurt bad enough that I won't be able to drag myself back to my car and plop my ass back in my coffin before sunrise.*

Thirteen nights had passed since the evening Preston and the other black vampires had left town. Since then, New Orleans had become a ghost city, much of it resembling the ruins of Atlantis, the roofs of houses and businesses poking above a lake of murky water up to fourteen feet deep. The National Guard and state police had closed off all the roads leading in, cordoning off the drowned city. Only soldiers were here now,

and a few groups of firemen and Army Corps of Engineers disaster recovery crews that had begun filtering in from other parts of the country.
They had their base station on the far side of the Mississippi River,
across the Crescent City Connection in Algiers, the only sizable neighborhood of the city which had escaped flooding. But this soldier was on
lone patrol duty, guarding the toney neighborhoods of the University
District from any leftover looters.

Hiding in the bushes at the edge of Audubon Park, Jules watched
the soldier, who leaned against the door of his sand-colored Humvee, pretend to aim his rifle at imaginary snipers atop the Gothic spires of Loyola
University on the far side of St. Charles Avenue. *The weekend warrior's
bored out of his skull,* Jules told himself. *Can't say I blame him none.*

But maybe he could get the soldier's boredom to work to his advantage? Jules figured his present appearance wouldn't come across as
especially threatening; nobody would be expecting to see a wolf at the
edge of Audubon Park, and in his wolf form, he resembled an extremely
obese, somewhat mangy German shepherd dog. The city was now crawling with abandoned, stray pets. The soldier shouldn't be too shocked to
see a German shepherd wandering about (although one as grossly obese
as Jules might raise some eyebrows). Maybe G.I. Joe was a dog lover.
Jules hoped so.

The soldier slung his carbine over his shoulder and ambled over to
another set of bushes. Jules waited for the man to finish taking a leak.
Should he jump him now, while the soldier's dick was in his hand and he
was concentrating on aiming? No; somehow, that notion just didn't sit
right with him. He wouldn't want a predator attacking *him* while *he* was
taking a leak.

He waited, impatient and nervous, as the soldier climbed back into
his Humvee. As soon as the man slammed his door shut, Jules scurried
out into the road. He knew he had to time this just right — get himself
hit before the big Humvee was rolling any faster than five miles an hour
or so.

He threw his massive canine body against the Humvee's bumper, wanting to generate the maximum amount of racket. Even at five mph, this was gonna *hurt*—! He was rewarded with a resounding THUMP! The impact sent Jules rolling across the asphalt.

The soldier slammed on his brakes. He threw his transmission into Park and jumped out of the Humvee. Jules, making sure to whimper piteously, picked himself up. Boy, was he gonna have some bruises well up by the end of the night... maybe he *should've* ambushed the guy while he was taking a whiz? He affected a limp as he hobbled toward the soldier, hopping awkwardly on three paws.

"Awww, boy, I'm so *sorry*," the soldier said. "What'd you run out into the road like that for, just as I was getting rolling? Good thing I wasn't going any faster..."

Wag your tail, wag your tail, Jules reminded himself. He also pinned his ears back, indicating he was hurt and scared, tucked his tail between his legs even as he wagged it. Actually, he *was* hurt and scared. He turned up the whining a notch.

"Geeze, I wish there was something I could do for you," the soldier said, compassion coloring his voice. "You hungry?" He glanced at Jules' flopping wolf belly and laughed good-naturedly. "You don't *look* like you need any food. But I'll bet you're hungry, anyway. Lemme see if I've got some spare K-rations you might like."

Still pretending to limp, Jules circled around behind the soldier as the man walked to the passenger side of the Humvee, opened the door, and leaned inside to rummage through the truck's front storage compartments. Jules waited until the man's head was less than a foot away from the metal dashboard. Then he leaped as high as he could manage and landed squarely on the soldier's bent back.

The soldier's forehead smacked solidly against the unyielding dashboard. Stunned, the man toppled onto the passenger seat. Jules knew he had only seconds to act before the soldier would recover his wits, think better about giving "doggy" a treat, and reach for his rifle. He had to do his presto-change-o and finish the job — fast.

As he'd done thousands of times before over a span of nearly a hundred years, Jules mentally reached out across the limitless ether of the null dimension to his stored proto-matter, his spare mass, which sat as a pool of gray jelly on the bottom of his coffin whenever he transformed into a creature (such as a wolf) smaller than his normal human form. With the strength of desperation, he yanked his proto-matter back to himself across the frigid, lightless vacuum.

His wolf body began quivering. Its edges grew indistinct and shimmery as a gray cloud settled around it. Within seconds, Jules was fully himself — his incandescently white naked self, since he'd stashed his clothes in the Caddy across the street.

The soldier rubbed his forehead and groaned, not realizing the naughty "doggy" had done a switcheroo. Jules grabbed him by the back of his collar and slammed his head three times against the dashboard, then once more for good measure. *Sorry, soldier boy — you're a nice enough fella, and I know you're just here doin' your job. Heck, I'm as patriotic as the next guy, or more so. But when it comes down to a choice between your life and Maureen's — buddy, that ain't no contest.*

Jules shook the man to make sure he was fully unconscious. He was out, his mental lights as dark as the lights of New Orleans. Jules noticed a trickle of blood dripping from a cut on the man's forehead. He was glad he'd eaten his fill while in wolf form; unsatisfying as that had been (and he sensed his guts rumbling ominously; he prayed he'd be able to hold out until he could get himself into the bathroom at Maureen's house), he'd wanted to make sure he wouldn't be tempted by any bloodlust while shanghaiing this soldier. Jules couldn't let himself sample even a taste. Maureen, his poor darling, needed every last drop of blood in this man's veins.

He turned off the Humvee's ignition and lights (no sense in attracting attention from other patrols), then dragged the unconscious soldier across St. Charles Avenue to the university parking lot where he'd left his Caddy. He shoved the man into the sedan's vast back seat. Then he headed back toward the Quarter along St. Charles Avenue, paralleling the streetcar tracks on the muddy, overgrown neutral ground. He didn't turn on his headlights, relying on his superior night vision to navigate the dark avenue and avoid fallen tree branches and downed power lines.

Jules parked in front of Maureen's house on Bienville Street. Parking, usually such a pain in the ass in the Quarter, had been a breeze since Antonia had blown through. He slung the soldier, still unconscious, over his shoulder (Jules hoped he wouldn't find it necessary to whack him over the head a few more times; after all, at the start of Operation Desert Storm, he had proudly placed a Support the Troops bumper sticker on the rear fender of his Caddy) and trudged up the steps.

He flung the door open. "Honey, I'm home!" he called up the stairs. "I've brought dinner!"

"Jules..." Maureen moaned weakly from the upstairs bedroom. "Hurry, honey... I feel *sick*..."

Jules hustled up the stairs as fast as his protesting knees (now blackened with bruises from his collision with the Humvee) would allow. Maureen had hardly eaten a thing for the past week. Unlike Jules, she was able to tolerate occasional small meals of solid food while in human form, thanks to the majority of her body having been "donated" from much younger vampires, female bloodsuckers who hadn't yet become totally dependent upon a liquid diet. But the ingestion of fresh blood was still critical to her digestive health and overall well-being. She hadn't had any blood since the night, two weeks earlier, when she'd fanged a would-be rapist on a rooftop in Gentilly.

She looked miserable. Her complexion had turned a waxy yellow. Jules noted with distress that she'd lost a significant amount of weight (and, to his eyes, she'd already been on the too-skinny side even before the storm had roared through).

He dumped the unconscious soldier onto the water bed. Maureen bobbed like a fragile twig on the surface of a stormy sea. "Babe, are you strong enough to feed?" Jules asked. Seeing Maureen looking this way had turned his intestines to strings of frozen link sausages. "If you're not up to it, I'll go and get a big bowl from the kitchen, and I'll cut open his throat for you. I'll — I'll even feed you with a spoon, if I have to... anything you want..."

"I — I should be able to do it," Maureen whispered, exhausted just from the effort of sitting up in bed. She glanced suddenly at the bruises covering his face and arms. "What — what *happened* to you, babe? You got yourself all banged up..."

"Aww, it's nothing," Jules insisted. "The important thing is, I found you a meal. Now you be a good girl and eat up, so you can get your strength back. Okay?"

Hearing her greedily gulp down warm gore was just about the sweetest sound he'd ever heard.

* * * * *

After that night, things didn't get any easier for Jules. He soon discovered that the local contingent of the National Guard had instituted a new policy of two soldiers per patrol, undoubtedly a response to the disappearance of the man Jules had shanghaied. This change made kidnapping another soldier nearly impossible — Jules figured he'd get more holes blown through him than the levee system had suffered during the storm.

There was only one place left in the city where he knew he could find blood (and not blood inside a soldier armed with an M-16). The only thing was, going there could potentially end up even more dangerous for Maureen than hunting soldiers would be for Jules. But the alternative was watching her slowly fade into a starving shadow of herself again.

So Jules dragged his weary behind out to his elderly Cadillac and headed for his least favorite patch of real estate in all of New Orleans... the Metairie Road estate of the High Krewe of Vlad Tepes.

Descending the Pontchartrain Expressway down ramp to Metairie Road, he had to sharply brake the car. The old sedan skidded through a cloud of brake pad dust and came to an emergency brake-assisted halt only after dipping its front tires and fender into a vast pool of water beneath the elevated expressway.

His hands shaking, Jules climbed out of the car. He had no idea how deep the water was down here. He knew his Caddy couldn't ford much more than about nine inches of standing water before flooding its engine. He figured most of Metairie Road would be high and dry. But that didn't help him a bit if he couldn't get the car through the water at the bottom of this off-ramp.

He took off his shoes and socks and placed them on the hood of his car. Then he rolled his pants legs up to just below his pudgy knees and stepped gingerly into the water. He didn't have to wade more than two feet from his car's bumper to learn the water got much deeper than nine inches.

"Aww, hell," he grumbled to himself. It was going to be one of those nights; and he hadn't even gotten near any of the snooty assholes of the High Krewe yet. He stripped off the rest of his clothes, stuffed them into a plastic grocery bag he found in his car's trunk, held the bag above his head, and waded out into the black water.

At the lowest point of the dip the exit from the expressway made, the water came up to the center of his chest, right about where his pair of man-boobs drooped onto his topmost belly fold. Then it began getting more shallow again. On the far side of the miniature lake, he paused to redress himself, noting with distaste how his button-down shirt clung to his pillowy arms and chest and how the seat of his trousers, always on the tight side, now soggily crept up his Grand Canyon of an ass crack.

He headed west along Metairie Road. A quarter moon weakly illuminated the collection of tombs and monuments arrayed in the sprawling Metairie Road Cemetery, which provided eternal rest to numerous heroes of the War Between the States and many of the city's most distinguished (and sleaziest) politicians and men of commerce.

He warily approached the security wall surrounding the High Krewe's estate, a compound made up of a dozen stately buildings — most important of which, to Jules' mind, was the large dormitory which housed approximately a hundred "blood cows," mentally deficient men and women, bred from an original contingent the High Krewe had taken over from a failing order of nuns in the mid-nineteenth century. The coven of vampires treated these hundred benighted souls as cattle, feeding them carefully balanced diets to ensure an ample, sustainable supply of high-quality blood.

He stared up at the cameras lining the top of the wall, security features dating back to those months, several years ago, when seven of the High Krewe's youngest members had disappeared, three of them, missing various body parts and sunken into comas, eventually being dumped in the woods surrounding the estate. The cameras didn't follow his movements now. They were dead, along with almost everything else within the walls. Had the system been live, it would've detected his clothes, if not the sizable vampire inside them.

Should he take the risk of ringing the bell? Would the bell even *work*? Assuming the bell would ring, the member of the High Krewe most likely to greet him at the gate would be Straussman, the butler — the man Jules had come to see. But there was a slight chance one of the others would come, instead. Jules didn't want to risk that.

That meant it was presto-change-o time again.

Jules once more stripped off his clothes (a clumsier task this time, due to everything being damp), stuffed them into his grocery bag, and threw the bag over the wall. He grimaced when it made a louder than expected rustling noise upon landing. Then he began concentrating on long, long fingers, leathery wings, a black button of a nose, and ears twice as tall as his head. The theme song from the 1960s *Batman* TV show insinuated itself into his consciousness, as it always did at a time like this. He tried as best as he could to push as much of his mass as possible through the null dimension and into the bottom of his coffin. Even so, after his form had finished its shimmering and shrinking, he was still left with a dreadfully un-aerodynamic belly sagging from his rodent midsection, a dead weight which would overburden his wings as badly as a brick would the wings of a hummingbird.

Experimentally, he tried flapping his wings. He remained as grounded as the parked Army Air Force squadrons at Pearl Harbor after the strafing Japanese Zeros had gotten done with them. *Mary, Mother of you-know-who — after all the training Doodlebug gave me in controlling my mass, I still can't get rid of this lard belly when I change into a bat?*

Still, even if flying remained beyond him, there was one very useful thing a bat, even a fat bat, could do that a human couldn't do nearly as well. And that was climb up a brick wall. Utilizing the sharp claws at the edges of his wings, he dug his nails into the seams between bricks and began the Herculean labor of hauling himself to the top of the wall. His tiny heart pumping faster and harder with each strenuous yank of his wings, Jules came close to passing out several times before he reached the summit. Only the thought of Maureen lying in bed, turning yellower and yellower, gradually starving into a wisp of herself, kept him climbing.

He rested at the top for a few moments. *Maybe I should just take a chance and jump to the ground*, he thought, dreading more exertions. His wings weren't strong enough to levitate him off the floor, but perhaps they could slow his fall enough to grant him a soft landing? *Naww, forget about it… that's probably a good way to break my neck. And then what would happen to Mo?*

So he took the long, hard, precarious way down, clinging to the spaces between the bricks. At least it was (somewhat) easier than climbing up had been.

He transformed himself back into his human form after he set foot on the ground, then quickly dressed himself. He'd made it so far without anybody spotting him. All of the buildings in the compound were dark; but that didn't provide him much in the way of cover, since every vampire here boasted night vision at least as good as his.

He remembered where Straussman's little room was, in one of the side wings of the primary residence mansion. Luckily for Jules, the butler's room had a door to the outside, so Jules wouldn't need to figure out a way to gain access to the mansion through one of the main doors. Either he'd find Straussman inside, or he'd need to find a nearby spot to hide while waiting for sounds of the butler's return.

He knocked lightly on the weathered oak door. He was rewarded by the noises of someone — Straussman, he hoped! — stirring inside.

"Who's there?"

Jules exhaled with relief; it was the butler's voice.

"Straussman, it's Jules Duchon. I've gotta ask you a big, big favor."

"I believe I know what it is," Straussman said. The tall, slender vampire, centuries older than his visitor, opened the door and glanced to Jules' right and left. "You'd better come inside. Quickly."

Jules squeezed himself through the door. He found the room he entered to be an even tighter squeeze. The butler's tiny room contained only space for his coffin, a side table, a bench, and a spartan wooden desk and chair. Straussman lived like a monk. Jules felt like the fat friar from *Robin Hood*.

"I assume, given the circumstances, you've come for blood," Straussman said in a low voice. "Blood from our farm."

"It's not for me, Straussman," Jules assured him. "I been livin' rough, eatin' doggy-style, if you know what I mean. I need blood for Maureen. You know as well as anybody that she can't pull the vampire tricks you and me can, 'causa the way Doodlebug and me had to bring her back from gettin' turned into a pile of dust. Now that she's made up of a bunch of assorted vampire parts, she's stuck in one form. Hey, while we're on that subject, are the High Krewe's patchwork dolls still lyin' in their coffins, stuck in comas, like they was when I saw them a couple of years back?"

"Mistress Victoria, Mistress Alexandra, and Mistress Flora Ann remain in their coffins, in a state of what can only be described as deep hibernation. I hand-feed them their blood rations twice each week. This is particularly... challenging with Mistress Flora Ann."

"She's the one who 'donated' her torso?"

"Yes. The blood ration must be divided between her head and each of her separated limbs."

Man, they stick Straussman with all the crap jobs, don't they? What does he do? Inject *the girl's arms and legs with blood? And when he spoons it into her mouth, where does it go, if she doesn't have a gullet or a stomach?*

"The Masters," Straussman said gravely, "will never abandon hope that the Mistresses' missing parts will someday be recovered, and that the girls will be made whole again." He reached out and clutched Jules' arm tightly. "They must never, *never* learn that Maureen has returned from oblivion. It could mean her life, Jules. You must understand that. And if they ever learn of the roles you and I played in Maureen's resurrection, and that your father-in-law and Rory Richelieu played, the sands remaining in the hourglass measuring the remainder of our existences would be few, indeed."

So Straussman was a poet? Maybe the butler spent more time reading the classics in the High Krewe's amazing library than he'd let on. "I get that, Straussman. I knew just comin' over here was a risk. I wouldn't have dragged myself out here to your hoity-toity playground unless I absolutely had to. Maureen's *starving*. She needs what you got here. She needs it *now*."

Straussman's grip on Jules' arm grew tighter. "Do you realize what you are asking me to do? The risk you are asking me to take? The emergency has turned the Masters viciously paranoid about our blood supply. Those of us who work the blood farm must now do so in pairs, and each member of each team is encouraged to spy and inform on the other, to guard against any cheating on blood allocations or purloining of the supply."

"But Straussman... she's your blood daughter. You were in love with her, once."

"And I love her still." The butler remained quiet for a few seconds. "All right," he said at last, a tone of fatalism darkening his voice. "Remain here. I will see what I can do."

Jules plopped himself down on the lid of Straussman's coffin. It looked roomier than the bench. The waiting drove him nuts. He kept checking his watch, swearing to himself that a half-hour had passed, only to find merely four or five minutes had elapsed since the last time he'd pressed the wristwatch's illumination button.

Finally, after an hour and a quarter (which had felt like the majority of the night), Straussman returned to his room. He handed Jules three pints of blood in plastic sheathes. "This is the most I dare give you. Now leave quickly. And do not come back to me asking for more, for I shall not be able to oblige you."

Three pints? That might be enough to get Maureen through a week, possibly a week and a half.

"Thanks, Straussman," Jules said, holding the bags of blood as though it were liquid gold. "You're a prince."

"No, I'm a sentimental old fool. Now go."

Jules left the room and silently crept toward the wall surrounding the estate. So he was good for the next ten days, if he put Maureen on the most miserly ration possible. If he could withstand her pitiful pleading for *a few swallows more.*

But what then?

Six

G AS for his Cadillac became harder and harder to find. It soon became obvious to Jules that he wasn't the only one in New Orleans siphoning gasoline from the tanks of the few vehicles which had been left behind in the great evacuation. At least a handful of diehards had remained in their homes, somehow avoiding the National Guard troops. If only Jules could locate those stay-behinds... it would be easier to spot them in the daytime, when they'd be out in the streets, scavenging from grocery stores. But Jules slept in the daytime. And his fellow stay-behinds slept at night, or they closed themselves up inside darkened houses or apartments, where Jules couldn't find them.

He made a mistake. A bad one. A few days after he'd wrung the precious last few drops of Straussman's gift blood from its plastic bags, he changed into his wolf form to sniff out and catch two stray dogs and a cat. Realizing he was placing himself on the SPCA's Most Wanted list, he slaughtered the three animals in Maureen's courtyard and collected their blood in a large sauce pan. Then he had Maureen drink it.

It went down easily enough. Jules figured it must taste kind of gamey, but Maureen was so ravenous, she probably would've slurped down a barrel of Bloody Mary mix if Jules had told her it had come from some guy's veins.

As fast as it went down her throat, it came right back up. Little devil-possessed Regan from *The Exorcist* had nothing on Maureen when it came to projectile vomiting. The walls of their bedroom were quickly coated with regurgitated animal blood, mixed with black bile.

Once she'd completely emptied her stomach, her ordeal left Maureen as weak as a newborn gerbil. Lying splayed on her waterbed, her long blond hair a sweaty tangle, her mouth and nose dripping with red vomit, she looked like a deflated sex doll that had just been gang-banged by the New Orleans Saints linebacker corps. Jules had made things worse... way worse.

He cleaned up as best he could, then got in his Cadillac and headed for the Crescent City Connection bridge and Algiers, on the far side of the Mississippi. That's where the people were — the firemen and Red Cross volunteers and disaster recovery crews. All guarded by soldiers. Lots of soldiers, with lots of guns and lots of anxious trigger-fingers, thanks to Jules' abduction of the soldier on St. Charles Avenue a few weeks earlier.

He found the base camp near the eastern end of General de Gaulle Avenue, on the grounds of Our Lady of the Holy Cross College. It was easy to find — the only spot for miles around with working electric lights, thanks to the banks of generators the Army and FEMA had set up. All those lights would only make things harder and more dangerous for him, he knew. But his memories of Maureen's helpless gasping and moaning overrode all thoughts of caution.

He slowly circled the campus in his car, headlights turned off. The grassy fields between the academic buildings were crowded with tents. The back of the campus, the area farthest away from the intersection of General de Gaulle Avenue and Woodland Drive, looked to be set aside for the Army National Guard; Jules spotted a couple dozen Humvees and two-ton trucks parked in neat rows, and the tents were all military-issue. The tents and vehicles arrayed on the other portion of the field were more motley, with fire and rescue vehicles parked next to police cruisers and fifteen-passenger vans marked with the emblems of the Red Cross and other voluntary agencies. The tents here came in all colors and sizes, with smaller ones probably bought at Wal-Mart and bigger ones sourced from FEMA. The insides of some of these tents were blue-lit by the screens of battery-powered TVs. Men circulated between the tents, carrying thermos jugs filled with coffee or more potent beverages (the latter being limited to just the civilians and any cops considered off-duty, Jules figured).

He needed only one guy. Just one victim. But how was he going to pick that one person off? He couldn't just waltz into the middle of the base camp, whack somebody over the head with a two-by-four, then drag him back to the car. There were too many guns around — not just soldiers with their M-16s, but cops with their duty sidearms, too. He'd have to be patient, much as it felt impossible to stay patient at a time like this. He'd have to wait until one of the sheep wandered away from the flock.

He parked his Cadillac in a lot fronting a drainage canal, a few dozen yards away from the low-lying green hill of a modest retention levee that ran along the length of the narrow, shallow waterway. Glancing around to make sure nobody in the civilian part of the base camp was watching, Jules walked over to a bus stop shelter at the edge of Woodland Drive. He figured he could hide in the shadows inside the shelter, where he'd wait for someone to get bored and take a stroll over to the levee. At least he'd have a bench to sit on while he was waiting and watching. A small blessing, but a blessing, nonetheless.

What he didn't expect to find was someone else already sitting there.

The man was staring upward at the sky, seeming to count the stars. He glanced around at Jules before the vampire could back away. He was a small man, in his late twenties or early thirties, about five and a half feet tall; Asian — either Japanese or Korean, maybe Chinese... Jules couldn't tell. He wore a vest issued by the International Red Cross. The big cross, made of red reflective plastic, forced Jules to look away before his eyes would start smarting and tearing up.

"Good evening," the man said. He definitely had an Asian accent. He stood and offered Jules a quick, polite bow. "I am Kenji Tezuka, from Kure, Japan. It is near Hiroshima, a city you may know. I have not seen you around base camp before. May I have the preasure of making your acquaintance?"

Not wanting to seem rude or hostile — especially not hostile; he wanted to set the man at ease — Jules forced himself to look at Kenji, despite the discomfort that cross caused him. "Sure thing," Jules said. "Nice to meet ya, Kenji. I'm Jules Duchon. I'm a, well, uh, a paramedic. In from, uh, St. Louis, Missouri. You're sure a long way from home. What made you want to come all the way to New Orleans?"

Kenji smiled eagerly. "It was Louis Armstrong who made me want to come." Jules noted how carefully he'd enunciated "Louis," apparently wanting to say the name exactly right. "I grew up enjoying very much the jazz of Louis Armstrong. And King Orriver, and Sidney Bechet. But mostly Louis Armstrong, for he was the greatest of the jazz trumpeters. So this makes me want to come to New Orrins. In Japan, we have many terrible storms, too. But called typhoons, not hurricanes. I have vorrunteered many times for crean-ups after typhoons in Japan. When I heard that a terrible storm had frudded New Orrins, home of Louis Armstrong, I went that very day to sign up with the Red Cross to come here. I ruvv New Orrins, because Louis Armstrong is my hero, my *sensei*. I pray trumpet too, you see, but my praying is very much that of a humburr beginner. In fact, when you came just now, I was rooking up at the stars and remembering how to pray the notes of a Louis Armstrong so-ro from 'Basin Street Brues,' a very fine Dixie-rand song. Do you know it?"

"Yeah, I know it." *Boy, I wish I could tell this guy I heard Louie Armstrong play that song live once... when Louie was still in his twenties, before he left New Orleans for Chicago, when he was still playing in bars on South Rampart Street and whorehouses in Storyville.*

Actually, Kenji's story had touched a chord fairly deep within Jules' heart. Sentimental about his home town, he had a soft spot reserved for anyone with a soft spot for New Orleans.

Maybe I should walk away... this is a swell guy, a prince, to have come here all the way from Japan to help us out. Maybe I should let him live a long, natural lifespan, huh...?

But then he thought about his wife, lying weak and helpless in her bed, having practically puked her guts out, thanks to him. This Kenji fellow was a gift from the vampire gods — gregarious, curious about New Orleans, eager to make a new friend in this strange place. It wouldn't be hard at all to entice him into straying away from the base camp. Who knew if another chance like this one would come around tonight? And he wasn't so certain Maureen could wait until tomorrow night for him to bring her fresh blood.

So Jules shoved his sympathy and budding fondness for his new acquaintance aside. He hardened his heart. *Pearl Harbor. Iwo Jima. Wake Island. Bataan Death March. Rape of Nan... of Nantucket? Uh, of whatever that city in China was that the Jap Army fucked over...*

He forced himself to remember all the yellow-faced, buck-toothed, *evil* Japanese soldiers and sailors from the hundreds of *Captain America* and *Human Torch* and *Sub-Mariner* comics he'd read during the war, how fiendish and rotten and sneaky the Japs had been, with their Samurai swords and submarines and secret scientific super-weapons.

Then he was ready to do it, conscience be damned.

"Hey, Kenji, you see that canal over there, the one that goes under that little bridge? You ever taken a look at it at night?"

"I have walked the revee arongside it during the daytime severawr times, but never at night. Why do you ask? Is there something odd about the canarr at night?"

"Heck, yeah. There's something you really outta see, bein' such a fan of Louie Armstrong. I like Louie, too. In fact, I've read his memoirs. You know he grew up here in New Orleans, right? Well, he wrote about these glowing fish in the canals. He used to fish for 'em as a kid, at night, when they'd be easy to see. But they only glow during the summertime, kinda like, y'know, fire flies, those bugs that only show up in the summer. Anyway, I seen some of them in that canal there. We really outta go take a look. You can tell your buddies back in Japan about 'em."

"Growing fish?" Kenji said. "I have never heard of this thing. You say Louis Armstrong would try to catch such fish as a boy?"

"Yeah. His family, y'know, they never had much money. Louie used to fish a lot, so they'd have something to eat."

"Very interesting... I wudd rike very much to see these growing fish. Prease take me to where you saw them."

"Happy to," Jules said. And indeed he was. He led Kenji out of the bus shelter and across the grass. They approached the lot where he'd parked his Cadillac. "That's my car," Jules said, unable to resist showing it off.

"That very big white car? What a big, fine car it is! So much *room* inside! We have no such cars in Japan, not rike that."

"It's a Cadillac Sedan de Ville. Louie Armstrong owned a Cadillac, too, when he lived in New York."

"Was it one rike this one?" Kenji said, peering in through the open windows.

"I think his was a little older, but yeah."

"How very rucky you are, to drive a car rike that of Louis Armstrong. He was the king of jazz."

Jules led him up the short slope of the levee to the flat path on top. "It might take us a few minutes to spot 'em," he said. "They shine pretty bright, but the water's muddy, and them fish are sorta shy, and wily, too. Soon as they hear anybody coming, they dart into weeds near the banks and hide. So let's be really quiet, okay?"

"*Ai!* I wirr be quiet, very quiet. Thank you."

And he bowed again. Jules wished he would stop doing that. It was only making him feel more guilty.

Pretending to search for the fish, Jules led Kenji a distance of about a city block, until he figured they were far enough away from the base camp that any sounds the Japanese man might make during a brief scuffle wouldn't be noticed. Overpowering the much smaller man shouldn't be too much of a chore. Then Jules figured he could drag him along the canal-side slope of the levee, away from the view of anyone in the base camp, open up the rear door of his Cadillac, and quickly stuff Kenji inside.

Jules halted. "Hey!" he whispered. "I think I saw one!"

Kenji eagerly scanned the dark water. "Where, Jures-*san*? I did not see—"

"You gotta be fast, Kenji. Over there. No, to the left. He ducked into those reeds there. I bet if you creep down to the edge of the water and watch really, really closely, you'll spot him when he swims out again. Just be careful not to fall in, okay?"

Kenji carefully stepped down to the canal's edge. Jules remained on top of the levee, about five feet higher than his companion. *In a few seconds, I'll rush him, knock him down, and bash his head a few times on that rock there.*

But then his heart began beating faster, and he felt sweat trickling from the pits of his arms. His mouth turned dry. His legs gave no indication they were in any hurry to move. *What's with me? Get with the program, Duchon. He's just some guy. Just another body full of blood — blood that Mo needs. C'mon, now. Concentrate! Pearl Harbor Pearl Harbor Pearl Harbor Pearl—*

A sudden flash of light behind him made Jules turn around. Someone with a flashlight was scanning the interior of his Cadillac! *What the hell*—? It was hard to make the guy out. But Jules thought he saw a rifle slung over the man's shoulder as he leaned inside the car, through the open window. A soldier?

Then the soldier shined his powerful flashlight's beam along the top of the levee, catching Jules full in the face. "Hey, you over there!" the soldier yelled. "This your car? I don't see a Corps of Engineers decal or a FEMA decal on the windshield. You got no business being here!"

Aww, fuck... What should he do? Kenji wouldn't stay down by the water's edge searching for a made-up fish all night. Was there some way he could get this soldier to buzz off? Or was his night's hunting blown, now that an authority had made such note of his Cadillac, probably writing down his license plate number?

The soldier turned his flashlight back inside the car. Jules saw him open the rear door and reach inside for something, something low, on the floor. He pulled out a necklace of some kind, a metal necklace that glinted in the flashlight's beam as the soldier held his find in front of his face.

Wait, Jules thought, his heart beginning to beat triple-time, *that's not a necklace. That's a set of* dog tags*! Fucking hell — that other soldier's dog tags must've gotten snagged on something and fallen off when I pulled him out of the back seat to drag him up to Mo's place...*

Even from a block away, Jules heard the soldier's stunned expletive as he read the name on the tags. "Holy *crap*...!" The soldier immediately swung his rifle off his shoulder and jammed the flashlight into a mount on the bottom of the gun's barrel. Then he pointed both flashlight and gun muzzle in Jules' direction. "Hey, *you*! Get your fat ass back here! *Now*!"

Seven

JULES found himself fleetingly wishing he and Mo had joined Preston on that long bus ride to St. Louis. He ran. *Run* was perhaps not the most accurate verb — he speed-waddled away from the soldier as fast as his overburdened knees and ankles would allow, praying he could somehow manage to outdistance the flashlight's beam.

"*Stop!*" the soldier shouted from next to Jules' car. "Stop, or I'll be forced to shoot!"

Fuck fuck fuck fuck— What could he do now? Where could he go? *Vampires don't need to breathe*, he reminded himself. He could hide in the canal, couldn't he? He could wade in and duck underneath the water and stay there until the soldier went away. Assuming the water was deep enough for him to hide his gargantuan bulk in. Assuming the soldier didn't call on his buddies to perform a full-scale manhunt, and they swarmed the area until sunrise, not letting him get back to his car and his coffin — and then he gradually boiled away into muddy dust under the rays of the sun, eventually becoming part of the canal's silted bottom...

Still, the canal was the only possible place to hide. Freaked out as he was, he told himself not to run down the slope; he had to be careful. Even with his night vision, he couldn't see where he was going too well. If he slipped on the muddy slope, he could pop a knee out of joint or bust a leg bone—

The impact of the first bullet and the sharp crack of its discharge reached Jules simultaneously. A rifle slug slammed into his upper back, just missing his spine. Big as he was, the blow wasn't enough to knock him off his feet. But the next two bullets, which hit his kidney and the fleshy part of his left arm, sent him tumbling down the levee towards the canal.

"*AAAH-OOWW*"! *Mary Mother of you-know-who*, he thought, *that* HURT! *Fucking soldier boy had to be a sharpshooter, didn't he?*

He landed face first in the muddy reeds. He felt the furnace-hot bullets burning inside his body. If he was to have any chance of surviving this night, he needed those bullets *out* of him — otherwise, his quick-healing ability would work so slowly, it might as well not work at all. He hated pulling a presto-change-o when he was covered in dirt or mud, like he was now; he always ended up with the most virulent acne imaginable. But a face-full of hot lead was a whole lot worse than a face-full of swelling zits.

Swooning with pain from his multiple gunshot wounds, he concentrated on canine thoughts. He heard footsteps rapidly approaching — Kenji's, or the soldier's? *Change, change!* He forced open the aperture to the null dimension and shoved the greater part of his mass through the sub-zero blackness into his coffin. As his rotund body shimmered and shrank and shrouded itself in an oily gray mist, Jules forced himself to remain insubstantial for an extra half-second, long enough for the three bullets to fall from the spaces which had formerly contained his upper back, his kidney, and his left arm. Only when he sensed the bullets land inside his now-empty pants did he allow himself to solidify into a big-bellied version of *Canis lupus*.

"Holy *shit*!" It was the soldier's voice, above him, on the top of the levee. "What'd I shoot — a *werewolf?*"

Close, but no cigar, Binkie, Jules thought. Quickly, he flexed his wolf muscles to make sure everything was in working order. He looked up in time to see the soldier aiming his rifle at Jules' shaggy head. A mix of terror and an instinct to self-preservation propelled Jules up the levee's slope, despite the impediment of his four legs being tangled in the muddy shrouds of his shirt and pants. He leaped onto the soldier before the man managed to get off another shot. They rolled head-over-heels-over-paws into the canal. The soldier lost his rifle. Jules took advantage of the man's disorientation to tear a savage gash from his throat with his elongated canine teeth.

He left the soldier bleeding and gasping in the water. It was truly a shame to see all that blood wasted — under better circumstances, maybe Jules could've hauled Mr. Sharpshooter's ass back to Maureen's house — but already he could hear sounds of rising agitation coming from the base camp, stirred up by the gunfire. He had to reach his car and get the hell out of here.

He didn't see Kenji. Undoubtedly, the Japanese Red Cross volunteer had fled back to the base camp. Ah, well, couldn't be helped. Jules had tried; he'd done the best he could for Maureen. Dragging his muddy clothes through the damp grass as he loped on all fours, Jules remained in wolf form until he got the side of his car. He didn't look forward to what came next. His wolf form wasn't torn up by bullet holes; his human form was (although the spent bullets now clinked together in the bottom of his pants). Turning human again would open him up to a world of hurt. Unfortunately, though, his Cadillac hadn't been designed for a wolf to drive. Not even by a wolf with an IQ in the triple digits (barely).

He didn't have much time. Soon the firemen and cops in the base camp would realize the gunshots had come from the levee, and they'd swarm around his car. He concentrated on his typical form — his once handsome, now doughy face; his shock of white hair (white ever since he'd transformed into several hundred white rats at the conclusion of his death-duel with Malice X); his great belly, with as many folds and ripples as the Gulf of Mexico had waves.

His remaining mass, stored in the bottom of his coffin, flowed back to him. But so did the agonizing pain which he'd managed to temporarily dump into limbo. The pain made it impossible for him to see straight; his agonized nerve endings pulsed like a psychedelic Lite-Brite set, powered by the entire voltage output of the Hoover Dam. Slumping weakly against the side of his car, he felt blindly for his door handle. How the hell was he supposed to drive in this kind of shape?

"Jures-*san*, ret me help you, prease."

Kenji? Jules thought he'd run away. He heard his passenger door open. Then he sensed arms — short arms, but a whole lot stronger than he would've expected them to be — pulling him into the seat.

Kenji ran around to the driver's side and jumped in. "Where are keys, prease?"

"In — in the pockets of my pants..." Jules had half a dozen questions he wanted to ask this guy. Starting with: why the heck did he want to help Jules? He felt Kenji digging through the wad of his pants, coming up at last with the keys.

"Where shudd I take you, prease?" the Japanese man asked.

"Back to — the French Quarter. You know how to get there?"

"No."

"At corner — turn onto Woodland, then go to General de Gaulle..."

Through the open windows, Jules heard a crowd beginning to approach from the base camp. Kenji nearly flooded the engine, jerking the big Cadillac from Reverse into Drive. But he got the old white barge moving before they could be surrounded by inquisitive cops and firemen.

Tires squealing, engine roaring, Kenji turned left onto Woodland Drive. Away from General de Gaulle Avenue. *That's all right*, Jules thought. *I can get him to take General Myer back to the bridge. The back way; we'll just go past a bunch of empty subdivisions. Shouldn't run into any cops.* At times like this, his decades of experience driving a cab came in handy.

Jules managed to get his eyes open and clear. He saw that Kenji was driving on the left side of the road.

"Hey — you're on the wrong side of the road," he croaked.

"But that is how we drive in Japan, Jures-*san*."

"We're not *in* Japan, pal." Jules saw Kenji make an effort to steer to the right. But a moment later they ended up on the left side of the road again. *Doesn't matter*, Jules told himself; *there's nobody else on the road*. "How come — you decided to help me out? Not that I don't appreciate it…"

"I — I saw you change, Jures-*san*."

He saw me change into a wolf? And that's why he wanted to help me?

"Wouldn't that just — scare you away?" Jules sputtered.

Kenji answered with another question. "Jures-*san*, are you what they wudd say in America as a 'superhero'?"

Despite his haze of pain, Jules smiled, remembering his long-ago nights spent in the costume of the Hooded Terror, protecting the docks and shipyards of New Orleans from Nazi saboteurs, his trusty sidekick Doodlebug at his side. "Yeah… long, long time ago, way before you was born, during the war…"

"Then you and I have very much in common, Jures-*san*. I am 'superhero,' too, but in Japan. My superhero name is *Bonsai Masutaa*. In Engrish, this is Bonsai Master. I make big things smawrr. It is a preasure to meet an American superhero, Jures-*san*. Thank you for the honor of your acquaintance. I can hardry wait to write my friends in Japan."

Eight

KENJI helped Jules get out of the car, then helped him to sit on the stoop in front of Maureen's house. Following Jules' instructions, he parked the Cadillac in a garage a block away, off the street, so no roving patrols of National Guard soldiers would spot it.

Kenji insisted that he be allowed to assist Jules into the house and up the stairs. He left his shoes on the front stoop, following Japanese habit. Before they reached the bedroom, Kenji asked in an eager whisper, "Your wife, is she a superhero, too?"

"Uh, sort of," Jules said. "Actually, she's in really bad shape now. Sick, very sick. I kinda don't think she's in any mood to entertain visitors..."

"We have doctors and nurses at the base camp. I could bring one here, prease? To help your wife?"

"I kinda doubt any docs or nurses you got there could do anything for her." *Unless they offered her their necks.* Jules wondered whether he could somehow finagle Kenji's offer into a blood supply. "Y'know, maybe one of them *could* help. See, she's got this condition, this weird blood condition. What she really needs is a blood transfusion. She needs them all the time, actually."

Kenji's eyes grew wide. "Needs brudd transfusion! What a terrible thing, to need brudd transfusion while being stranded by a typhoon!"

"Jules, who's that you've got out there with you?" Maureen's voice, from within the bedroom, sounded tremulous, weak, and desperate with hunger. "Have you brought me my *dinner*, honey?"

Jules stuck his head through the doorway, making sure that Kenji stayed in the hall and out of Maureen's sight. "Uh, no, Mo, not exactly... this is a *friend*. His name's Kenji. He's a Red Cross volunteer. From Japan. He helped me out of a *major* jam tonight—"

"Japan? I don't care if he's from *Saturn*, Jules! I can *smell* him! I'm *starving*! I need BLOOD! And I need it NOW!"

From behind Jules, Kenji said in a low voice, "For someone who is so sick, she sounds very energetic..."

"Jules, he smells *delicious*!" Maureen shouted. "Shove him in here with me and lock the door! I WANT BLOOD!"

Jules realized that letting Kenji inside the house, given the state Maureen was in, hadn't been his brightest idea. True, not more than an hour ago, he'd had every intention of dragging Kenji's prone body into Maureen's bedroom and letting her have her way with him. But that was then. Since then, the slight Japanese visitor had saved his ass. Big time. Not only that, Kenji was a superhero. He said he made big things small. Jules wasn't sure he knew what that meant, exactly. But he knew he didn't want to find out by seeing Kenji test his ability on Maureen.

"Uh, Kenji," Jules whispered, pulling his companion away from the door after shutting it, "if you know what's good for you, you'll high-tail it *out of here*. I'll make excuses to Maureen — I'll say I tried grabbing you, but you broke away and ran down the stairs—"

"*Jules!*" Maureen shouted. "What are you *whispering* out there? Hurry the hell up! If I turn any more yellow, they'll shove me in a butter churn, whisk me up, and sell me in the dairy aisle as whipped spread!"

Jules pushed his visitor towards the stairs. "Go, go, *go*—"

"But if your wife is so sick, what is the hurry for me to go? Wirr you not need herrp—"

"She wants to *drink your blood*, you *idiot*!"

Now Kenji stared at him with an expression of almost comical perplexity. "Drink my *brudd*? Jures-*san*, prease pardon my asking, but is your wife a *demon*?"

Jules shook his head. "No, no, not a demon. Oh, she can be a *devil* sometimes, but that's different."

"But different how? Are not 'devirr' and 'demon' the same thing?"

"What I mean is, she's not *evil*. She's just *hungry*. Starving, actually. See, Kenji, Maureen and me... we're *vampires*."

"But you said you are superhero, rike me—"

Jules rolled his eyes. "Yeah, yeah. Well, you can be both a superhero *and* a vampire. Do they have vampires in Japan? Do you know what a vampire *is*?"

"I think so. It is rike Berra Ru-gosi?"

"Yeah, that's right. Drinks blood. Turns in a bat or a wolf. Can't stand sunlight. Sleeps in a coffin, usually."

"I have heard stories of such beings in Japan. From rong ago. When the superheroes drove the criminawrs and demons and monsters out of Japan, in the decades after the Pacific War, they must have driven out the vampires, too. Although I have heard many rumors that not awr the demons and monsters were driven out of the home eye-rands; some stayed and became superheroes themservs, working onry for good, not evirr."

"JULES DUCHON! BRING ME MY DINNER!"

Jules winced. "If you don't get out of here right *now*, I'm afraid she's gonna come charging through that door and jump on your neck—"

Kenji's face tightened as he struggled with a decision. "You say she is starving? That she needs to drink brudd?"

"Yeah, right," Jules said, staring nervously behind him at the door.

"Wirr she die if she does not drink brudd?"

"She will eventually..."

"Then I wirr give her some of my brudd for her to drink," Kenji said with a sense of conviction.

Jules' mouth fell open. "You'd do that? You'd really *do* that?"

"*Hai.* I ruvv New Orrins. You are New Orrins superhero, rike I am Japanese superhero. I must herrp to save your wife. Do you have a knife in this house? And a pot in which to boi-urr water?"

"You want to cut yourself? Wouldn't it be easier and quicker to just, y'know, let her drink it straight from your neck?"

Kenji grimaced. "Too many germs that way. A knife is better, once steri-rized in boi-ring water. Then I wirr put my brudd into a cup for her to drink."

Jules ran to the bedroom door and flung it open. "Honey! Great news! Blood is on the way! Just be patient a few minutes longer, okay?"

"Be *patient*?" Now it was Maureen's turn to look perplexed. "Jules, what are you *babbling* about—?"

"Don't have time to explain, hon!" he said, gallivanting down the stairs. "I've gotta get some water boiling on that camp stove down in the kitchen!"

"JULES! I'm not having a BABY, Jules! Why are you boiling water?!?"

Things became clearer for Maureen a few minutes later, when Jules proudly brought her a thirty-two-ounce Big Slurp plastic mug from Circle K, filled to its brim with Kenji's blood. Jules had seen with his own eyes that Kenji, superhero or not, was definitely something more than plain human; after wincing when he'd drawn the knife across his left wrist, then holding his wrist over the mug until it was full, Kenji had pressed his torn skin together for ninety seconds, and his wound had healed. Sort of like Jules' own healing ability (when it was working right).

"Here ya go, honey!" Jules said with a flourish, handing her the huge plastic mug. "Bottoms up!"

Kenji entered the room behind Jules, his eyes locked on Maureen's face, obviously eager to see what effect imbibing his blood would have on his hostess.

Maureen took a sip. "Hey..." she said, her cracked lips spreading into a smile, "this is really *good!*" She took another sip, then another. "I mean, really, *really* good!" She chugged down the remainder of the blood, ravenously licking her lips. "This stuff's *amazing*! This is the best damn blood I've ever drunk! The best blood in the whole *world!*"

Jules caught Kenji smiling with obvious pride. He turned back to his wife. Already, she was looking better than she had; normal color (for a vampiress) had begun returning to her sunken cheeks. "Yeah," he said, pleased and relieved, "when you're really starvin', whatever you scarf down tastes like champagne and caviar, huh?"

Maureen shook her head. "*No*, Jules, that's not it. You don't get it. What I mean is, that's not *ordinary* blood. That's *super* blood!"

Kenji smiled again. "Yes, 'super brudd,' that is right! I torrd your husband, Jures-*san*, I am a superhero from Kure, Japan. That is near Hiroshima, a city you may know."

"What was your name again? Jules told me, but I was rather distracted."

"I am Kenji Tezuka. My superhero name is *Bonsai Masutaa*. In Engrish, this is 'Bonsai Master.' If I may ask, would you rike to drink more of my brudd? I see that it makes you feerr much better."

Maureen's eyes grew wide. "*Would* I...? But, but," she stuttered, "you just gave me nearly a whole *quart*. Not that I want to look a gift horse in the mouth, but is that *safe* for you?"

"*Hai.* It is, how you Americans say? 'No prob-rem.' My body makes more. I was terring Jures-*san* that I vorunteer many, many times after typhoons in Japan. I am big hero at awr the brudd drives. I give brudd, drink juice, then get back in rine to give brudd again."

Maureen reached out and grabbed Kenji's hand (this seemed to make her visitor very embarrassed). "Kenji, you are a *prince*! I am *so* glad

Jules didn't let me do anything nasty to you! It's not every night that Jules and I get to meet such a sterling example of humanity!"

Fifteen minutes later (Jules had to get water boiling again on the little propane camping stove on his kitchen floor; Kenji was a stickler when it came to "steri-rizing" that knife), Jules and Kenji returned with another mug of blood. Maureen looked even better than she had a quarter hour earlier. Her normal color had fully returned. She looked very... relaxed, Jules thought; relaxed and happy, maybe even... *tipsy?*

"C'mere, Jooooles," she purred, patting a space on the waterbed next to her. "I wanna snuggle while I have some more of that blood. C'mere, lover boy..."

Huh? What's up with her? Jules wondered. Maybe she was just relieved at having been rescued from starvation? Exceptionally grateful to him for finding Kenji?

She patted the bed again, more insistently this time, so he sat down next to her. She started playing with his hair while taking small, slow sips of blood, savoring both the taste of the blood and the feel of Jules' wavy white locks. She leaned over and began sucking, then nibbling on his ear. Her nibbles turned to bites. "*Oww!*" Jules said. "Not so *hard*, babe! That *hurts!*"

Maureen reared back in bed and laughed her biggest, horsiest laugh. She had no dainty, ladylike laughs in her repertoire — only snickers, sniggers, giggles, contemptuous "*HAs*", and that big, horsey guffaw. "Oh, Jules! I *love* you, hon! I feel so *good*... do you know that I can feel my *hair?* The hair on my head? Even all the hairs on my legs, 'cause I haven't shaved in weeks... *Sorry*, Kenji, that's 'too-much-information,' I know..." She brayed once more. "I'm like a, what d'you call it? A sea anemone? One of those things in an aquarium that's, like, all covered with red linguine noodles? And all the noodles wave back and forth, back and forth in the stream of bubbles that shoots out of the air hose in the aquarium tank? You ever seen one of those?"

"Sea anemone is very popurar in Japan," Kenji said. "To eat. Very de-ricious."

She looked at him sweetly. "Kenji, you wanna sit on the bed with Jules and me? It's really *comfortable*... Jules is like a great big *pillow*..."

Kenji smiled tightly, reddened, and stared down at his socks. "I wudd rather stand here, thank you. I am comfortable standing. But thank you for inviting me. You are a kind hostess."

"*Hostess*!" Maureen shouted suddenly. "I know what I want! *Hostess Twinkies*! You gotta get me a box of Twinkies, Jules! And — and there's *other* stuff I want, too! Guacamole Doritos, the green kind! And Sour Cream and Chives Ruffles! And those elf cookies that are covered in fudge, what are they called? *Keebler*, right? Isn't that the brand? Whatever — you can get me the generic store brand of fudge cookies if you can't find Keebler. And I want Little Debbie brownies, the ones that come individually wrapped, those are *awesome*—"

Jules extricated himself from his wife's sloppy embrace. Ever since her resurrection a few years ago, Maureen had guarded her new, svelte figure with fanatical determination. Now she wanted to pig out on junk food? "Uh, Mo, sweetie, you're actin' really, y'know, *weird*... Are you okay?"

"'Okay?' I'm *way* better than 'okay,' hon. I'm freakin' *super-duper*! And I'll be even super-*duperer* once you go out and get me my snacks. Okay? Will you go get me my snacks?"

"Babe, I'm big-time grateful to our pal Kenji, believe me; but I think drinkin' his blood mighta done somethin' to your head. It's like you just chugged down a fifth of Vodka—"

"I *know*!" Maureen beamed. "Isn't it *wonderful*? I'm *high*, Jules! I'm high as a kite! Tell you what — you be a good boy and head out and find me my snacks, and I *promise* I'll save some of this super-duper blood for you. You've really gotta try some, sweetie! Do we have a deal? Do we?"

Jules squirmed. "Babe, I don't think it's such a good idea, leavin' you by yourself. Not when you're in a state like this—"

Maureen grabbed his shoulders with the strength of a bull gorilla. "JULES! GO GET ME MY SNACKS! OR YOUR NAME IS MUD, MISTER!"

* * * * *

Jules and Kenji walked uptown along South Rampart Street, looking for a downtown convenience store which hadn't been completely cleaned out by looters in the days following Hurricane Antonia's passing.

"Your wife, she is very commanding," Kenji said. Jules noticed his companion tried making that sound like a compliment.

"Yeah, isn't she? Tell the truth, she's not any less 'commanding' when she's *not* high as a kite."

They passed a dark Holiday Inn, its side decorated with a fifteen-story-tall mural of a clarinet. Kenji eyed the mural with happy appreciation. "Jures-*san*, was this the prace of the birth home of Sidney Bechet, greatest of the Dixie-rand crarinet prayers?"

"Don't think so," Jules said, glancing up at the mural. "Actually, I don't think *any* of the birthplaces of the jazz greats from way back are still standin'. This whole area, where this hotel is and City Hall across the road there, and the empty place where the State Office Building used to be, and over by the Superdome? See it all? This all used to be a big, sprawling, run-down neighborhood, way back when. This was the neighborhood where Louie Armstrong grew up in, in fact. But it looked entirely different back then."

"Did the neighborhood get destroyed in your Civir War?"

"No, Kenji. The Civil War was back in the 1800s, somewheres around then. And New Orleans didn't get messed up in the Civil War."

"Was there a great fire, which burned down awr the birth homes of the jazz *sensei*? Back in Japan, Tokyo suffered many great fires. That is a reason why so few very ord buildings stirr stand."

"No, pal, it wasn't a big fire that did it. We did it ourselves. Didn't realize what we was gettin' rid of, I guess. If they'd managed to preserve

Louie Armstrong's birthplace, could you imagine the tourist attraction that'd be?"

"I wudd go visit, most certainry," Kenji said.

They walked another couple of dark blocks and came to the intersection of South Rampart Street and Perdido Street. A boarded-up three-story structure with a dignified but crumbling stone facade sat on the corner. To Jules, the building looked like a once-wealthy dowager who'd lost her family fortune and decided to let her appearance go to hell. "That's pretty much all that's left of the old neighborhood, that one old building there," Jules said, pointing across the street. "The Eagle Saloon and Oddfellow's Hall. That's one of the places Louie Armstrong used to blow his trumpet, when he was a teenager. Another couple of years, it'll probably get knocked down for another parking lot, just like all the other old buildings that used to stand around here."

Kenji stared at the building with dawning reverence. "Ohh, you must *save* it, Jures-*san!*"

"Me? I barely got two quarters to rub together, pal. I drive a cab for a livin'. Least I do when there are tourists around."

"Then I must return someday soon with my friends. We wirr earn money, and we wirr buy that buirding, and we wirr make it back into a jazz crub, where peopurr can come hear good music."

Jules smiled and clapped Kenji on the shoulder. "Nice idea. Hope it works out." *Boy oh boy, Kenji... you thought World War Two was tough? Try opening a business in this town!* But he wasn't in a mood to bust Kenji's bubble. Let the man have his dreams. "Tell you what — you turn that joint into a jazz club, and I'll pass out coupons to every fare who steps into my cab. I'll even discount my rate, special, for drivin' 'em over here. I'll get Maureen and my mother to stand on the corner there wearin' old-timey costumes and hand out leaflets."

"You wudd do that? Thank you, Jures-*san*." Kenji bowed. "I wirr terr my friends of your worthy promises."

They walked another block. Jules spotted a convenience mart that sold sodas, beer, snacks, and cheap souvenirs. Unlike other stores they had passed, which had been broken into and looted, this one was guarded by a sturdy roll-down metal security door, and its windows were armored with a screen of steel mesh.

"Hey, Kenji," Jules said, "I'm really curious about that super-power you said you have. Makin' big things small. I never seen that done before. You think you could give me a demonstration?"

"*Hai*. What wudd you rike me to make smawr?"

"How about that metal door there?"

Kenji walked to the roll-down security door and placed both of his palms flat upon it. He closed his eyes and appeared to concentrate hard. Then his hands began glowing with a phosphorescent green light. It spread to the metal of the door in a rapidly expanding radius.

The hairs on Jules' arms and the back of his neck tingled and stood on end. He stared more closely at the security door. It didn't seem that Kenji was projecting energy into the door — it looked more like he was sucking some kind of energy *out* of it.

The green glow spread to cover the entire surface of the roll-down door. Then, with a sudden POP! — a rush of air into a briefly created vacuum — the door vanished. Or had it? Jules glanced down at the sidewalk. There was the roll-up door, motorized mechanism and all, reduced to six inches tall. A toy version of itself.

"Well, give me wings and call me a five hundred-pound skeeter!" Jules murmured, kneeling down to take a closer look at the miniaturized door. "You did it. You really did it. I always thought that stuff about Japanese superheroes was just a bunch of hooey to sell manga comics and anime videos. But you really *do* have a super-power."

"Of course," Kenji said. "Wudd I make something rike that up?"

Kenji's hands continued glowing green. The green glow slowly climbed his arms. "Uh, Kenji," Jules said, staring nervously at the glow, "what now? It looks like that energy's takin' you over..."

"Oh, it does me no hurt," Kenji said. "With it now, I can do any of three things. I can absorb it into my body, and it makes me stronger for a day or two. Or I can pass it arong to my friends, Emiko or Shogo. They are superheroes, too. We are a superhero family. Emiko, my sister, her superhero name is *Anime Onnanoko*. In Engrish, that is Anime Girr. Shogo, my cousin, is *Kawaii Kowai Otoko*. In Engrish, that is Cutie-Scary Man."

"Sounds better in Japanese, I bet," Jules said.

"Or I can do this, the third thing." He held his arms straight up and pointed his palms at the stars. The green energy shot out of his palms in a series of Roman candle-like bursts. It soared high into the sky, to twice the height of the Holiday Inn hotel, then soundlessly exploded into a chain of flower-like green puffs which blotted out the moon and most of the stars surrounding it.

"Whoa," Jules said, watching the expanding petals of green energy lengthen into filaments, expending themselves and gradually fading from sight. He sniffed the air. It smelled vaguely like lime-scented Right Guard deodorant spray. "I'll bet you're a really popular guy on New Year's Eve."

"Many companies hire us to do this at times of festiverrs and openings of new stores."

Jules turned back to the convenience mart, now denuded of its steel security door. Kenji had saved Jules the trouble of ripping apart the roll-down door. He'd probably also saved the owner's insurance company some money; Jules was sure he would've caused a whole lot more damage removing the door his way than Kenji had caused doing it his. Jules wrenched the remaining door's handle loose with comparatively little effort. "Okay. Time to go get Maureen's snacks. Don't want to leave her alone for too long."

He stepped inside, squeezed behind the cash register counter, located a couple of large plastic bags, and then began pacing the store's aisles, grabbing bags of chips and boxes of cookies. "Hey, Kenji? You want me to grab you some beer? Sorry they don't have any of that *sake* stuff you Japs drink, but you do like beer, right? If we're gonna throw a party, might as well throw it for all of us. You got a brand of beer you like? Kenji?"

He looked around him. He didn't spot his companion. He went back to the door. Kenji had remained outside, staring down at the sidewalk, his hands clenched into fists at his sides.

"Kenji? Anything the matter? I asked what kinda beer you like."

Kenji did not look up at him. "I must aporrogize, Jures-*san*," he said gravely. "By using my superpower, I have rured you into a crime. I have made you do this bad thing. I have brought shame upon you and your famirry."

"What? You mean liftin' these snacks? Kenji, it's *okay*. The whole city's been flooded out, almost. It's like the end of the world, kinda. I mean, like, in *The World, the Flesh, and the Devil*, did Harry Belafonte get his knickers in a twist over grabbin' whatever food he could find? In *The Omega Man*, did Chuck Heston give a shit about liftin' his groceries? No, he was too busy fightin' albino zombies! Hell, he made it a habit of stealin' Ford convertibles outta showrooms in downtown LA, and he was the movie's *hero*. Now, I'll admit I ain't no Chuck Heston — who is? — but I figure in the long run, ain't nobody gonna miss these bags of Doritos too much. A man's gotta do what a man's gotta do. So what kinda beer do you want? Pick one that tastes okay warm."

Kenji, still staring downward, waved his hand in front of his nose as though he were warding off a swarm of gnats. "No no no no," he said. "This is not the action of a superhero, Jures-*san*."

Jules sighed. He dug his wallet out of his pants. "Will it make you feel better if I leave the owner some cash to cover it?"

Kenji looked up and smiled slightly. "*Hai*, Jures-*san*. That wirr make it better. Do they have a beer cawrred Kirin?"

Kenji had to make do with a six pack of Rolling Rock ("I rike the green botterrs"). Maureen was thrilled with the stash of goodies Jules brought home. She immediately set about satisfying her munchies, tearing packages open with happy abandon. She also directed Jules to the big mug of intoxicating blood she had left for him on the nightstand.

"Kenji, pal," Jules said, "how about you crack open one of them beers while I try out this super-duper blood of yours that Mo's raving about?"

Kenji bowed. "*Hai*, Jures-*san*. Thank you for your hospitarity. It is good to drink with friends."

"Our pleasure, Kenji, darling!" Maureen giggled through a mouth full of Guacamole Doritos. "I'm having so much *fun!*" She licked her green-dusted fingers clean.

Jules took a cautious sip of the blood. *Damned if it isn't as delicious as Mo said it was*, he thought. He took another sip, then another. He swallowed a big mouthful after letting it linger on his tongue a few seconds. *Better slow down*, he told himself. *No sense in overdoin' it, not till I got some idea how this stuff's gonna affect me.*

He stared out the window next to the bed. A big bottle fly crawled across the glass pane, attracted by the light of the candles inside. Jules lazily started thinking about *The Fly*, one of his all-time favorite movies. Not the remake; the original version, from the Fifties. The one that ended with the little fly with the human head and arm, trapped in a web as a spider moved in for the kill, screaming in a shrill voice, "Heeeellp meeee! *Heeeeeellp meeeeee!*"

Jules took a closer look at the bottle fly. It had his mother's head and was wearing her favorite gingham house dress. It waved at him. It was holding a teeny-tiny frying pan with teeny-tiny fried eggs in it.

He closed his eyes and shook his head. Then he opened his eyes and took another look. The bottle fly was a typical bottle fly again.

Whoa...

He decided to try an experiment. He cleared his mind and waited for an image to appear or for words to drift through his head. The phrase "crab claws" floated through that cramped region of his brain dedicated to verbal processing and abstract reasoning. All right; maybe he was getting the munchies, too. *Crab claws. Okay. Crab claws. I'm gonna look down at my hands now and see if they've changed to crab claws.*

He stared down at his hands with their fat fingers, each joint puffed up like a plump marshmallow with excess white flesh. They looked just as they had for at least the past five decades or so. Not a bit of difference.

"Hon, how are you feeling?" Maureen asked. "Is anything *interesting* happening?"

He glanced over at his wife. She had become a five-foot eight-inch long crawfish. She lolled in bed with a bag of Chips Ahoy! cookies in her claw, each of her antennae stalks puncturing three marshmallows, as if she were heading for a campfire, intending to make some s'mores.

"Aaak..."

"Jules, are you *okay*? Are you choking?"

He clenched his eyes shut again and shook his head, more desperately this time. When he dared open his eyes again, Maureen was back to her typical, if not normal, self. He grabbed the side of the water bed mattress and clenched it tightly. *Don't think*, he told himself. *Until this crazy blood wears off, don't think about* nuthin'. *Shouldn't be that hard — Mo always complains I hardly got two thoughts to rub together in my head...*

Still, he didn't like how Maureen was staring at him. Now Kenji was doing it, too. He needed to do something to get the attention off him. Why were they staring at him? They could be staring at anything in this whole room, or anything outside the window, like that damned stupid bottle fly... but they were staring at *him*. He needed to do something fast, before they stared at him another second. "Hey..." he managed to mutter. His lips felt weird, as if they'd become water balloons filled with Vaseline. "Hey, Kenji, how're you doin'? How's that beer?"

"Oh, it is very fine, Jures-*san*. Very fine."

"Not too warm for ya?"

"Warm is fine, is okay. Sometimes we drink our beer rike this in Japan. I was thinking about something, Jures-*san*. A question I want to ask you. I aporrogize if this is too forward. You told me you are a paramedic from St. Rouis. Yet your wife has this house. Do you have *two* houses, one here, and one in St. Rouis?"

Maureen laughed her big, horsey laugh. "Kenji, darling, Jules was *shitting* you. He's never been in St. Louis in his life, or his un-life, neither. Paramedic? HA! Jules couldn't explain the difference between a paramedic and a para*chute*. He was telling you a fairy tale, dear."

Ordinarily, Jules would take umbrage at Maureen's unflattering insinuations about his intellect. But tonight, getting offended seemed like too much effort. He let himself settle more deeply into the pillows on the bed. "Maureen, there's a difference between tellin' a fairy tale and, y'know, *strategic disinformation*." He was proud that he remembered that lingo from reading the newspapers during World War Two. "What I told Kenji, that was me guardin' my secret identity. Since Kenji's a superhero himself, I'm sure he knows all about that."

Kenji's face lit up. "Ah! So you were protecting your civiran secret identity! I have heard of such things with American superheroes. Bat-Man, he is rearry Bruce Wayne. Spiderman, he is rearry Peter Parker..."

"But Aquaman's just Aquaman," Maureen said. Then she belched and giggled.

"In Japan," Kenji said, "we superheroes do not have secret identity. We have superhero name, but everyone knows who we are when we are not dressed in costume. Jures-*san*, did you have a costume?"

"Sure I did! My superhero name was the Hooded Terror. So... can you guess what my costume was?"

Kenji thought about this some. "A... hood?"

"Yeah, that's right! A hood!"

Maureen thought this was hilarious. She laughed so hard that she peppered Jules' face with flecks of Doritos. This got Jules guffawing. Then even Kenji joined in.

Everybody had to pause to wipe their eyes. "So... so I ran around in this... this *hood*—" Everyone laughed again, including Jules. "And... and I beat up on Nazis who were tryin' to blow up the Higgins Boats plant, or freighters loadin' up with supplies at the docks. I beat 'em up, then I drank their blood."

"Did Nazi blood taste different from American blood?" Maureen said.

Kenji's hand shot into the air, holding a green beer bottle. "Rike difference between Heineken and Ro-ring Rock!" he said.

This time they laughed so hard and so long that Jules and Maureen both begged Kenji for mercy, but he kept repeating his punch line, and they all kept on laughing. Until the sky started to lighten, and Jules reluctantly closed the bedroom's storm shutters, told Kenji the party was over, wished him a safe drive across the bridge, and tossed his new friend the keys to his Cadillac.

In the months that followed, parties at Maureen's and Jules' house became a weekly tradition. Kenji not only continued donating his own blood to his friends; he also started a blood drive among his fellow Red Cross volunteers, telling them he had met a reclusive hemophiliac in the French Quarter.

So this was how Maureen got through the great Antonia Disaster. Jules and Maureen, listening to their shortwave radio, would occasionally hear news stories about mysterious occurrences of wrecked barges and fishing boats, which had floated ashore during the storm and blocked critical roads, disappearing overnight, without the Army Corps of Engineers having hauled them away. They knew their friend Kenji, the Bonsai Master, had secretly been behind it.

Kenji diligently delivered blood to his friends, although as the weeks passed he fretted more and more about the partners he had left behind in Japan, his sister and his cousin, whose powers could not function normally for very long without Kenji's presence. The Army Corps of Engineers repaired the broken levees and pumped the city dry. Wide swathes of New Orleans stank like rotting catfish left to putrefy in the sun. But as soon as the flood water had been pumped out and the levees had been declared at least nominally safe, the people began to return to their homes, a few hundred at first, then thousands. At last, nearly three months after his arrival in New Orleans, Kenji bid his friends farewell.

But he promised them he would return.

Nine

A new celebration in every neighborhood, every day and night: that's how things rolled for a time after the storm refugees began returning home. Excuses for a party (or at least a beer or two) abounded. Residents reoccupied lightly or moderately damaged homes. Beloved neighborhood businesses reopened their doors, their renewed activity bringing with it a sense of rebirth for the surrounding streets. The Big Easy, left for dead only months before, began sluggishly stirring to life.

The single reopening that Jules looked forward to the most was the night the Trolley Stop Café began serving their giant omelets and bottomless cups of coffee again. The modest restaurant, with its homey streetcar paraphernalia (it was located only steps from the St. Charles Avenue Streetcar Line), generous portions, wisecracking wait staff, and late-night operating hours, was a big favorite of the city's cops and taxi drivers. Even more importantly to Jules, it had been the place where he and Maureen had celebrated their wedding.

He tried convincing Maureen to go with him to the big reopening, but she begged off, saying she was tired, and she wasn't anxious to immerse herself in what would undoubtedly be a standing-room-only crowd. So instead, Jules insisted that his mother and Doc Landrieu accompany him. Edna had emerged from her long hibernation apparently cured of her bloodlust; at minimum, it had gone into remission. Still, her husband insisted on keeping a close eye on her consumption choices. At the Trolley Stop, Jules steered his mother toward a potato and onion omelet and away from a steak, which he suspected she would have ordered rare to the point of bleeding.

He returned home in an exhilarated mood. His reunions with so many friendly acquaintances among his fellow cab drivers and the Trolley Stop staff had gotten him almost as high as he'd been after swilling down a pint of Kenji Tezuka's extraordinary blood. He found Maureen sitting on one of the couches in the parlor, reading a romance novel. "Mo, you shoulda gone with us! I can't tell you how *great* it was to see everybody — even the assholes I can't stand! The coffee's just as good as it ever was. Amos couldn't fault it, and you know how picky he is about his java. Hey, I even saw Erato..."

That perked up Maureen's ears. "Is he talking with you again?"

A little air leaked out of Jules' balloon. "Naw... I still freak him out," he said, sadly. "He made sure to stay on the far end of the bar from me. I waved at him, but he pretended not to see. Still, just knowin' he's back in town again, back in his house, back drivin' his cab, it made me feel good. No matter how much he avoids me." Jules had been forced to reveal his true nature to his friend just prior to Jules' and Maureen's wedding. Since then, Erato, a devout Christian, had not spoken a word to his former buddy, repulsed, Jules figured, by a combination of religious revulsion and understandable, human fear.

"Hey," Jules said, grabbing his wife's hands, "how about we go to the Trolley Stop tomorrow night, just you and me? It might be less crowded. It'd bring back memories of our wedding night..."

Jules felt Maureen's fingers twitch in his grasp. She pulled her hands away. "I, uh... I don't think so, Jules. I just haven't been feeling social. I haven't been sleeping well. Not since Kenji left town."

"You miss his special blood that much, huh?"

"It's not just that. I've been having nightmares. Awful nightmares."

"I know you been thrashing around a lot in the middle of the night. It's been wakin' me up. How come you haven't told me about these dreams till now?"

"I — I didn't want to worry you."

"What kinda nightmares you been havin', Mo?"

"Mostly about being deprived of blood. Being trapped in my bedroom while I'm starving. I went through some awful nights, Jules, before you met Kenji..."

Jules turned a deep shade of crimson. "Y'know, babe, I did the best I could for ya. I even got my hide shot fulla hot lead, tryin' to find you a meal..."

"I know you did, honey. But I've been through a trauma. And the nightmares aren't only about me starving. I've had stranger, more terrible dreams. About Victoria and Alexandra and Flora Ann attacking me with knives, trying to retrieve their — *my* body parts. In other dreams, I seem to wake up in my own bed, with you next to me, and my arms and legs are pulling away from me, trying to detach themselves from my torso, trying to tear my head off my neck... so my arms and legs can go back to their original owners."

"Jeeze... you think maybe you oughta talk with somebody? Talk with a professional?"

"Now *who* would I talk with, Jules? I can't very well go see a mortal psychiatrist, can I?"

"Well... I mean, there's Doodlebug. Now that the airport's open again, I'm sure he'd be willin' to fly in."

"Doodlebug is a *guru*, Jules. A spiritualist. Not a medical professional."

"Then how about your father-in-law? I know Amos was a coroner in his first life, not a head-shrinker. But a doctor's a doctor, right?"

Maureen shook her head. "I don't want to pester Amos. He's got his hands full with your mother right now. I'm hoping the nightmares will go away by themselves. Once things get back to normal." She bit her lower lip. "Things *will* get back to normal, won't they? I know you've been complaining how slow the taxi business has been. I'd hate to have to go back to hostessing at my old club or some joint like it... but our funds have been getting low. And with so few fares to victimize, you've barely been bringing home enough blood for the two of us..."

"That's what I wanted to talk with you about, Mo. I know we been livin' on the edge ever since Kenji went back to Japan. But I got a plan of how to change all that. I came up with a *great* idea tonight. Lemme tell you all about it."

She stared at him dubiously. "What *kind* of idea, Jules? Aside from getting married, most of your ideas haven't worked out all that well..."

"This one's gonna be different, babe. Even Amos thinks this is a great idea." He scooted next to her on the couch and put his arm around her shoulders. As the excess flesh on his leg cascaded familiarly over her thigh and hip, he felt her thigh muscles quiver with revulsion, as though they'd been enveloped by a giant jellyfish. Similarly, her shoulder and arm jerked away from him. "Hey," he said, "I'm just tryin' to be affection-ate, Mo. What gives?"

Now it was Maureen's turn to blush. "I — I'm sorry. It's not you, Jules. I just haven't been myself lately. It's not only the nightmares — my body's been doing some weird things..."

"You get yourself checked out by Doc, okay? No excuses, young lady."

"Okay... I will." She made an effort to snuggle into him, but Jules could tell her body resisted her, squirming and jerking away from him at the slightest contact. After a few seconds, she gave up and scooted away, to the far edge of the couch. She blushed again. "How about telling me all about these big plans of yours?" she said with forced enthusiasm.

"Yeah, sure. See, you ever wanna know what's goin' on in this town, the people you gotta talk with are the cops and the cabbies. They got their fingers on the pulse. So, anyway, there I am at the Trolley Stop counter tonight, shootin' the bull with all my old buddies. Some of them start talkin' about all these grants FEMA and the Small Business Association are givin' out. Them two agencies, they're shovelin' money out the door like crazy, to anybody who wants to start a small business in New Orleans. Part of the disaster recovery. You don't got to have no prior experience runnin' a business or nuthin'. You just write up a business plan, and they write you a check."

"Do you have to pay this money back, Jules? Because for you, that could pose a problem."

"See, that's the beauty part. They wanna encourage hiring, gettin' everybody who returns to New Orleans back to work. So if you can show you've hired at least three employees, and if you keep 'em on your payroll for at least a year, the loans from the government get forgiven. They get turned into grants, and you don't hafta pay 'em back. So it's, like, free money."

"Jules, you've never been anybody's boss before. You can barely manage to boss *yourself*—"

"Just hear me out, will ya? You seen them dudes in black top hats and white face makeup walkin' around the Quarter at night, leadin' crowds of people around, tellin' 'em stories?"

"You mean the tour guides? The ones who lead ghost tours of the French Quarter? Those so-called 'haunted tours'?"

"Yeah, those guys. They're basically, what, professional bullshitters, right? They charge tourists fifteen bucks a head for what's pretty much a buncha dumb-ass bullshit about haunted houses and ghosts and stuff. Well, who's the best bullshitter you know? *Me*, right?"

"*You* want to lead ghost tours?"

"Not ghost tours — *vampire* tours! Picture this — I can dress up in a cheesy Count Dracula costume and put on white makeup and have fake blood drippin' from the side of my mouth. Tourists'll figure I'm an actor pretendin' to be a vampire, right? When really, I'll be a vampire pretendin' to be an actor pretendin' to be a vampire. Get it? I can come up with plenty of great bullshit stories about vampires in the French Quarter, but I can mix in real stories, too, about the Malice X gang and the High Krewe. The customers, they won't know the difference. And, y'know, I'll make it educational, too. So them tourists get good value for their money. 'Cause I was actually alive durin' the early days of jazz, and I remember Storyville, and the French Quarter before it got turned into a tourist trap. So I can tell them real history, eyewitness stuff."

Maureen sniffed. "How are you supposed to find customers?"

"That's what the grant money'll help with. We'll advertise on the Internet. I can get a bunch of them laminated leaflets made up and pay restaurants to stick 'em in display boxes by their cash registers, and concierges at hotels to hand 'em out. Here's the thing. We'll advertise ourselves as 'the *Real* New Orleans Vampire Tour.' For customers who are willin' to give a blood donation, we'll only charge three bucks a head, when all our competitors are chargin' fifteen or twenty bucks a head."

"A *blood donation?*"

"Yeah! It'll make us unique. Maybe we'll even get written up in big magazines, like *The National Enquirer*, or featured on Oprah's show, or somethin'. Say you wanna take the tour. You can either pay full price, twelve bucks, or you can pay just three bucks and let Doc Landrieu, a licensed professional doctor, withdraw a pint of the red stuff. All part of 'the *Real* Vampire Experience.' We say to our customers, wink-wink, the blood's for us vampires to gulp down later, wink-wink. In small print, it says all blood donations go to the Crescent City Blood Bank. Which, of course, doesn't exist. 'Cause, wink-wink, us vampires are actually takin' the blood home with us and storin' it in our freezers. You get it, Mo? Once I get this goin', we'll have us a sweet set-up like the High Krewe's, or Doodlebug's out in California. A regular, dependable supply of blood for us, without us havin' to go out and murder anybody."

Maureen crinkled her brows, but she looked a smidgeon less dubious than she had before. "So who are these three employees you'll be keeping on the payroll for at least a year?"

"Well, there's Doc, for one. He'll be the main phleb — , uh, y'know, blood withdrawal guy. You can help Doc out with drawin' the blood, and also help me out with leadin' the tours. Folks like them sexy female vampires, y'know. And Mom can sell souvenirs, vampire T-shirts and whatnot. You know the sorta shirts I'm talkin' about — 'My Parents Went on a *Real* New Orleans Vampire Tour and All I Got was This SUCKY T-shirt!' That kinda thing."

Maureen crossed her arms tightly. "Do you think this could actually work, Jules? It *sounds* good, but so many of your schemes have had unhappy endings..."

"Honey, this is practically a surefire thing! Have you ever seen any of those ghost tour guys go outta business? How many ghost tours can a tourist go on, though? Now, a *Real* New Orleans Vampire Tour — that'll be unique! And folks'll figure they're doin' a good deed while they're havin' their fun, what with givin' a blood donation. Like I said, even Doc thinks this is a good idea. And Doc's nobody's fool."

"But what if tourists don't come back to New Orleans? What if everybody assumes the *entire city* got flooded out and destroyed, even though the French Quarter and Uptown hardly got damaged?"

"You leave that up to the Tourism and Marketing Board, hon. I'm sure FEMA's givin' them a shitload of money to promote the hell outta New Orleans and convince the tourists to come back. We can get in on the ground floor, see? Maybe other attractions won't be startin' back up again; maybe their owners are gonna stay in those other cities they evacuated to. We can help pick up the slack. Don't you wanna be part of the rebuilding of New Orleans, Mo? Don't you wanna do your civic duty? Not takin' that free money FEMA's handin' out — under the circumstances, it would be *immoral*. Anti-American, even."

"Well... if you put it that way... I suppose I can't very well say I won't help. Especially not if Amos and your mother are going to be involved, and since I'll be drinking some of whatever blood you manage to bring home. But I want to help in my *own* way, Jules. As a full, equal *partner*. Don't you *dare* suggest I work as your flunky. I can't even be your employee, unless it's just on paper, for the sake of earning that grant. It wouldn't be healthy for our marriage, believe me."

Jules held up his hands, palms out, in a sign of surrender. "Yeah, yeah, *sure*, babe. However you wanna work it. I'm flexible. So, you got any ideas about how you could help out the family business?"

Maureen rubbed her porcelain chin. "Oh, I'm sure I'll think of *something*, Jules."

The idea Maureen came up with combined several of her interests and talents: show business, advertising, and silly old horror movies. She realized her old profession, stripping, was no longer an option. The surgical scars left over from Doc Landrieu's piecing together of her patchwork body put a damper on that; whereas there existed a significant population of men who would pay good money to see a grossly obese woman take off her clothes, the number of men aroused by the sight of post-surgical scars could comfortably fit in an old-fashioned phone booth. If stretch marks were generally a no-no with the managers of profits-seeking titty bars, then train track scars straight out of *The Curse of Frankenstein* were definitely beyond the pale. She could waitress just fine with her scars covered up, but she had decided that waitressing and hostessing were beneath her. Maureen had been a minor star on the New Orleans stripping circuit for decades, and she had gotten used to being the center of attention.

However, she knew of one profession for which two of her rather unique attributes — her lurid scars and her inability to be photographed or visually broadcast — would be assets. Horror hostess. True, the market for horror hostesses was exceedingly small, but Maureen figured there was always room for one more good one. Hadn't Elvira, Mistress of the Dark, hit the big time? Maureen figured she possessed oodles of advantages over someone like Elvira. First of all, she was a real-life horror herself, not a pretend horror, and she slept next to a worse horror. Her whole life was one big, long special effect. An hour of research on the Internet revealed dozens upon dozens of terrible old horror movies which had fallen into the public domain and were available to be freely exploited; virtually all of them she had watched multiple times over her long decades with Jules, enough times that she had memorized much of the most atrocious dialogue.

A dumpy old office building squatting in the shadows of the elevated Pontchartrain Expressway, at the corner of Canal Street and Claiborne Avenue, just a few blocks from Maureen's home, housed a public access cable TV studio. In the wake of the storm, the studio (a barely watered offshoot of the cable monopoly which operated in New Orleans) had lost many of its regular programmers. It had multiple slots to fill, many of those slots in the late-night hours. Once she got her horror hostess idea in her head, Maureen was all over the station manager, like fleas on a mule. After a couple of nights of badgering him, she had her own three-hour slot, six nights a week, from eleven at night to two in the morning.

She told Jules she would interrupt her showings of the terrible old horror movies (which would benefit from as many interruptions as possible, actually) with frequent commercial breaks, during which she would flack tickets for the *Real* New Orleans Vampire Tour and also sell promotional items and vampire souvenirs. Most importantly, she would make the tours a regular part of her broadcasts; she'd have Jules bring his groups to her studio at the close of each tour, at which point the customers could make their own disparaging remarks about whatever miserable movie was being shown and pose on camera with the horror hostess (and then purchase DVD copies of the episode in which they had appeared).

"See, honey," Maureen explained to her husband, "that'll make your *Real* New Orleans Vampire Tours even *more* exciting and unique. I mean, who doesn't want to be on a TV show? I'll bet we'll make even more money off DVD sales to tour customers than you make off tour tickets. And it's what they call 'holistic marketing.' I learned all about that from Mike Dumbowski, my last manager over at Jezebel's Joy Room. Mike always said you have to give your customers multiple opportunities to buy things from you, lots and lots of reasons to spend money. That's what's holistic about it — 'whole-istic,' as in, you get them to spend their whole wads with you before they leave. Amazon Dot Com got to be a multi-trillion-dollar company that way. That's what Mike said."

"Amazon Dot Com, huh?" Jules rubbed the side of his head. "I dunno about this, Maureen... Straussman, your blood-daddy, warned me to be extra careful about keepin' you under wraps, makin' sure the High Krewe's Triumvirate never find out that you're back from your grave. I'm not so sure havin' you host your own cable TV show's the best way to keep you undercover, y'know?"

Maureen stubbornly placed her fists on her hips (which, Jules couldn't help but notice with pleasure, had become a bit more expansive since her frequent pig-out sessions resulting from drinking Kenji's blood). "Jules Duchon, I *refuse* to live my life cowering in fear from Bestoff, Krauss, and Katz. Besides, those old fuddy-duddies would no more turn on a cable TV horror movie show than they would dance around Jackson Square dressed in feather boas, listening to acid rock on their iPods. It's just not going to happen."

"Yeah, but what if some of the younger vampires in the High Krewe tune in some night? What if they recognize their comatose sisters' body parts?"

"Jules, I'll hardly be recognizable! I'll be wearing costumes that'll cover my entire body, and thick makeup all over my face, and a wig, and contact lenses, so I can be seen on TV. I'll use a stage name, all right? How about 'Morganna the Marvelous?' That sounds like a horror host-ess."

Jules couldn't help but see the excitement on his wife's face. He hadn't seen her this enthused about any activity since they'd made love on their wedding night. He hardly had the heart to continue arguing with her. Besides, he knew he had as much chance of winning that argument as he did of winning the Powerball lottery. Probably less.

"Oh... all right," he said.

She flung her arms around his neck. Just as quickly, her arms sprang off him, as though his skin were electrified.

"Uh, Mo, you really need to get that checked out..."

"I will, I will, I promise." She gave him a quick peck on the cheek. At least her lips didn't seem to think he was a leper. "Oh, *thank you,* Jules! This is going to be so fantastic! I'm going to be a TV star!"

Ten

EVEN in famously corrupt, shadowy New Orleans, government business was generally conducted in the sunlight, or at least during daytime hours. For a group of vampires seeking to establish their own business, this posed a problem.

Making use of his numerous contacts at City Hall, and subtly deploying threats of an Americans with Disabilities Act lawsuit when he had to (mentioning that both his son-in-law and daughter-in-law suffered from an acute, morbid sensitivity to sunlight), Amos Landrieu cajoled the necessary representatives from FEMA, the Small Business Administration, the City of New Orleans Health Department, and a myriad of city business licensing bureaus to conduct their interviews, paperwork reviews, and signings of documents with Jules and Maureen in a series of after-sundown meetings. The next six weeks blurred together for Jules into a nail-biting nightmare of bureaucratic hang-ups; if it weren't for the steadying hand of Doc Landrieu on his shoulder at all times, Jules would've screamed "the *hell* with this *shit!*" approximately three dozen times and would've fanged at least that many bureaucrats.

But, incredibly enough, after six weeks had passed, Jules found himself the owner and operator of his own small business. His mother claimed this was a heaven-sent miracle, due entirely to the rosaries she had convinced her kind neighbors to recite on Jules' behalf (she would've recited them herself, she told her son, only nowadays she couldn't touch a set of rosary beads without setting her hands on fire).

Jules, always on the superstitious side, had Maureen, his mother, and Amos all kiss the start-up grant check for good luck before he deposited it in the bank. Then he, his family, his cab driver buddies, and Maureen's stripper and bartender friends from Jezebel's Joy Room spent the next two weeks carpet bombing the city's reopened hotels, restaurants, bars, and coffee houses with leaflets and laminated cards advertising the inaugural tour of the *Real* New Orleans Vampire Tours Company. Jules spread around the payola as necessary, doing his best to keep the bribes for concierges and managers to less than eye-smarting levels. Amos gathered the necessary phlebotomy equipment. Maureen ordered the initial run of souvenir T-shirts, paid a group of local high school computer nerds to build a website, and prepared scripts and costumes for her initial week of TV episodes, scheduled to coincide with Jules' first week of tours. Edna busied herself knitting from sundown to sunrise, creating dozens of adorable, if somewhat creepy sock monkey vampire dolls and vampire tea cozies.

Finally, the big night arrived.

Maureen, already dressed in her TV costume but not having yet made herself up, grabbed her bulky makeup bag and cast a worrying glance at the phlebotomy chairs and cots which crowded her parlor. "Jules, you won't let any of the tourists make a mess in here, will you? Doc's had practice with those arm-stickers, hasn't he? I mean, he's not going to accidentally spray someone's blood all over my curtains...?"

"Don't you worry yourself none, Mo," Jules said. "I won't let nobody make a mess. Besides, Mom'll be in here sellin' her souvenirs. She'll watch everybody like a hawk; you know how she is. And Doc's as good as they come with that blood-drawing stuff. You just keep your pretty head focused on your show, okay? Break a wing tonight, babe."

"You mean break a *leg*, Jules."

"I mean a *wing* — a bat wing. You're a vampire, right, 'Morganna?'"

"Yes, but a vampiress who can't change into a bat anymore."

"Well, whatever... just have a great show, hon. Enjoy yourself, and everybody'll enjoy it along with you. What movie are you puttin' on to-night?"

"*The Last Man on Earth*, with Vincent Price."

"Oh, that's a *good* one. Ol' Vince against a whole planet full of vam-pires. Great choice, babe. You can never go wrong with Vincent Price, that's fer sure. Well, I'll see you in a few hours, hon. I'm sure the custom-ers'll be jazzed about gettin' to appear on TV."

He gave her a kiss on the cheek, taking care not to touch her any-where lower than her chin (she still hadn't gotten that weird jumpiness checked out, but he mentally excused this, knowing how busy they all had been). When she left the house, he avoided glancing out the door, not wanting to see yet if anyone had gathered on the sidewalk outside to wait for the start of the nine o'clock tour. He didn't want to jinx matters by looking. He kept the curtains drawn, fighting an impulse to take a peek.

He paced the parlor, obsessively adjusting the positions of the phle-botomy chairs and cots, and disturbing his mother by fiddling with her display of vampire sock monkeys, tea cozies, and souvenir buttons and shirts. At last, at eight-fifty, he couldn't take the uncertainty anymore.

"Doc," he said, his voice taut with anxiety, "take a look outside for me. Tell me how many people are out there. I can't look myself. It might ruin things."

Amos obliged his son-in-law by momentarily pulling aside a curtain. "Hmmnn... not bad, Jules. Not bad, at all, especially not for an opening night. I count twenty-three customers waiting for our tour. A few are dressed up as vampires themselves—"

"Oh!" Jules said. "Thanks for remindin' me! I almost forgot my cape!" He rushed to a closet and pulled out a jumbo-sized black cape, lined with red satin fabric. He'd had to special-order it from an online costume shop that specialized in costumes for the big and husky; even they hadn't had his size in stock.

"There are three odd birds out there, Jules," Amos said. "They look like they got directions to the wrong costume party. I'd say they're Japanese, judging from the symbols on their outfits. Two men in superhero costumes, and a young woman in a frilly dress and bonnet made from the same shiny, synthetic material. I suppose we'll just have to expect a certain level of eccentricity among our customers... no skin off our noses. It doesn't matter what they chose to wear, so long as a decent number of them are willing to donate blood..."

"Wait a minute," Jules said. He strode to the window. "You said there are three Japs out there, dressed in superhero costumes—?" He pulled the curtain aside so he could see. "Holy mackerel! That's *Kenji*! He's wearin' his Bonsai Master outfit. And I'll bet those other two are his sister and his cousin. Doc, they came all the way from Japan! Kenji's the guy who got Maureen through the disaster!"

"The Red Cross volunteer you told me about?"

"Yeah! That's him! What a swell surprise this is!"

Unable to contain his excitement, Jules flung the front door open, starting the tour six minutes early. "Greetings, folks!" he boomed from the top of his stoop. "Welcome to the *Real* New Orleans Vampire Tour, the only tour in New Orleans that's run by real vampires. I invite y'all to enter my abode. I hafta say that, y'know, in case there are any other vampires out there among you. Accordin' to our lore, a vampire can't enter someone's home without havin' first been properly invited. Oh, and here are some ground rules. If you're wearin' a cross or a Star of David or some other religious necklace, please be considerate and tuck it inside your shirt. No tossin' holy water on your tour guides; you may think it's a gag, but *I* don't. And if you gotta use a mirror... aww, heck, I guess there ain't no good reason you *can't* use a mirror. Just don't expect to see *my* reflection, that's all."

The crowd, including several children, climbed the steps and shuffled into Jules' front parlor and dining room. Jules directed them to line up in front of the souvenirs table, where his mother sat, armed with a cash register and a credit card swiper. "Tickets are twelve bucks for adults, six bucks for kids ten and under. Of course, if you want the full vampire experience, you can donate a pint of blood, which lets you buy a discounted ticket for only three dollars. That's the way to go, folks. Dr. Amos Landrieu is a licensed phlebotomist, one of the best in the business. We call him 'Mister Painless.' When he sticks ya, you won't know what hit ya." Amos waved from the corner, where he waited with his blood extraction equipment.

One of the customers, a man in his mid-twenties, chuckled. "So, like, this blood donation thing isn't just a gag? It's for real?"

"Sure it's for real," Jules said. "A vampire's gotta *eat*, don't he?"

"I guess... So what do you *do* with the blood, anyway?"

Jules did an exaggerated double-take. "*Drink it*, of course! What *else* would a buncha vampires do with blood? Use it to water our petunias with? Sheesh!"

A curly-haired boy of about eight years, the son of a couple in their mid-thirties, approached Jules. He wore a Disney Store sweatshirt with a picture of the White Rabbit from *Alice in Wonderland* on its front. "So *you're* a vampire?" he said, staring at Jules' massive stomach, then up at his pudgy face. He said it in the same tone as he would've while inquiring whether Jules were truly Santa Claus — the tone of a too-smart-for-his-years child whose bullshit detector was set to maximum sensitivity.

"Sure I'm a vampire," Jules insisted. "You wanna see my fangs?" He bared his teeth for the youngster.

"Ooooh, *nice* fangs!" piped up a young woman dressed in her own vampire outfit. She shot Jules a thumbs-up.

"Anybody who wants to buy a discount ticket," Jules said, "sit your-selves down on one of them blood extraction chairs or lie down on a cot, and Doc Landrieu will be right with ya. A cup of delicious Florida orange juice is included in the price of a discount ticket. The rest of you, line up and pay my mother. Oh, and while you're waitin' for the brave blood do-nors to get finished up, spend some time perusin' our line of exclusive vampire souvenirs."

Nine of the twenty-three customers chose the discount option. Among them were Kenji and his two companions. Jules eagerly walked over to where his friend had sat on one of the phlebotomy chairs. "Man oh man," Jules said, "what a *surprise* to see you back in town! Great to have you back, Kenji! Maureen's gonna be *thrilled!*"

Kenji smiled. "It is good to see you, too, Jures-*san.* Arroww me to introduce my sister, Emiko, and our cousin, Shogo. I spoke of them when I was in New Orrins rast time."

"Harrow!" Emiko said cheerfully, flashing Jules a dazzling smile. "I am excited to be in New Orrins and meeting new friends." Even though petite, skinny Japanese girls weren't his type at all, Jules had to admit to himself that she was one of the cutest little gals he'd ever seen. She wore a flouncy Little Bo Peep-style dress made of a shiny silver fabric embroidered with red roses, with a matching silver bonnet on her head.

Shogo stood, bowed to Jules, and sat back down on his cot. "It is good to meet you," he said solemnly. His face was far more impassive and less readable than that of either of his cousins. *Kinda inscrutable*, Jules thought. "Kenji has told me much about you and your family. I am eager to rearn more." Shogo stood a good five inches taller than Kenji; not extremely tall by American standards, but he towered over his older cousin. Like Kenji, he wore a form-fitting body suit made of a shiny synthetic fabric, with silver torso and upper sleeves and bright red lower sleeves and pants legs, set off by shiny calf-high black boots.

Doc Landrieu went to work, quickly and efficiently, his fingers aiming the phlebotomy needles with supernatural precision, guided by their unnatural sensitivity to blood; he managed to hit the proper vein precisely on the first try each time. Customers smiled with relief as they realized the procedure was far less painful than they'd anticipated.

"So Kenji," Jules asked, "how did you find out about my new business? This is our first night in operation, y'know."

"Oh, I know," Kenji said. "I read about your new tour guide business on the Internet, of course. That is why we came to New Orrins now, not rater. I wanted to herrp you get started, if I cood. And Emiko and Shogo were becoming bored with our jobs in Kure. They, rike me, are interested in working as *tarento* in New Orrins."

"'Talent-oh'? What's that?"

"No, Jures-*san*. *Tarento*. In Japan, *tarento* are, how you cawr them? Entertainers. You, running this tour business, are kind of *tarento*. Maureen, with her new TV show, she is most definit-ry *tarento*. Remember, I terr you before, I pray the trumpet? My sister Emiko, she is singer. My cousin Shogo, he pray the drums. I torrd them you know many jazz musicians here in New Orrins. If it is not too much for me to ask, Jures-*san*, as we have not known each other for very rong, do you think you cood herrp us meet jazz musicians and find jobs? I have torrd my sister and cousin what a good man and a good superhero and vampire you are, and they are excited to work as *tarento* and pray music here in New Orrins, home of jazz."

Jules was touched that Kenji would have such faith in him, that he and his relatives would make the long, expensive flight all the way from Japan based mainly on a hope that he would help them. "Well, sure I'll help, Kenji," he said. "I'll do whatever I can, pal. Hey, after what *you* did for Maureen and me a few months back, I owe you one, buddy. Shit, I owe you three or four. Now, I gotta warn ya, some of the clubs we had around here before the storm, they ain't opened back up yet. But on the other hand, lots of musicians who lived here before the storm are still in exile in other cities, 'cause their houses got flooded out. There's a lot less competition in town than there was before Antonia. So, fewer jobs, fewer musicians? Maybe it all balances out? Who the hell knows? Anyway, my old buddy, Porkchop Chambonne, he's back in town. I'm sure he'd be happy to try to hook you guys up. Maybe you could play a benefit concert or two to get started, to get your names out there."

Kenji's face lit up. "Ahh, Porkchop Chambonne! *Hai*! He is great *sensei* of Dixie-rand jazz, Porkchop Chambonne. We have heard of him in Japan. We who ruvv jazz pray his music very much. It will be great honor for us to meet him. Thank you, Jures-*san*. Thank you!"

Jules got a warm feeling all over. What a terrific night this was turning out to be! A night he'd remember for the rest of his undead existence. He cleared his throat to get the crowd's attention. "Hey, everybody! Gimme your ears for a minute. We got us some special guests here tonight. I wanna introduce you all to Kenji, Emiko, and Shogo. They're superheroes, *real* superheroes who came all the way from Japan. And not just superheroes, but superheroes who play old-style jazz! How about *that*? They're here in New Orleans to learn how to become professional musicians. So if you're in town for a while, make sure to check the music listings, and go out and hear them play!"

Kenji waved to the rest of the group. "I am Bonsai Master," he said. "I pray the trumpet. I am very happy to be here with my good friend, Jures-*san* the vampire tour guide."

Emiko waved next. She flashed her thousand-watt smile, which seemed to melt most of the men in the room (and some of the women, as well). "Harrow! I am Anime Girr! I sing many wonderful American songs! I hope to see awr of you at our performance! Thank you!"

Shogo did not smile. He did, however, stand and bow to the crowd. "I am Cutie-Scary Man. I pray drums, awrso. I am preased to be here in New Orrins with my famirry."

The young woman in the vampiress costume waved excitedly at the Japanese trio from one of the phlebotomy cots, where Doc Landrieu had just removed the needle from her arm and placed a Band-Aid over her vein. "Wow! Japanese superheroes, too? This tour has, like, *everything*!"

Amos handed her a cup of Florida orange juice, then pushed his cart of equipment over to Kenji, Emiko, and Shogo, his last customers. Before he got started on them, Jules pulled him aside. "Doc," he whispered, "make sure you label their blood and put it aside from the other bags in the freezer. That's top shelf stuff, pal. We're gonna save it for special occasions."

A few minutes later, once souvenirs had been purchased and Amos had finished his work, Jules led his tour group out onto the street and shepherded them towards Jackson Square. "Now, who here has read some New Orleans history?" he asked.

About half the crowd raised their hands.

"Well, I'm not sayin' that what you've read in the guide books and history books is *wrong*... it's just not *complete*, that's all. See, there's a whole missin' layer of New Orleans history that they leave out. *Vampire* history. That's what I'm gonna be sharin' with y'all tonight — the secret vampire history of New Orleans."

The eight-year-old boy wearing the White Rabbit sweatshirt raised his hand. "Yeah, kid?" Jules said. "What ya wanna know?"

"If you're a vampire, then how come you're so *fat*? I've never *heard* of a fat vampire before..."

The boy's mother practically turned purple with shame. "*Matthew*! You say you're sorry this instant!" She turned to Jules. "I am *so* sorry... Matthew's a sweet child, but he's very smart, and sometimes he asks questions he shouldn't..."

"Oh, that's all right, ma'am," Jules said. "No harm done. Actually, it's a good question. Kid's got a right to be curious; I don't mind. See, kid, I got changed into a vampire way back in 1917, right before the U.S. went into World War One. You know about World War One, don't you?"

"Sure I do! That was the war to make the world safe for democracy."

"Yeah, right. Smart kid. So I been a vampire for almost a hundred years now. All that time, I been drinkin' the blood of people here in New Orleans. Now, y'all bein' visitors, you been goin' out to eat in our restaurants every day and night, haven't y'all? Delicious, right? But what makes our New Orleans food so delicious? Lotsa butter, lotsa duck fat, lotsa fatty andouille sausage. Everything fried up in a spicy batter. Get me? And the size of them *portions* — look out! So, anyway, you are what you eat. For almost a hundred years, I been drinkin' the blood of folks who've wolfed down mass quantities of New Orleans food. All them lipids and cholesterol in the blood, it tends to put a few inches on a man's waistline." He patted his belly appreciatively. "Hey, maybe I'll lose a little weight, leadin' all these tours around the Quarter. Stranger things than that've happened around these parts."

He led the group down Chartres Street toward Jackson Square. "Anyway, you're not here to hear about my eatin' habits. You're here to learn about the secret vampire history of New Orleans. So let me get back to that. Those a you who've read some New Orleans history know them French guys Bienville and Iberville founded the City of New Orleans way back around 1700 or so. What you *don't* know is *why*. Why the heck would a buncha French la-de-dahs wanna found a colony in some mosquito-infested hell-hole of a swamp out in the middle of nowhere? Huh? Why? You ask them historian guys, they say the French wanted to control the mouth of the Mississippi River. I call baloney on that.

"The *real* reason? It was 'cause the French wanted to get rid of their *vampires*. French vampires had started overrunnin' Paris and Versailles and all a them hoity-toity places. Napoleon, he knew his army wasn't strong enough to kill all of them vampires. So he made a deal with the head French vampire, whose name was Jacques Q. Stowe. Napoleon said he'd stop makin' war on the vampires if the vampires would agree to move to a new colony in North America. To sweeten the pot, Napoleon said he'd send a buncha mortal Frenchmen as colonists, too, so the vampires would have plenty of human blood to drink. The vampires, figurin' they'd have plenty of Indians to drink blood from, too, on top of the French colonists, said, 'Heck, yeah, we'll take that deal.' So Napoleon had all of the vampires loaded in their coffins onto sailing ships, and off they sailed to the new colony of Louisiana—"

"It *couldn't* have been Napoleon," the White Rabbit-wearing boy insisted. "Napoleon didn't become ruler of France until after the French Revolution in 1789. You said New Orleans was founded in the *early* 1700s. King Louis the Fourteenth was ruler of France then. Not Napoleon."

Jules glared at the boy. "It was Napoleon, kid."

"But it *couldn't* have been Napoleon!"

"Who's the tour guide here? Me, or you? Look, walk with me another block, and I'll *prove* it to you." A block later, Jules paused in front of a stately French town house, wrought iron balconies running the length of its second story. "This here's the Napoleon House. It's a bar and restaurant now, but way back when, it was actually Napoleon's *house*, where he'd stay when he'd come to check out his colony. Hardly anybody knows this, but if you go down to the secret sub-basement under Napoleon House, you'll find a big stone slab in the floor. That stone slab covers a tomb. The tomb of the vampire Jacques Q. Stowe. He rebelled against Napoleon, welshing on their deal after he arrived in New Orleans. So Napoleon had him staked through the heart and entombed beneath Napoleon's own house, so he could keep a close eye on his enemy. Tell you what, kid. We'll wait right here while you go inside. If you can find the entrance to the secret sub-basement, move the stone slab, open Stowe's coffin, and pull the stake out of his rib cage, I *promise* you he'll back up every word I just said. We got us a deal?"

Matthew shook his head vigorously. A few persons in the tour group laughed.

Jules led them another block toward Jackson Square. Then he pointed to an iron horse-hitching post near the corner. "Lemme have everybody's attention," he said, pointing grandly at the post. "Y'all are standin' in the presence of one of the most historical sites in all of New Orleans. I'm talkin' that humble little horse-hitchin' post right there. What's so special about that post, you might ask? And if it's so special, how come there's no City Landmarks Commission Historic Sites plaque? Well, it's special 'cause it's the spot where Marie Antoinette died. Where she *really* died."

"But Marie Antoinette died in France, her head chopped off by the guillotine—" Matthew piped up.

"I *knew* you was gonna say that, kid," Jules shot back. "But this time, I got ya covered. See, after the French Revolution started, Marie Antoinette knew she was basically toast. So she arranged for one of her maids to take the fall for her. It was that poor maid, the one disguised as

Marie Antoinette, who made the snarky remark about cupcakes and got her head chopped off, not the real Marie. Meanwhile, the real Marie had friends over here in Louisiana, even though by that time it was under the control of the Spanish. So she arranged for a ship to take her and her treasure to New Orleans, where she figured she could live out the rest of her life in style, far away from the rabble-rousers back in Paris. She had herself a grand ol' time here in the Crescent City for about six months, usin' a different name. But then she crossed paths with Count Vince du Varney, who was secretly the high priest of all the vampires in New Orleans. She fell under his spell, and he drank her blood and changed her into a vampire.

"Well, as somebody who'd been, y'know, suckin' the blood of the peasants for years, so to speak, it wasn't any big change for Marie to start suckin' their blood fer real. She liked it. And, bein' an aristocrat already, she fit right in with the vampire aristocracy. Everything was fine and dandy with our Mizz Antoinette, till she had her fateful meetin' with this here hitchin' post. She'd been havin' herself a hellavuh night, out carousin', drinkin' the blood of half a dozen Spanish sailors who'd gotten liquored up on Tequila. All that booze in their bloodstream made her pretty tipsy herself. Somewheres about an hour before sunrise, she was walkin' right along where this hitchin' post stands, weavin' back and forth 'cause of all that Tequila, and 'cause she was wearin' about thirty pounds worth of wig on top of her pretty head. You know the style I'm talkin' about — the beehive hairdo that stands four feet tall. Well, she lost a shoe, and when she leaned down to grab it, her beehive hairdo got tangled in the hitchin' post. No lie. She tried pullin' away, but the more she pulled, the more her hair got tangled in the post. She didn't wanna yank all her pretty curls out, and she didn't wanna mess her nails untanglin' knots.

"So, drunk as a Cajun skunk, she sat next to the post until the sun came up. And y'all know what sunlight does to a vampire. The next day, all the townspeople found of her was an expensive hoop skirt, a buncha jewelry, a pair of shoes, and a four-foot-tall wig tangled in the hitchin' post. Oh, and a big pile of dust, too. Moral of the story, ladies? There's more important things on this here planet than your hair and your nails. Keep that in mind the next time you walk past a hitchin' post."

Jules pulled Kenji aside. "So, pal, how'm I doin'?" he whispered. "Are you enjoyin' the tour so far?"

"It is very interesting, Jures-*san*," Kenji said. "Very educational. Most herrpfur for us who are new to New Orrins."

"Good."

Jules led his group into Jackson Square, the heart of the French Quarter. An equestrian statue of General Andrew Jackson, victor of the Battle of New Orleans, stood in the middle of a small, meticulously land-scaped park, which was surrounded by a cobblestone promenade. The wide promenade provided space for strolling musicians, painters, quick sketch artists, mimes, jugglers, fortune tellers, and Tarot card readers. The square was surrounded on two sides by the Pontalba Apartments, the oldest apartment buildings in the South, and on a third side by St. Louis Cathedral, flanked by the Cabildo and Presbytere buildings, home to the city's government during its early years.

Jules led his group to the Presbytere building. Its arched entrance, lined with slender columns, sheltered an open arcade which held several historic displays. Chief among these displays was what appeared to be an iron flounder, nearly fifteen feet long and seven feet high.

"Folks," Jules said, "you are now lookin' at the tomb of Count Vince du Varney, high priest of the New Orleans vampires. See, President Thomas Jefferson wanted to buy Louisiana from the French, who'd just gotten it back from the Spanish. But as a condition of the deal, Jefferson said the French had to get rid of all the vampires then runnin' around New Orleans. Now the French, they'd had plenty of experience with vampires, and they knew they couldn't get rid of *all* a them. So they figured if they could catch the leader and make an example of him, the rest of the vampires would fall in line and lay low, least until after the Americans bought the place."

Jules spotted Matthew, the White Rabbit kid, paging furiously through a guidebook he'd grabbed from his mother's purse. He started talking faster. "Anyway, a posse of French soldiers caught du Varney in his coffin. They stuck a stake through his heart, chopped off his head, and stuffed his mouth full of garlic, which, bein' French, they had plenty of. But they needed to make a permanent example of him. So they had this here weird iron coffin made in the shape of a fish, 'cause that's a Christian symbol, y'know. And they stuck it here, on the front arcade of the Presbytere, right next to St. Louis Cathedral, where the power of the church's holiness would help make sure du Varney never got resurrected. Also, they stuck it in a spot where the sun would hit it every afternoon, heatin' that iron coffin up to a couple hundred degrees, keepin' it nice and uncomfortable for du Varney, in case his spirit was still hangin' around—"

"That's not a coffin!" Matthew shouted in his high, reedy voice, having found the page of the guidebook he'd been looking for. "That's a *submarine*! A primitive, experimental submarine from the Civil War! It says right here in my book that this submarine didn't get pulled out of the mud at the bottom of Lake Pontchartrain until the 1870s. And it didn't get put on display at the Presbytere until almost *a hundred years later!*"

All eyes turned back to Jules. Jules scowled angrily at the boy's parents. "Hey, I'm bein' heckled mercilessly here!" he complained. "Can't you get that mouthy kid of yours to shut the hell up? He's ruinin' the tour for everybody else—"

"He's not ruining it for *me*," the young woman in the vampire costume said, crossing her arms. "I think *he's* very well informed."

"Yeah," a young man sporting a bushy goatee said (he'd had his eye on the woman in the vampire costume throughout the tour). "Don't tell the kid to shut up. He's a paying customer."

"Yeah?" Jules said belligerently to his challenger. "Well, the small print on the back of my brochures says I got a right to expel anybody from my tours who causes a disturbance, payin' customer or no payin' customer."

The young man with the goatee (obviously relishing the attention, particularly the newly appreciative attention from his costumed female companion) ostentatiously placed himself between young Matthew and Jules. "If you put *him* out, you'll have to put *me* out, too. And I'm warning you right now, I'm a stone cold *activist* on Twitter, man. You put *me* out, and I'll drop your business *dead*. I'm talking *boycott*, mister. You'll be as popular as apartheid, dude."

Eleven

THE standoff between Jules and his first-ever group of customers threatened to grow ugly, as ugly as a Bourbon Street gutter at the end of a Saturday night.

Kenji pulled Jules aside. "Ahh, Jures-*san*, I do not mean to terr you your business. But in Japan, we have a saying: 'In fight between customer and businessman, no one wins.' My famirry and I, we are *tarento* in Japan, we work for many businesses. May I herrp you in this difficurrt situation? Take their minds off confrict between you and rittuww boy?"

"You wanna try with this bunch?" Jules said, feeling deeply affronted by the lack of support he'd gotten from anyone but Kenji. "Be my guest, pal."

Kenji turned to the small crowd. "Harrow, everyone!" he said cheerfully. "Now that we have reached the center part of the *Ree-awr* New Orrins Vampire Tour, it is my preasure to give you a show of the Acme *Tarento* Tremendous Power Trio. We come from Kure, Japan, which is near Hiroshima, a city you may know. To make a show for you of our super-powers, we need a vorrunteer. Being a vorrunteer is safe and causes no pain, but it can be, how you say? Disconcerting. Like being on fast rorrer coaster ride. Also, vorrunteer will roose weight. Would anyone rike to vorrunteer for our show?"

Several hands shot up, all from tour guests who could be described as being on the north side of portly. Kenji selected the portliest gentleman, a white-bearded man in his fifties who wore sandals and a too-tight Green Bay Packers jersey.

"Prease come forward," Kenji said. His hands began glowing green, the same color they had the night when Jules had asked him to shrink the convenience store's security gate. "Thank you for being vorrunteer. You shudd ask your friends to take many pictures soon. You wirr want to remember what happens now."

Kenji touched one palm to the man's chest and placed the other on his back. "Oh, *myyyyyy*..." the portly man said, a look of astonishment overcoming him as the green energy spread from Kenji's hands across the man's body. "This is so *straaaaange*..."

The timber of his voice grew higher and squeakier. He suddenly began shrinking. As he shrank, the green energy drained from his body into Kenji's hands and arms. The man's clothes shrank along with him, the rate of diminishment accelerating until he reached a size of merely six inches tall, at which point the shrinkage abruptly halted.

Kenji held the man above his head, steadying the dizzy, newly shrunken volunteer by gently grasping his legs in his fist. "This is why I am cawrred Bonsai Master," Kenji said modestly. "I have power to make big things smawrr."

The audience gasped. Then they began applauding with great gusto. Whispers of "How did he *do* that?" and "Most amazing special effects I've ever seen!" and "Do they do it with holograms?" floated through the crowd. Other people, unconnected to the tour, began congregating from far corners of the square, wanting to see what sort of new act had caused such a commotion. Even a couple of the mimes wandered over.

"Each member of the Acme *Tarento* Tremendous Power Trio has their own super-power," Kenji continued. After shrinking the man in the Packers jersey, the residual energy from his stunt — the mass he had absorbed from the volunteer and transmuted into an energy state — had spread from his hands and arms to the entirety of his body; it now shined greenishly through the silver and red fabric of his uniform. Jules wondered whether he would shoot that energy into the sky again, like he had that night several months back. Also, if he did, would the shrunken tourist remain tiny for the rest of his life?

Kenji set the doll-sized man gently down on a park bench. "Now you will see the power of my sister, Anime Girr."

Emiko stepped forward. "Harrow, friends!" she said. Her expansive wave and greeting struck Jules as almost magical; if nothing else, she was one hell of a crowd charmer. "Who thinks our vorrunteer is very cute now? Or, as we say in Japan, is *kawaii*?"

A few tour participants tentatively raised their hands.

"My power is to make him much, much more *kawaii*. Who here has a favorite *kawaii* anime character? Or cartoon character, as you say in America? But must be a *cute* cartoon character, not ugrry. Must be *kawaii*."

The young heckler Matthew began jumping up and down. "Me! Me! Pick *me*! I have a favorite cartoon character!"

"Okay, rittuww boy," Emiko said, gesturing for him to come forward. "Who is your favorite character? Can I take a guess? It is that rabbit on the shirt you wear?"

"Yes!" Matthew said, a mischievous grin on his face. "Make him just like the White Rabbit from *Alice in Wonderland*! And let me take him home as a toy!"

"This is a Disney firrum? I am not knowing it well. But I know *another* rabbit. Oswarrd the Rucky Rabbit. Oswarrd is very *kawaii*. He is awrso from Disney. We have Oswarrd at Tokyo Disneyrand. I make the man rike Oswarrd, okay?"

Jules dimly remembered Oswald the Lucky Rabbit. The character had starred in a brief series of movie shorts back in the late 1920s, right around the same time Mickey Mouse had been introduced. Jules thought he might've seen an Oswald cartoon the same night he'd watched *Wings* with Gary Cooper at the Saenger Theater on Canal Street.

"Well... okay, I guess," Matthew said, a touch of disappointment in his voice.

"Oh, you will *ruvv* Oswarrd, I know!" Emiko insisted. "But to make the man rook rike Oswarrd, I need the herrp of Bonsai Master, Kenji-*san*."

Kenji stepped forward. He and Emiko bowed to one another. Then Emiko coyly pulled back her bonnet and tilted her face up toward her brother's. Kenji, still glowing brightly green, gently touched his two index fingers and middle fingers to his sister's cheeks. In a rush, as though it were a living thing hunting sustenance, the energy flowed out of Kenji's body through the tips of his fingers and into his sister's face. It pooled in her lips, making them glow so brightly that Jules found them painful to look at.

Emiko adjusted her bonnet so that it sat prettily atop her head once more. Then taking steps so tiny that her feet never left the cobblestones, swaying softly and gracefully from one side to another, a kind of dance Jules thought might have something to do with *kabuki* theater, Emiko approached the park bench where the minuscule man stood. She lifted the tiny figure to her face, cradling him in both hands as though he were her precious kitten, the dearest possession of a magically entrancing little girl. Then she kissed his tiny cheek.

Like quicksilver driven by an electric jolt, the green energy leaped from her lips into the tiny man's body. He quickly began changing. Jules stepped closer to get a better look, pressing against three dozen other people who were doing the same. The man's skin grew a coat of smooth, black fur. His torso grew rounder. His fingers became round and plump, and one digit on each hand shrank into his palm and disappeared, leaving only three fingers and a thumb on each hand. His eyes became large, black saucers on a white, pie-like face. Most impressively, two great slender ears grew from the top of his head, each black ear half as tall as the remainder of his body.

Emiko kept her lips pressed against his cheek until his transformation was finished. At that point, all the glowing green energy had left her lips. The stunned volunteer, now changed completely into an image of Oswald the Lucky Rabbit, glowed as green as a kryptonite meteor from a Superman cartoon.

Emiko held her new Oswald triumphantly above her head. The crowd burst into wild applause.

"Thank you very much for the crapping!" Emiko said. "Crap, too, for our brave vorrunteer! Now I will give him to *Kawaii Kowai Otoko-san,* the Cutie-Scary Man."

She bowed to Shogo, then handed him the glowing green Oswald the Lucky Rabbit. Once he had the thoroughly disoriented volunteer in hand, Shogo bowed back to her. Shogo held the tiny, transformed tourist in both hands and lifted him high above his head, as though the cartoon rabbit were a sacrificial offering to the sky god. Then, without uttering a word, he closed his eyes tightly, appearing to concentrate with all his will. The green energy drained from the itty-bitty Oswald into Shogo's hands, arms, and shoulders. It spread rapidly throughout his body, glowing beneath his uniform just as it had Kenji's. Seconds later, he transformed into a seven-foot-tall version of the figure he held. To Jules, he looked like a Disneyworld character enactor who'd been dipped in luminescent green paint.

"Now, I am Cutie-Man," Shogo said. He wiggled his long ears and displayed a gap-toothed, cartoon-style smile. He set his miniature twin, no longer glowing green, back down on the park bench. After a few experimental bounces on his oversized hind legs, Shogo closed his eyes once more and pressed his front paws tightly together (Jules thought he looked like he was praying in an anime church). The green energy field surrounding him shimmered, as though it had been disrupted by an outside electrical current. Jules smelled that lime ozone scent he remembered from the first night Kenji had demonstrated his super-power.

Shogo began changing yet again. Now his smooth black fur grew gnarled and matted. Knotted muscles and sinews, like those of a body building champion, erupted from his arms, legs, and neck. His forepaws and back paws sprouted sharp, curved claws, looking like a giant ground sloth's enormous talons. Twisted horns now towered over his floppy ears. His eyes began glowing a demonic orange color. For Jules, the most impressive change came when his *kawaii* buck teeth transformed into fangs which would put Dracula's canines to shame.

"Now, I am *Scary-Man!*" Shogo cried. He leaped twelve feet straight into the air. His second leap sent him hurling over the heads of the startled audience. His third leap, just outside the gates of the manicured park, landed him atop the equestrian statue of General Andrew Jackson.

"Prease, give much crapping for Cutie-Scary Man!" Kenji exhorted the audience. After a few seconds of stunned silence, they complied. "Now Cutie-Scary Man will restore our brave vorrunteer to his originar form." He gestured for Shogo to come back to the plaza. Shogo leaped off General Jackson's horse, then shambled over to the bench where the tiny Oswald still stood.

Shogo touched his two index fingers to the shrunken tourist's shoulders. The green energy fled Shogo's body. As his body stopped glowing, Shogo's fur, horns, droopy ears, fangs, and extra muscles receded, and he returned to his normal, handsome-but-somber appearance.

The green energy now made the tiny tourist glow exceedingly bright. His subsequent transformation was even more dramatic than Shogo's. Not only did he lose his Oswald the Lucky Rabbit features, but he simultaneously grew, as the energy which had originally been borrowed from his body as mass and then transformed into an energy state resumed its original composition as bone, muscle, fat, skin, and blood. Twenty seconds later, the man no longer glowed, and he stood his original five feet, eleven inches in height.

There had been *some* changes, however. Standing atop the bench, the tourist disbelievingly pawed his belly, squeezing fat folds which had formerly been much more abundant. "Hey!" he said. "My shirt... it's *hanging* on me now. This morning, I could barely pull it on! I must've lost, oh, twenty-five, thirty pounds! This is *amazing*! I thought I'd be *gaining* weight on this vacation!"

As soon as this sank in, two-thirds of the crowd erupted into shouts of "Do me! Do *me!*" and "I been tryin' half my life to lose just twenty pounds…"

Kenji waved aside their demands. "That is awwr for tonight from the Acme *Tarento* Tremendous Power Trio," he said. "We thank you much for your apprause and enjoyment. Now I turn you back to my friend Jures-*san*, who wirr continue your tour."

Jules did his best to regain the group's attention. But his audience had been too stirred up by the Japanese superheroes' performance to pay any mind to Jules' fractured fairy tales about vampires in New Orleans. He wasn't too taken aback by his lack of success in regaining the crowd's focus; during the pauses between his futile attempts to spin his yarns, he listened in on the fervent debates which swirled through the crowd, arguments over whether what they had seen had been the result of laser lights, holograms, a new, secret Japanese entertainment technology not yet released in America, or hallucinogenic drugs embedded in a mist that had been surreptitiously sprayed throughout the crowd. *Oh, well,* he thought, *at least none of 'em can complain they ain't been entertained.*

Jules could tell that Kenji was more than a little embarrassed by having stolen the limelight from his host. The vampire tried to reassure his friend. "Kenji, pal, don't sweat it," he whispered to him as they approached Canal Street. "You done good. *Real* good, in fact. I'm not ticked off at ya, not a bit. After tonight, word-of-mouth on this tour's gonna be through the roof. Up into outer space, even. I'm gonna hafta turn folks away."

They finished the tour at Maureen's public access TV studio, where she was half-way through her screening of *The Last Man on Earth*. The tourists happily posed for pay photos with the horror hostess and the members of the Acme *Tarento* Tremendous Power Trio.

"Oh, Kenji, dear, it's so *good* to see you again! What a marvelous surprise!" Maureen, excited by the size of the tour group, hurried from person to person, wanting to make sure that each and every tourist got a chance to be on camera and talk about their experiences on the tour.

She had Kenji and his sister and cousin introduce themselves to the TV audience. With all her frenetic activity, she began sweating through her makeup. Without thinking a thing of it, she swabbed her face with a wash cloth that one of the technicians fetched for her from a bathroom.

The tourists who bought photographs taken alongside Maureen didn't notice until after they'd returned to their hotels (or, in some cases, until after they'd flown home) that they had posed next to a woman without a face — just a mass of false hair levitating over a pair of contact lenses floating above a random smear or two of lipstick.

If they gave much thought to this at all, they figured it had been just one more weird special effect at the close of a night which had been chock full of them. What a town New Orleans was, even after the storm!

Twelve

"WHEW!" Maureen exclaimed, collapsing onto her waterbed. "Are you as exhausted as I am?"

Jules flopped onto the bed next to her. "Probably *more* tuckered out," he said. "That's three nights in a row for me of traipsing around the French Quarter with my group. My achin' legs are a darn good reminder there was a *reason* I took up drivin' a cab, instead of chasin' down my victims on foot..."

"Maybe I didn't walk around the Quarter a few hours, like you did. But still, having to be constantly *on* in front of the cameras, coming up with quips to make about those silly movies, then posing for pictures with your tourists... it's even more tiring than dancing at Jezebel's used to be. That is if you can call what I did 'dancing'... it was more like wiggling to music..."

"'Wiggling' or 'dancing,' whatever it was, *I* liked it... kinda miss it, in fact..."

"Well, that's sweet of you, Jules." She rolled over and gave him a peck on the cheek. But when her arm grazed against his, her limb jerked away from him. "Oh! I *hate* that! I wish my body would stop doing that!"

Jules frowned. "You still ain't talked with Doc about it, have you?"

"Oh, Jules, you know how *busy* I've been... I'll get around to it, honey, I promise..."

"How've you been sleepin' lately? Still havin' any nightmares about bein' stuck without no blood? Hey, you gotta admit, my idea of startin' our own business has been workin' out *great* so far. I mean, we been runnin' tours just three nights now, and already we got enough blood stored up in our freezer to last us almost two weeks, longer than that if we're careful. So them nightmares of yours, they should be a thing of the past. When it comes to blood, doll, we're on easy street now."

Maureen sat up. Jules noticed her perturbed look. "No, I haven't been having nightmares about starving. Not lately, not since I got so busy with my TV show. But I've been having *different* dreams, and they've been almost as bad..."

"What're these new ones like?"

"I don't want you to take this the wrong way, Jules... I know you preferred it when I was a bit, well, *larger*..."

"Yeah? So?"

"Well, I've been having nightmares about being *fat* again. In my dreams, I'm lying in my coffin, and I'm even fatter than I was right before Malice killed me. And I'm getting fatter and *fatter*, until I can hardly *fit* in the coffin anymore. Until I can barely *breathe*. I don't know... maybe I'm having these dreams because of all that junk food I scarfed down during those 'party' nights we shared with Kenji, huh? What do you think, Jules?" She glanced over at him lying next to her. He noticed her see something which made her wryly smile. "Jules Duchon, did you just get a *woody*?"

Jules' eyes darted to his pants. Sure enough, his trousers looked like an overstuffed pup tent. "Awww, babe, I sure wish there was somethin' we could do with that there woody... but I'm afraid if I tried touchin' ya anywhere but your face, your knees would hammer my privates and your nails would scratch my eyes out. Y'know, if you'd gone and talked with Doc a week or two ago, when I asked ya, maybe he woulda come up with a cure by now, and we *could* do something fun with that woody..."

"Don't make me feel *guilty*, Jules! I *said* I'd get it checked out. As soon as I'm not so busy, okay?" She got up from the bed and walked over to her dresser, where she'd posed a group of Japanese anime action figures. "Aren't these little figures just *darling*?" she said, obviously in a hurry to change the subject. "It was so thoughtful of Kenji and the others to bring them for us from Japan. Which one do you think is the best likeness? I think they got Emiko's face pretty close, but Shogo's figure just *nails* that bad-boy personality of his. What do you think?"

Jules pushed himself off the bed and lumbered over. "Yeah, the Shogo figure's the best one. The Kenji figure, it don't look a thing like him, except for the costume. Might as well be a Japanese Ken doll."

"How did their performance in Jackson Square go over tonight?"

"Just as good as it did the last two nights. Kenji said he and the others'll help us out for the next week or so while we're buildin' up our business. In the meantime, I'm gonna get them together with my buddy Porkchop Chambonne and see if he can hook them up with some music gigs. Ain't it a gasser, though? I mean, here they've got the best act in town, what with their super-powers shtick, and yet all they wanna do is play Dixieland jazz."

Maureen picked up the Shogo action figure and fiddled with its arms. Her fingers lingered on the figure's face. "Oh, you know what they say about the grass always being greener on the other side of the fence..."

"Hey," Jules said, chuckling, "you know who showed up at our door again tonight before the tour? That bratty little know-it-all, Matthew, draggin' his parents with him. Remember him? The kid who wore the White Rabbit shirt the first night? He wanted to do the tour all over again, but his dad said no. Boy, I sure dodged a bullet. That kid was *murder*."

"Did Kenji and his relatives donate blood again tonight?"

"Yeah, they did. I told 'em they needn't feel obligated, but they did it anyway. Third night in a row. Guess they can give blood as often as they feel like. And you know how polite them Japanese are. Sheesh.

Y'know, I'm surprised that when them Jap Zeroes and dive bombers was over Pearl Harbor, their pilots didn't radio, 'Ahh, Uncurr Sam-*san*, prease would it be arrowable for us to sink your batturships?'"

Maureen laughed. "Oh, Jules, you're so *bad*! That's *awful*. But true. They are terribly polite."

"Hey, I got me an idea," Jules said. "Seein' how we've both earned us some fun time, and fun time with ol' Woody's temporarily outta bounds, how about we dip into our stash of superhero blood?"

"Oh, I don't know that I'm in the mood to get all silly tonight. And I really should lay off the junk food, or my fat nightmares are gonna turn *real...*"

"I wasn't thinkin' about sippin' more of Kenji's blood. We already know what that does. But how about tryin' out some of Emiko's blood, or Shogo's? It might affect us the same way as Kenji's blood does. Or — hey, who knows? It might do somethin' different, and even *more* fun."

"You don't think that's too risky?" Maureen said.

Jules shook his head. "Hon, 'risky' was when you insisted we stay here in New Orleans after the flood. We had no idea how we was gonna get ourselves through that, and if it hadn't been for Kenji, we might notta. But this? This is *experimentin'*. Mankind never woulda left the trees if it hadn't been for experimentin'. We'd still be eatin' berries and crackin' open squirrels' heads for brains, and you'd be munchin' on little chiggers you'd pull outta my hide. Get me? We can't chicken out now. Not before we learn what that blood is good for. Right?"

"Oh, I suppose if you put it that way..." Maureen grinned. "Actually, I *am* up for some fun. Go get us some superhero blood out of the freezer. Heat up a pot of water on the stovetop and stick the bags in it for a couple of minutes. Don't put it in the microwave, okay? Not even on the defrost setting. Ruins the flavor."

"Sure thing, Mo."

A few minutes later, Jules reentered the bedroom, carrying two bags of defrosted blood and a pair of mugs. "You wanna try Emiko's blood first?"

"That'll be fine, Jules. Oh, goody! I can hardly wait!"

Jules poured them both blood from the plastic bag with Emiko's name written on it. "Well, here's lookin' at ya, kid!"

"Should we both drink at the same time?" Maureen asked cautiously. "Maybe one of us should go first, to see what happens?"

"Naww... let's jump off the cliff together. Bottoms up, babe!"

They clinked their mugs together, then drank simultaneously.

"What do ya think?" Jules asked.

"It's good... sort of like Kenji's blood, only sweeter..."

Jules felt the blood burn his esophagus as it headed for his stomach. "Whoa! Watch out for that aftertaste! It's got a *kick!*"

Maureen scrunched up her face. "Ooohh, Jules... I don't feel so good... I need to lie down..."

Jules felt out of sorts himself. Neither of them had experienced anything like this when they'd imbibed on Kenji's blood. He helped Maureen settle back into the pillows. She looked extremely queasy and uncomfortable. "Babe, you need me to fetch a bucket?"

She grimaced. "No — no, I don't feel like I'm gonna barf. This feels more like the old days, when I could still change into a bat... that feeling I'd get right before the transformation, like my body was about to turn into pudding. Only this is a lot more *intense—*"

A green glow began to illuminate the room. It came from Maureen's stomach. Before he could say a word, a sudden green flash blinded him. He felt the waterbed give way beneath him. He was instantly deposited onto the floor, with only deflated sheets of plastic and shreds of bedding between him and the hardwood flooring. His nostrils filled with that now-familiar odor of lime-scented ozone.

"*Mo!*" he shouted, still unable to see. "Are you *okay*, babe?" His vision began returning, but his eyesight remained clouded by a screen of oscillating green spots. He reached for his wife. His fingers blindly located her lying on the floor. She felt... *different*. Billowy, overstuffed, voluptuous — like she used to—

"*Jules!*" she screamed. "Jules, I'm FAT again!"

Jules frantically rubbed his eyes, trying to clear them. Most of the waterbed was gone, he saw. Not just deflated — *gone*. It hadn't sprung a leak; there wasn't a puddle of water anywhere, and the soil which surrounded the waterbed remained dry.

Then he saw his wife. There was a whole lot more of her to see. Naked, she now took up nearly a quarter of the room. His old sweetheart had returned, every luscious pound and fleshy roll of her.

"Mo... you look *gorgeous*!"

"'Gorgeous'? I'm *hideous*! And look at *you*!"

"Huh? Whadda ya mean, 'look at me?'"

"Look at yourself!" Her new jowls quivered with shock and indignation. "Just *look*!"

Jules stared down at his hands. They weren't hands anymore. They were paws. Big, plump paws, covered with white, fluffy fur. His legs, also covered in white, fluffy fur, now bent at a strange angle, and his furry feet were five times the size they had been formerly. He pawed the top of his head, dreading what he would find. Sure enough, he touched a pair of long, furry, floppy ears. "Uh, oh..."

"You're a big *rabbit*, Jules! A big *white rabbit*!"

"Maybe drinkin' that blood wasn't such a good idea, huh...?"

"*Now* you tell me!"

Staring at his enlarged wife, Jules felt a powerful stirring in his loins. *What a time to be gettin' horny!* he rebuked himself. But then he recalled what rabbits did best (aside from hopping and delivering Easter eggs). And the feelings he was experiencing so strongly then made perfect sense.

He loped over to her side and nuzzled her expansive belly with his pink nose, his nostrils oscillating with excitement. "Jules! What are you *doing*?" Maureen cried. But he didn't let her objection stop him from nuzzling and licking and pawing her irresistibly tantalizing flesh.

"I'm bein' a *rabbit*, hon," he murmured between licks and nuzzles. "Doin' what comes naturally..."

His befuddled brain made hazy note of the fact that her body no longer recoiled from him. He climbed on top of her. "Oh, Jules," she whispered passionately into one of his huge, drooping ears. "This is *very* weird, but I *like* it..."

They went with it.

After a brief intermission of post-coital cuddling, they went with it again.

"I can keep this up all night, y'know," Jules said, rather smugly. "Least I'm pretty sure I can. You know what they say about rabbits."

"Oh, yeah, I know what they say, my great big Mr. Thumper." She fondled his damp rabbit privates and, growling, chewed lustily on one of his ears. But then the sex-crazed smile faded from her face. "We really need to *do* something about this, Jules. And by 'doing something,' I don't mean fuck more."

"Why the hell *not*? We got us a months-long dry spell to make up for!"

She abruptly sat up. "Jules, be *serious*! We can't *stay* like this! We have to figure out what happened, then find a way to reverse it! There's no *way* I'm willing to stay fat, no matter how much you adore me this size!"

Jules' ears drooped (along with another part of his anatomy). Fun time was over, damn it. "Well, I guess we can start by figurin' out what happened to our bed."

"The bed! That's right! My gosh, it's almost all gone!"

"If I had to take a guess, I'd say your clothes, the bed covers, the big plastic bags that used to hold the water, and all that water that was in the bags, it's all now part of *you*."

"Part of *me*?"

"Sure! All that extra mass you're wearin' hadta have come from *somewheres*. It's not like you had a whole buncha spare proto-mass lyin' around in the bottom of your coffin, like I do whenever I change into a bat or a wolf. I'm guessin' that when you drank Emiko's blood, you temporarily gained her super-power to convert mass into energy, and energy into mass, and play with it like it's Silly Putty. You converted all the mass you was touchin' into more of you. Me? I didn't need to suck in no extra mass when I changed." He patted his fur-covered belly. "I had *plenty* of raw material to start out with."

"But why did I turn *fat*? Why didn't I turn into, oh, I don't know, a big pussycat or something?"

Jules thought about that. "Hey, right before we drank Emiko's blood, weren't you tellin' me about your nightmares? The ones where you turned big and fat in your coffin again?"

Maureen's face lit up with a sudden *ah-ha*! "And *you* were talking to me about that obnoxious little boy who wore the White Rabbit shirt!"

"That's *gotta* be it! Emiko's blood is like our Red Kryptonite!"

"Are you talking nonsense from one of your comic books, Jules?"

"Yeah, but it's not nonsense. See, Red Kryptonite is this kinda Kryptonite that has unpredictable, weird effects on Superman. I read somewheres that the guys at DC comics who wrote the Superman stories back in the 'fifties, they used to go out and get hammered at lunchtime, and they'd come back to the office and write a story about the weirdest transformation for Superman they could think of — him turning into a superbrain from the future, or growing a lion head, or becoming Caveman Superman — and they'd just blame it on Red Kryptonite. Only with us, see, it's not a buncha drunk-off-their-asses comic book writers who decide what we get changed into. What does it for us, it's gotta be whatever we were thinkin' about most strongly, just before we drank the blood."

"How did Superman change himself back to normal?"

"Sometimes Jimmy Olsen used a super-science ray to do it, or Superman found some doodad in his Fortress of Solitude that worked like an antidote. Usually, though, the weirdness just wore off by the end of the story, so long as Superman stayed away from Red Kryptonite."

Maureen frowned. "But what if *our* changes *don't* wear off? What if we're *stuck* like this, forever?"

He reached for her pillowy thigh again. "We could have ourselves a buncha cute little bunnies—"

"*Jules!*"

He sadly withdrew his paw. "Well, here's one thing we could try. Now that we know, or at least we're *kinda* sure, that the transformations are controlled by whatever we're thinkin' about most strongly, we could concentrate on what our old selves looked like, and then take another big swig of Emiko's blood."

Maureen shook her head. "I'm too *scared* to do that, Jules. What if I think something *wrong*? What if drinking more of her blood just makes my transformation *worse*? I mean — what if I end up sucking up the mass of this whole room, or even the whole second story of this house, and I end up *eight thousand pounds?*"

A four-ton wife? That might be a little much for even a six-foot-tall vampire rabbit to handle. Jules didn't believe there could ever be too much of a good thing, but still...

"There's got to be another way," Maureen said quickly. "Didn't you turn yourself into a hundred and fifty white rats after you killed Malice? And didn't you somehow manage to combine all those little bodies back into one big Jules body again? Maybe if you just *concentrate* really hard, you can force yourself to change back. And if you can manage it, then you could teach *me* to do it, too."

"But this is *different*, Mo. Back then, that was all vampire stuff I was dealin' with. And Doodlebug had given me a week's worth of trainin' in how to turn myself into multiple bodies. This? This is weirdo Jap superhero stuff. I mean, this is Twilight Zone, Tokyo-style..."

"Just *try*, Jules!"

Jules closed his eyes. Maybe if he turned himself into a bat first, his body would remember how to change back to human form, and it would happen automatically when he retrieved his spare proto-mass from the bottom of his coffin? Turning from a rabbit into a bat shouldn't be so hard; they were both members of the rodent family, after all. And after having spent nine months as a hundred and fifty rats, Jules knew *plenty* about rodents.

Come on, bat form, he mentally urged. *Black wings, long black fingers, radar sense, little stubby legs... Bat-Man! Bat-Man! Nah-nah nah-nah nah-nah nah-nah, nah-nah nah-nah nah-nah nah-nah, Bat-Man! Bat-Man!*

He waited for oily gray smoke to surround him. "Is anything happenin' yet?" he asked, hoping to hear that his voice had turned squeaky and batlike.

"Nothing, Jules. You look like you're trying very hard to go to the toilet."

Bummer. Okay, so the bat business wasn't working out. Maybe he should just aim for his human form straight off? He wished he had a photograph of himself he could stare at. The only thing was, the most recent photo which had been taken of him was of Jules at the age of twelve, dressed in a too-tight sailor's suit. And that old photo was somewhere in his mother's treasure box over at Doc Landrieu's house.

He did the best he could. *Big fat man with white hair. Who was that actor from Cannon, the old TV detective show? I'm kinda a better lookin' version of him, maybe a little bigger, though. Let's see... there's late-career Marlon Brando; he was a big tubba lard in that romance picture he did with Meryl Streep. Or Orson Wells, from when he was doin' them wine commercials...*

He had a hard time concentrating on the faces and bodies of even those famous fat actors, though. This rabbit form of his wasn't making his task any easier. All he wanted to think about, really, was making litter after litter of cute little bunnies with Mo...

He tried another minute, then gave up. "Nothin' doin', hon," he said, sadly. "'Fraid your idea's a bust."

"Ohhh," Maureen moaned, "if only we had our *own* Fortress of Solitude, like Superman's, stuffed full of antidotes!"

Antidotes. Maybe that was the key word? There was still one type of Japanese superhero blood they hadn't tried. Shogo's. Both times Jules had watched the three Japanese superheroes do their shtick, Shogo had closed the loop. His use of his power had come last; it always seemed to return everything and everybody back to normal.

Jules stared at the bags of blood sitting on Maureen's dresser, where he'd left them. Maybe a sip of Shogo's blood would do the trick? It made more sense than taking a sip of Kenji's blood. If he did *that*, he'd probably end up a stoned white rabbit, a figure straight out of a Jefferson Airplane song.

"I'm gonna try me a little sip of Shogo's blood," Jules said. "Maybe that'll work as an antidote."

"Do you think that's *safe*?"

"Here's my way of thinkin'. Shogo's always the one who closes out their shows. After he finishes usin' his powers, the volunteers who Kenji shrunk to mini-size and who Emiko turned into cartoon characters get returned to normal. Right? So it makes sense that his blood would, y'know, counteract the effects of his cousins' blood. Don't it?"

Maureen looked uncertain. "I... I *suppose* so... that *seems* to make sense..."

"I'll take an itty-bitty little sip, just to be on the safe side. Then we'll see what happens. All right?"

Maureen cautiously nodded her head. Jules poured himself a tiny amount of Shogo's blood into his mug. Having paws instead of hands made handling the bag of blood awkward. He wanted to cross his fingers, but he worried about burning himself. Besides, he didn't have fingers to cross anymore, not really. Instead, he tossed Maureen the Shogo action figure.

"What's this for?" she asked.

"Rub the top of his head for luck. I'd ask ya to rub my lucky rabbit's foot, but I'm afraid that would get me all hot and bothered again, and we'd spend the rest of the night fuckin'."

"Okay, I'm rubbing…"

Here goes nothin', he thought. He raised the mug to his rabbit lips. Shogo's blood didn't taste nearly as good as either Kenji's blood or Emiko's had. It had a sour taste, and an especially bitter aftertaste. At least it didn't burn his throat going down, like Emiko's blood had.

"Are you feeling any different?" Maureen asked anxiously.

"Not yet," Jules said.

He heard the front door downstairs open. "Jules? Maureen? Either of you home?" It was his mother. What was *she* doing here?

"We're upstairs, Mom," he called down to her. "But this ain't a good time for no visit—"

"You two go on about your marital business," Edna called up the stairs. "Don't mind me! Just pretend I'm not here. Anyway, I just came over to count out our receipts for the night. I forgot to do it earlier. I think we're doing really well so far, don't you? I know I'm selling a whole lot more of these vampire sock monkeys than I thought I would. I've gotta find more time for my sewing! I'm sure glad we're making a little extra cash on the side. I've been wantin' a new vacuum cleaner for the longest time. Amos keeps insistin' that the vacuum cleaner we've got is perfectly good, and he doesn't see no sense in spending money on a new one. But the one we've got is as weak as a three-month-old baby with the runs. Y'know, *you* used to get the runs all the time when you was a baby, Jules.

I think it's 'cause you used to eat all the dust bunnies off the floor, after you learned to crawl. I used to hafta pull *everything* outta your mouth — knittin' needles, pencils, dried-up mouse turds... You was an eatin' *machine*, boy, even at the age of nine months—"

Jules covered his ears (not that this was easy, given their size). His mother's yammerings made his want to punch his rabbit fist through the wall. "Mom! Could you *please* go *away* and come back *some other time?*"

"I'm not botherin' anybody or anything!" his mother called up at him. "Am I? And is that any way to talk to your sweet old mother, who's slavin' away every evening to help you run your business?"

Jules saw red. He almost rushed out of his bedroom and hopped down the stairs in order to shove his mother out the front door. "Count your money some other time, Mom! Maureen and I are havin' sort of a *crisis* up here, okay? Can't we have us some ding-dabbed *privacy?*"

"A *crisis?*" Edna called up the stairs. "What *kind* of crisis, Jules? You don't sound like yourself. I don't think you're well, boy. I'm comin' up there, right now!"

"Don't you *dare*, Mother!" Jules shouted. "If you do, you'll be *sorry!*"

Jules and Maureen heard Edna hurrying up the stairs. Maureen grabbed the remnants of the bedcovers to throw over herself. Jules rushed to the door to slam it shut and lock it.

But he was too late. By the time he started pushing the door closed, his mother had already inserted her head and neck through the doorway.

"*Maureen!*" Edna shouted, not yet seeing her son. "What you gone and *done* to yourself, girl? You's as big as a house! Naww, make that a housing *development!*"

She squeezed herself into the room. Only then did she see Jules. "AAAAAHHHHH!!!" she screamed. "I'm seein' things! I gone senile! It's *Harvey!*"

"Who the fuck's 'Harvey,' Mom?" Jules sputtered, furiously tapping the floorboards with his giant right foot.

"The big rabbit from the movie *Harvey*! The one with that darlin' Jimmy Stewart! Is that *you*, Jules?"

"Damn right it's me, Mom! Didn't I warn you not to come up here?"

"What you *done* to yourself, boy?"

"Mo and me drank some blood we shouldn't have. We're tryin' to work things out, and *you* ain't helpin' none by bein' here. Now get the hell *out*, will ya? We don't need no distractions!"

"Jules!" Maureen shouted at him. "What's *wrong* with you? You don't have to be such a *beast* to your mother! Can't you see she's in *shock*? She's just worried about you, that's all!"

"Tha-thank you, Maureen," Edna said, trembling. She turned back around to stare at her transformed and glowering son with terrified eyes. "I — I thought bunny rabbits was *sweet* and *gentle*! But you — you sound like a monster, Jules! Like a *were-rabbit*!"

So now his mother was calling him *names*? "You women are *gangin' up* on me, ain't ya? When I'm at my lowest, you're tryin' to shove me down even *lower*!" He grabbed the bedroom door and yanked it open so hard that its hinges pulled away from the wall. "Well, Mom, if *you* won't leave, then *I* will! I'm outta here, Maureen! Don't bother leavin' the lights on for me!"

"Jules, don't *go*!" Maureen pleaded, her eyes wide. "You're not in your right mind, honey! I think — I think drinking Shogo's blood has done something *bad* to you!"

Jules thumped down the stairs. The damn steps were too small for his feet. So he leaped over the last six steps, landing with a great *WHACK*! on the hardwood floor. "I'll go see my pals at the Trolley Stop, that's what I'll do," he muttered to himself. "Maybe Erato'll talk to me now. Wait a minute — why should I hafta *beg* that sonofabitch to talk with me? Is he so much *better* than me that he can't be bothered to acknowledge a hello? And after I done gave him money for his kid's college education? Fuck him! That's right — fuck *him*, and fuck all them *other* losers who spent years snipin' at me 'cause of my weight, laughin' at me from behind their cups of coffee!"

He looked up. Maureen had managed to descend half-way down the stairs. "Don't *go*, Jules!" she repeated, stretching her round arms to him. "If you leave, I'm scared you'll do things you'll always regret! Shogo's blood — it's turned you *evil*, honey!"

"Evil, *schmevil*," Jules growled up at her. "How evil can I *be*, Maureen? After all, I'm the goddamned *Easter* bunny! Tell you what — you keep that old harpy upstairs out of my fur, and maybe I'll FedEx you a giant box of chocolate Easter eggs. Make sure and enjoy 'em, lard ass!"

"*Jules!*"

He fumbled with the front door's knob, his furry paws making him clumsy. He finally got the knob turned, then kicked the door open. Fresh air, at last! He'd thought he'd suffocate in the stuffy, constricting atmosphere inside that house. Those yammering women had been sucking up all his air.

He hopped over the stoop's steps to the sidewalk, then hopped a block west to the quiet stretch of street where he'd parked his car. Too late, he remembered that he'd left his keys back in his bedroom. He'd rather have a blind Chinaman depilate his entire body with a pair of rusty tweezers than go back inside that house. He stared down at his massive feet, each more than a yard long. There was no way those feet would manage to manipulate the Cadillac's accelerator and brake pedals, anyway.

Well, who needed the car? He got around just fine, hopping. And why head straight for the Trolley Stop? Why set his sights for the evening so low? Revenge on Erato and that crummy crew of cabbies could wait. Why not have himself an all-out, no-holds-barred *reign of terror*? He was a vampire, wasn't he? And now, he was a vampire *rabbit*, a predator much faster and even deadlier than before. What had his mother called him? Harvey the Horrible? Tonight, he would live up to that name... or down to it.

He felt a stirring in his rabbit loins again. *In between tearin' some heads off some necks, I'm gonna screw every chubby gal in this town,* he told himself. *And if I can find 'em, some fat bunnies, too.*

Thirteen

"K ENJI!" Maureen screamed into the phone. She'd nearly lost her sanity during the couple of minutes it had taken the night clerk at the Residence Inn (a new trainee) to locate the Japanese guests' telephone number and connect her. "You've got to come over here *immediately*! You and the others! Jules has done something *terrible* to himself! He drank some of Emiko's and Shogo's blood, and it's turned him into a *vicious seven-foot-tall rabbit*!"

"Call Amos! Or let *me* call him!" Edna insisted, grabbing for the phone. *"He'll* know what to do!"

"Just a *minute*, Edna!" Maureen said, slapping her mother-in-law's hands away. "I've got to give Kenji the address here so they can give it to their cab driver!" She put the receiver against her cheek again. "Kenji, please hurry! There's no telling *what* Jules is up to! If there's ever been a time for superheroes to leap into action, it's *now*!"

After Kenji assured her they would be over as quickly as possible (and in costume), Maureen handed the phone to the older woman. Edna frantically dialed her home number. "Hello, Amos? It's Edna. Yes, I *know* I sound out of breath. *Yes*, there's an emergency! No, *no*, it's not me. It's *Jules*. He's turned himself into a *monster*, Amos! A *rabbit* monster!

"Yes, I said 'rabbit monster.' Eight feet tall with them ears, and a temper as bad as King Kong's — if King Kong was a rabid bunny instead of a gorilla. How did he manage it? Oh, you know him! He was like a darn stupid teenager, experimentin' with wacky weed! Not marijuana, no — wacky *blood*! Superhero blood from those Oriental friends of his! Maureen says he and she tried out different kinds, for a kick. Some kick! She done turned herself back into a big fatso. He turned himself into a big, white bunny rabbit. Then he tried reversin' the spell by drinking that other fellow's blood, the quiet one — Shogo's. But it turned him *evil*, Amos! My son's out there on the streets somewhere, hoppin' around and making a public menace of himself! You got to *do* something!"

* * * * *

Forget about the Trolley Stop, Jules told himself. *If I wanna go on a rabbit rampage — and I DO — the best place to do it this time of the night is Bourbon Street. That's where the crowds are gonna be.* Smaller crowds than before the hurricane and the flooding, for sure. But heavier concentrations of tourists than he'd find anywhere else in town at two o'clock in the morning.

He hopped along empty Iberville Street until he reached Bourbon Street. Upper Bourbon was virtually deserted; the only person Jules saw as he turned the corner was a stray celebrant stumbling out of a twenty-four-hour drug store with a can of energy drink, undoubtedly trying to counteract his acute inebriation just enough to drive himself home. The man took a last swig from his energy drink, then tossed the empty can into the overstuffed maw of a full garbage container. The can bounced off the pile of refuse and clattered into the street. The man watched it roll down the gutter. It stopped rolling when it struck Jules' yard-long bunny foot.

The drunk took a look at Jules. He shook his head wildly and slapped at his eyes. Then he turned on his heels and stumbled back inside the drug store, possibly reasoning that just one can of energy drink had not done the trick, no siree Bob.

Great, Jules grumbled to himself. *I can't even get a good rampage started right. What's the first thing I do? Scare a would-be drunk driver off the street before he gets in his car. Some menace I am!*

He needed to go deeper into the Quarter, to the parts of Bourbon Street with the overpriced titty bars and karaoke joints and gay hangouts. After dark, Bourbon Street was closed to vehicular traffic and turned into a pedestrian mall. The pink, green, and red neon lights of Larry Flint's Hustler Club, the Sho Bar, the Famous Door, Lipstixx Gentleman's Club, and dozens of other tourist traps beckoned to him, stirring the rabbit fury that boiled within his furry chest.

The stench of spilled beer, lingering cigar smoke, discarded fast food leftovers rotting in garbage cans, and rank human sweat invaded his sensitive pink rabbit nose. Vile goop stuck to the bottoms of his oversized feet, making him hate the sloppy, disgusting tourists even more. Who asked them to use New Orleans as their open-air toilet? Sure, the city desperately needed their money, but did it need it *this bad*? And that crappy music they listened to — here in the Big Easy, you could hardly turn over a rock without finding a world-class musician, but *these* bastards wanted nothing better than to hear covers of "Proud Mary" and Jimmy Buffet's greatest hits while swilling their overpriced, watered-down booze.

Jimmy Buffet, for Varney's sake! Jules felt his remaining wisps of kindness and charity wasting away again in Margaritaville. He wanted to puke a strawberry daiquiri.

He hopped beneath the wrought iron balconies of the Royal Sonesta Hotel. A middle-aged man wearing nothing but a pair of athletic shorts leaned over one of the balconies, his TV blaring the baleful techno pop of a pay-porn channel through an open sliding door. The man, beer in hand, grew apishly excited when he spotted Jules on the street. "Hey! Hey! Easter bunny! Hey, up here!"

Jules made the mistake of pausing and glancing up. The man leaned even further over the railing and held out his hands, grasping for Carnival beads. *"Throw me something, mister!"* the man bellowed.

"Fuck you, asshole!" Jules bellowed back.

"Oh, no beads for me?" the man said. "I gotta show you my tits? Well, this is the best I got, bunny!" The man turned around, thrust his ass towards the railing, and dropped his shorts.

"And *this* is the best *I* got!" A bunny snarl gathering in his throat, Jules leaped at the second story balcony. His front paws smashed into the railing, knocking it off its moorings and hurling the startled tourist, shorts bunched around his ankles, tumbling back inside his hotel room, wailing.

Now that *felt good*, Jules told himself when he landed on the beer-damp pavement. He'd gotten his rampage off to a semi-decent start. He scanned the street for other targets. A young couple, both clutching plastic cups the size of ice buckets, darted out of a take-out daiquiri shop (which assailed Jules' large ears with the noise pollution of canned Jimmy Buffet songs) to gawk at him. His altercation with the "throw me something, mister!" guy had attracted attention from other pedestrians further down the block, as well.

Jules waited until a large enough audience had gathered. He wanted this next stunt to benefit from some eyeballs... before he sent those eyeballs, severed and bloody, bouncing down the street. He spotted a Lucky Dog hotdog cart sitting on the curb in front of the daiquiri shop. The lids to the bins filled with heated water that kept the dogs hot were open, spilling the aroma of obscene, unmentionable meat byproducts into the already dicey air surrounding Jules' nose.

I always wanted to do this, Jules told himself. *Imagined doing it for years. And now I finally can*! He backed up for more running space, then took a tremendous leap in the direction of the Lucky Dog cart. He turned his body in midair so that his massive feet aimed at the center of the six-foot-long fiberglass wiener. His rabbit feet kicked the cart with the force of a steam-powered jackhammer.

The wiener cart, along with its sheltering umbrella, soared inside the daiquiri shop. The fiberglass missile smashed open an entire row of five swirling daiquiri machines, flooding the floor with a mixture of strawberry, blueberry, pineapple, chocolate, and banana rum-flavored slush. Catsup, mustard, and pickle relish splattered the cash registers and the panicked employees. Hot dog water from the distended cart shorted out the speakers which had been playing the grating beach bum tunes. Loose Lucky Dogs rolled across the filthy floor onto the sidewalk. A large gray rat, feeling itself lucky, darted out from the shelter of a garbage container, grabbed one of the wieners with its teeth, and happily dragged it down into the gutter.

The crowd standing on the street drank in every second of the multicolored mayhem. Then they turned to Jules and clinked beer bottles together or applauded.

"This ain't no fuckin' SHOW, people!" Jules bellowed. To make his point even more blatantly, he picked up the garbage container which had sheltered the hungry rat and hurled it in the direction of the tourists. Not a hundred percent certain that this was an OSHA-approved movie stunt staged by a bonded production company, the crowd scattered and fled down Bourbon Street.

A NOPD squad car, light bar swirling red, siren bleating an ear-splitting warning, turned onto Bourbon from Toulouse Street. The driver pushed his way cautiously through the fleeing crowd. He slammed on his brakes when he saw Jules ahead of him.

Jules took a running leap high into the air. He landed squarely on the roof of the squad car, his five-hundred-pound weight ruinously denting it. Before the stunned cops could open their doors and escape, Jules jumped up and down on the battered roof three more times in rapid succession, caving it in and bending the Crown Victoria's door frames so severely that the two cops were trapped inside, squished against their collapsed seats.

A young man wearing dreadlocks, dark sunglasses, and a Bob Marley T-shirt gave Jules a Black Power salute from a nearby sidewalk. "You go, rabbit!" he said, beaming. "Fuck the cops! Rabbit versus pigs! Outtasight!"

Jules jumped off the crippled squad car. What next? His appetite for destruction had barely been whetted. He wished he were two hundred feet tall so he could go the full Godzilla. But no sooner had the image of the famous Japanese dinosaur flitted through his rage-clouded brain, Jules heard a familiar Japanese accent politely command him from behind.

"Jures-*san*, you must prease stop this at once! You are not in your right mind! This is no way for a superhero to be acting, not even when he is a rabbit!"

Jules whirled. "So you found me, huh, Kenji? Are you and the Super-Friends gonna try and stop me? I *hope* so. 'Cause it's gonna be *fun* takin' the three of you apart."

Kenji's hands began glowing with a green light. "This is not you speaking, Jures-*san*. Not trury. These words are from a madness caused by Emiko's and Shogo's blood. Let us herrp you, prease. Come with us back to the house of Maureen-*san*, your wife…"

"Or *what*?" Jules said. He stared at Kenji's glowing hands. "Or you'll shrink me down to the size of a toy stuffed bunny? Well, I got news for ya, Kenji, old pal — you can't *shrink* what you can't *touch*!"

Having said that, Jules leaped over the heads of the Japanese super-trio. Then, to emphasize his point, he leaped back over their heads in the opposite direction. "I can keep this up all night, kids!" he bragged. "Faster than Bugs Bunny! More powerful than Oswald the Lucky Rabbit! Able to leap tall Jap superheroes in a single bound!"

He leaped over them a third time, then a fourth. Kenji remained unperturbed. "Bring him to the ground, Anime Girr," he commanded his sister.

Emiko peeled off her wide, flouncy skirt, revealing a set of form-fitting silver tights beneath. She tossed her skirt to a surprised onlooker a few yards away. Then, displaying the strength, speed, and skills of an Olympic-level gymnast, she catapulted herself onto the damaged squad car, utilized its hood as a trampoline, somersaulted into the air, and landed a roundhouse kick on Jules' Adam's apple when he was at the apex of one of his leaps.

Jules landed hard on his back, choking and sputtering. Kenji immediately straddled him and slapped his glowing hands against Jules' white-furred chest.

Here comes Toyville, Jules thought. But to his surprise, nothing happened. The green glow failed to spread from Kenji's hands into Jules' body.

"*Iai!*" Kenji exclaimed, clearly shocked. "What is this? My power has no effect on him!"

"So yer — *cough* — best trick, it don't work on me, huh? Too bad, so sad, Samurai Sam!"

He tossed Kenji off of him, then rolled away to the curb. While Jules was struggling to get to his feet, Kenji turned to his cousin. "Shogo! Hold him!"

The third member of the Acme *Tarento* Tremendous Power Trio responded with alacrity, grabbing Jules' arms and twisting them behind him. "Real *cute*, Cutie-Scary Man," Jules grumbled. "You ain't gonna be able to hold me fer long, Shogo. Without that power transfer from your cousin, you're just an ordinary wimp. I'll toss you like a mixed salad."

Kenji used his power to shrink a garbage container down to the size of a shoebox. Then he gently placed his power-charged hands on his sister's face, so the glowing green energy could flow into her lips. "Turn him *kawaii*, Anime Girr," Kenji told her. "Then wirr we reason with him, when his rage is gone."

"*Hai!*" Emiko responded.

Seeing her rush his way, Jules broke free of Shogo's grip. He shoved the Japanese superhero against the brick wall of a T-shirt shop and prepared to leap away from Emiko's touch. But before he could gather his strength for the jump, she performed a swift set of tumbles across the asphalt, then sprang out of her final somersault to wrap her arms around his long, furry neck in a tight embrace.

She kissed his rabbit mouth. Jules sensed the heat from her energy-infused lips radiate against his face. It excited him. Despite knowing the jeopardy he was in, he couldn't help himself. His rabbit instincts took over. He embraced her tightly — *va-va-va-VOOM!* — pulling her slender, girlish body into his plush, squishy rabbit belly and chest. His rabbit member grew stiff as a ripe carrot. *This is nice,* he told himself. *Reee-aaally nice...*

He gave her some rabbit tongue.

"*Eeewww!*" she shrieked, pushing him away. He saw her scan his face for any signs of a change. But what she saw in his expression was bunny lust, not at all *kawaii.* "*Nani?* What? I did not turn him *kawaii?*" She pressed her fingers against her lips, which still glowed green. "The energy — it remains with me, not him! I have *fai-urred!*"

Kenji grasped a time-share booklet vending machine with his glowing hands; it quickly shrunk to something which could easily be crushed underfoot. His hands glowed with double the brightness and intensity they had only seconds before. "Jures-*san!*" he cried. "You have seen what I can do with my energy, how I can shoot it into the sky so that it exprodes rike big bombs. Do not make me shoot this energy at you! I do not want to destroy you! Surrender! Come with us back to the house of Maureen-*san!*"

"Do your *worst,* Kenji," Jules sneered. "I'm bettin' you're too *chicken* to use that blast power of yours here. Miss me — and with the way I can jump around, there's a good chance you *will* — and you'll end up blowin' up half of Bourbon Street, barbecuing hundreds of workers and tourists. Won't *that* be great for U.S.-Japan relations. You wanna take that chance, Mr. 'I Ruvv New Orrins'? *Do ya?*"

Steely-eyed, Kenji pointed his blindingly bright hands at Jules. But then Shogo stepped between them. "No, Bonsai Master-*san!*" he said. "Prease, awrrow me to hand-urr him." He flipped open a canteen-sized container attached to his belt, then removed a toylike figure of Felix the Cat. The figure glowed as brightly green as Kenji's hands.

"What is this?" Kenji asked, staring uncomprehendingly at the tiny figure. "What have you there?"

"It is for emergency," Shogo said. "Such as now. I have brought my own *otaku* from Japan. From this *otaku*, I can draw my power." Shogo held the glowing figure above his head, closed his eyes, and concentrated. The green energy flowed from the figure down his hands and arms and throughout his body.

A blinding green flash forced Jules to close his eyes. When he opened them, he saw that Shogo had taken on the likeness of Felix the Cat, a brick-throwing cartoon character Jules remembered well from cinema's silent days.

Shogo handed the *otaku*, no longer glowing green, to Emiko. "Take care of him," he said. "I wirr restore him in a few moments, once I am done here." Shogo again closed his eyes (which were now big black circles missing a triangular slice). He pressed his jet-black palms together in front of his chest. Then he underwent a second transformation, far more sinister than his first. His stubby cartoon hands and hind paws sprouted claws of needle sharpness. His stick-thin arms grew bulky with fresh muscle. His pointed black ears, formerly cartoonish triangles, grew tall and twisted like a devil's horns. His square white teeth became fangs. His eyes, when he reopened them, glowed as red as the boiling heart of a volcano.

"Now," he said, "rett us see if the Cat can vanquish the Rabbit!"

Snarling a high-pitched feline snarl, Shogo hurled himself at Jules, moving even faster than the incredibly quick Emiko had moments before. Jules managed to leap out his way, but just barely. As soon as Jules landed, Shogo reversed direction with amazing catlike agility and bounded upon his back. Shogo sank his claws into Jules' furry shoulders and poised himself to tear Jules' neck open with his teeth.

"That *hurts*, goddamn it!" Jules reached behind him, grabbed "Felix" by the scruff of his black-furred neck, and tossed him with all his strength at the plate glass display window of Fritzel's European Jazz Pub.

The window shattered. Shogo vanished into the club's dark interior, emptied of customers for the night. Jules glanced down at his raked shoulders. He knew he should flee before Shogo, who posed a genuine threat, reemerged. But the sight of his own blood dripping down his white fur drove him to new heights of fury. "I'm comin' for ya, Shogo!" he screamed. Then he leaped through the remnants of the window into the jazz pub.

He landed on a small stage, cluttered with standing microphones and instrument holders. Chunks of broken glass littered the polished wood surfaces of an upright piano. Jules scanned the dark spaces of the club's interior for his foe. He was at a disadvantage — Shogo, almost entirely black, blended in with the darkness, while he, white as bone china, stood out against the light streaming in from the street.

Still, he could rely on other senses besides sight. His ears stood fully erect. His nose twitched. "I can *smell* ya, you rat fink," he said. "You stink like kitty litter…"

He cautiously stepped off the stage and pushed his way past tables heaped with stacked chairs. Then he saw a glint of light off varnished wood, a flicker of swift movement. He whirled. Shogo was swinging a *giant violin* at him—?

The massive bass guitar exploded into expensive splinters when it crashed into Jules' head. Jules fell into a group of tables, stunned. A pile of stacked chairs toppled onto him.

"Ohhhhh…" Jules moaned. "Sneak attacks… you Japs… always quick with the sneak attacks…"

Shogo grabbed him by the scruff of his neck. Jules felt himself being dragged back onto the stage. Then, with a crowd of tourists looking on from the sidewalk, the monstrous Felix the Cat smashed Jules' rabbit skull into the keys of the upright piano, twice, three times. Jules' face played distended chords way more *avant-garde* than the Dixieland and ragtime melodies typically played on that particular instrument.

Shogo dragged Jules back out onto the street. The onlooking crowd retreated before him, in awe of his brutal work. A pair of waiters, who had run over from the Clover Leaf Grill a block away to catch the action, began a laudatory chant of "Cat-Man! Cat-Man! *Cat-Man!*"

Barely able to keep his eyes open, feeling his face swelling into a huge, pulsating bruise, Jules saw a familiar car pull up. Doc Landrieu jumped out of the vehicle. "Let me through!" he said. "I'm a doctor! A doctor of veterinarian medicine! That animal escaped from the zoo!"

Was Amos here to help him escape his tormentors? Or was he here to help capture him? Jules' muddled mind, fading in and out of consciousness, couldn't decide.

As soon as he spotted the hypodermic needle in his father-in-law's right hand, Jules knew it was the latter. *So much for family loyalty...* he mentally grumbled as twenty cubic centimeters of animal tranquilizer sent him tumbling into bunny dreamyland.

* * * * *

Curious to see how this American crowd would react, Shogo decided to dare a very un-Japanese display. With his foe sprawled unconscious on the dirty street, Shogo placed his foot on Jules' chest and clasped his cat's paws together above his head in a gesture of triumph.

The crowd cheered. The two waiters from the Clover Leaf Grill, dressed in green aprons stained with hamburger grease, cheered the loudest, whooping it up while leaping up and down like a pair of junior varsity cheerleaders at a middle school football game.

"Cat-Man! Cat-Man! *Cat-Man!*"

Shogo motioned for Emiko to bring him the *otaku*, the tiny, living Felix the Cat whom he had given her for safe keeping. She set the *otaku* on the street before him. Shogo knelt beside the miniature figure and placed his two index fingers on its head. He closed his glowing red eyes to concentrate once more. The familiar green energy sparked forth from his fingertips and infused the tiny Felix. Seconds later, Shogo had resumed his normal form, and the *otaku* stood revealed as a Japanese man in his late twenties, who clutched his now too-large pants to keep them from falling down around his ankles.

"Where am I? What is this place?" the man babbled in Japanese, looking wildly around him.

"You are on Bourbon Street, in the city of New Orleans," Shogo replied.

"I thought I was still in Kure...?" the man said, bewildered. "Am I truly in America, in New Orleans, the city of jazz? Will I meet Louis Armstrong?"

"I do not think so," Shogo said.

Kenji approached the man. "What is your name?" he asked.

The man's eyes widened. He quickly bowed. "I am Akira Iwabe, Bonsai Master-*san*. A humble follower and admirer of the Acme *Tarento* Tremendous Power Trio. I have collected all of your action figures, in all their versions, from the very oldest to the newest. Can you tell me, please, how much time has passed since I have last been in Kure?"

"My team and I left Japan one week ago," Kenji said. He glanced disapprovingly at Shogo. "I do not know at which of our demonstrations in Kure you were transformed into a *kawaii* figure, and then stored away by my cousin..."

"I volunteered at the grand opening of the Sun Bright Cherry Blossom Shopping Center," Akira said.

"Ahh. Then you have been in storage with Cutie-Scary Man as a *kawaii* figure for the past month," Kenji said.

"No!" the man said in shock. "I had no idea — what must my parents be thinking? I said I would only be gone for a few days!"

"I will purchase for you a return ticket to Japan, Iwabe-*san*. I apologize for any inconvenience which the actions of my team have caused for you and your family. It is most regrettable."

Akira bowed once more. "Illustrious Bonsai Master-*san*, I am unworthy to accept your overwhelming generosity. I shall find work here in New Orleans and earn enough money to purchase my own return ticket."

"You do not need to do that. It was the actions of my own family which have taken you from Japan without your knowledge or consent. You must allow me to buy for you the return ticket."

"But I *cannot*, exalted superhero-*san*! I am unworthy of such a gift, from such a person!"

"Worthy or unworthy, you must accept. I am responsible for the actions of my team. I must return you to your family."

Akira bowed a third time (most awkwardly, due to his need to hold up his pants). "Of course, then, I shall accept your most generous gift of a return ticket. Am I permitted to tell of this experience? This will make me a most famous person among my fellow superhero *otaku*, if I may tell of it…"

Kenji returned the man's bow. "You may tell of it, Iwabe-*san*. But only among your friends, please."

Shogo silently scowled at the respectful tones with which his cousin and superior addressed the *otaku*. Personally, he considered the superhero fanboys and fangirls, those obsessive collectors of action figures, video clips, and homemade anime pamphlets, to be somewhat less than human, certainly not worthy of being addressed as a social equal.

He had two other shrunken *otaku* stored away in his luggage. Considering the disapproving glance Kenji had cast upon him and his cousin's words of contrition and regret, Shogo knew he would need to find a more secure hiding place for those two remaining *otaku*, power sources which he had furtively squirreled away at various events in Kure after having falsely assured Kenji and Emiko that he would restore the *otaku* to their normal forms.

A pair of NOPD squad cars turned onto Bourbon from Dumaine Street. Four officers emerged from their cars and approached the spot where Jules lay unconscious, being tended by Amos Landrieu. "Mister, who do you think you are — George of the Jungle?" the senior cop barked to the physician. "That's a dangerous animal! We had reports it was tearing up Bourbon Street! What authority do you have to handle it?"

"I'm the lead veterinarian from the Audubon Zoo," Amos said. "This animal has been sedated, and I'll be returning him to his enclosure in our Australian exhibit. He's a very rare albino kangaroo, the only one on display in North America."

"*Kangaroo?*" the cop said dubiously. "Looks like a big-ass *rabbit* to me."

"Oh, don't be ridiculous, officer," Amos said, smiling (he quickly covered his mouth, not wanting to accidentally reveal his fangs). "There's not a rabbit in the world that grows this big. He's a kangaroo, very rare. I'll admit he has some rabbit-like features, but that's normal in the mutant albino variety."

"Okay, whatever, just so long as you got him under control," the cop said. He glanced at the old Mercedes-Benz. "Hey, how come you didn't bring a wild animal wagon or something?"

"Oh, that's my fault — I misplaced the keys. I got woken up in the middle of the night with a report that our white kangaroo had escaped. Not wanting to waste time searching for the keys to our animal transport van, I brought my personal vehicle. Would you and your men be so kind as to help me move the animal into my back seat? I want to get him back to my clinic as quickly as possible to check for any internal injuries he may have suffered during his escape. He's on loan from the Sydney Zoo in Australia, so we must take very good care of him."

Shogo watched the four policemen, Amos Landrieu, and his cousin Kenji maneuver the bulky, quarter-ton form of Jules Duchon into the back seat of the old Mercedes-Benz. But then the crowd demanded his attention, thrusting napkins and matchbook covers and souvenir menus at him to autograph, and peppering him with questions.

"Where did you come from?"

"Are you a *real* superhero?"

"This wasn't just a stunt for a movie, was it?"

"Can I take your picture? Will you pose with me? Will you pose with my brother-in-law?"

"Are you here to help New Orleans rebuild?"

"Are you kind of like, y'know, Jesus, only Japanese?"

"Do you have an agent? Here's my card..."

The two waiters from the Clover Leaf Grill pushed the others aside. Each grasped one of Shogo's arms. "*This* man gets his pick of any items on our menu, for *free*," the taller of the two waiters said. "He saved us all from that awful, terrible, vicious bunny creature!"

"Will you come with us to the Clover Leaf Grill, Mr. Cat-Man?" the other waiter said. "You are one *fine-looking* superhero, you know that? I just *love* those boots. You put Christopher Reeves *himself* to shame. And I'm talking Chris Reeves in his *prime*."

Shogo nodded his head, pleased with the adulation. "I will go," he said.

"Wonderful!" the first waiter said. "Let's make it a party! Hey, everybody, y'all come to the Clover Leaf Grill, too! Free Cokes, on the house! This is Cat-Man's night!"

The crowd cheered him again. Shogo felt good. It had been very satisfying, defeating a monster. A worthy use of his special powers — much, much more satisfying than cutting a red ribbon at a new shopping center, or standing next to Kure's mayor at the opening of a new bridge, or putting on yet another staged performance with his cousins. For years, Shogo had suffered bitter pangs of envy at the thought of his illustrious predecessors' careers — those post-war superheroes, blessed by fortune, who had made their names and reputations battling demons, monsters, and criminals of science. He had assumed he was forever trapped in the boring, thrill-less existence of a corporate and city mascot, all the supernatural menaces of Japan having been vanquished before he had even been born. And, seeing no alternative, he had mostly resigned himself to his unfair fate.

Yet, here in New Orleans, here in this far-off land of the *gaijin*, he had found his own monster to vanquish. He had achieved martial glory of the sort of which he had only fantasized. He had earned the adulation of a crowd — not by putting on a show or cutting a ribbon, but by risking his own life in the quest to protect others from bodily harm. These people who surrounded him now were not fawning *otaku*, who fed upon Shogo's made-up exploits to fill their empty lives. These were people he had *saved*. People who owed him their very *lives*.

This adulation was different from any he had ever known. He liked it. He liked it very much.

And he wanted more of it, he decided.

Much more.

Fourteen

"MAUREEN. Let me *out*, Maureen."

Jules' voice, bottled within the walls of his coffin, sounded muffled, as though his mouth were stuffed full of Easter chocolates. Maureen shifted her position atop Jules' piano case-sized coffin. To help the long, trying hours pass, she'd been watching the progress a wolf spider had been making climbing the wall of her basement. She prayed her immense weight would continue to be an adequate safeguard against her husband's escape. Doc Landrieu had assured her that the ropes tying Jules' limbs tightly against his torso and the chains surrounding the coffin itself would be proof against her temporarily insane hubby's breaking out, and that she didn't need to act as additional ballast. But she hadn't felt Jules would be truly secure without her four hundred pounds atop his coffin. And she'd wanted to be near him during this time of his suffering.

"C'mon, Mo, be a sport. Let me out."

"Not until you're back in your right mind, Jules."

"Oh, but I *am* in my right mind, doll. Rightest mind ever. Couldn't be righter. Righty-oh, righty-hoe!"

"I wish I could believe that, Jules. *How* I *wish* I could…"

"Maureen… you want my rabbity love, don't you, baby? I *know* you do. You want it *bad*. I'm *soooooo* positive you want my rabbit love shaft between those big, plush thighs. Once you've had a taste of hare, other guys had best beware… ain't that right, babe?"

Maureen dabbed tiny droplets of sweat away from her forehead. "Oh, Jules, you aren't making this any *easier*, sweetheart…"

"You think this is easy for *me*? Bein' trussed up in my own coffin like a Thanksgiving turkey, uh, rabbit?"

"I know it's hard, honey. But Amos is working from sundown to sun-up, searching for a cure—"

"Maybe I don't *wanna* be cured. Yeah, it's hard, bein' cooped up in here. But you wanna know what *else* is hard, what stays hard *all the time*…?"

"Oh, Jules! Do you *have* to start *that* up again?"

Amos Landrieu descended the stairs. "How is our large-footed friend doing this evening?" he asked. "Has his behavior shown any signs of moderating?"

"Oh, he's just as *ornery* and *nasty* as ever," Maureen complained. "How I *wish* he'd never experimented with that sip of Shogo's blood! He did it for *me*, Amos… because he knew it was a torment for me to remain at this size. But if I'd had the tiniest inkling of what that blood would do to him, I *never* would've let him drink it, *never*, even if it meant I had to stay four hundred pounds for the rest of eternity…"

"Oh, that's so *sweet*, hon," Jules purred from inside the coffin. "How about you let me outta here, and I'll reward you with some hot make-up fucking?"

"You hear how he is," Maureen said, clenching her hands together. "Have you made any progress at all?"

Amos sighed and shook his head. "Not much, I'm afraid. I've been analyzing samples of all three Japanese metahumans' blood, trying to sort out the similarities and differences. The factors are incredibly complex, way beyond the capabilities of my rather limited equipment to analyze in any reasonable amount of time. Perhaps if I had access to the National Institute of Health's supercomputers, I might be able to make some headway. Or if I could tap into the research Kenji told me about, research the scientists from the Japan Self Defense Forces have done on tissue samples from their population of superhumans. But that's classified material, unfortunately."

"Does that mean there's no hope?"

Amos patted her hand. "I didn't say that, my dear. If nothing else, there's a good possibility that the passage of time may return matters to normal. After all, remember the effect drinking Kenji's blood had on you both?"

"It made us high, Amos."

"Yes, but did you *stay* high? No. The effect was temporary. It's very possible that the effects of Emiko's and Shogo's blood will also prove to be temporary. Oh, another thing. Since I was examining the effects of Kenji's blood anyway, as well as checking out your tissue samples and Jules', I also took the opportunity to look into that problem you've been experiencing regarding your limbs and torso, their strange willfulness."

"You mean the fact that Victoria's legs, Alexandra's arms, and Flora Ann's torso all found ways to express their revulsion for my husband?"

"Uh, yes. I can't be certain, not at this early stage, but I strongly suspect that your repeated imbibing of Kenji's blood lead to the awakening of a sort of limited, residual consciousness within your borrowed body parts. A kind of reflection of the personalities of those parts' former owners."

Maureen's shoulders quivered, as though Alexandra's arms were stunned by this news. "But — but that doesn't make any *sense*, Amos! It wasn't until at least three weeks after Kenji returned to Japan that I started experiencing any sort of fussiness from my parts when Jules would try getting affectionate..."

"You didn't let me finish what I was saying. The strange willfulness of your borrowed body parts wasn't a primary effect of your drinking Kenji's blood. The inebriation or 'highness' was. The awakened sentience of your limbs and torso has been a kind of withdrawal symptom. During the weeks you spent subsisting primarily on Kenji's blood, your body grew accustomed to its unique qualities. Your limbs' distressing bouts of independence are, in a way, a protest against your denying them the benefits of imbibing Kenji's blood. So far as I know — and again, I must emphasize that I am only at the bare beginnings of my investigation — the only way for you to obtain relief from your body parts' expressions of independence would be to go back to regularly drinking ample portions of Kenji's blood. Just as a heroin addict can quell his withdrawal pains by shooting up again."

Maureen furrowed her brow. "That *still* doesn't make sense, Amos. I didn't drink any of Kenji's blood last night. And yet, after Jules turned himself into a big rabbit, my body parts didn't, uh, protest at all when he, you know, got all lovey-dovey with me..."

Doc Landrieu rubbed his chin thoughtfully. "That may be due to a personality quirk shared by the three young women vampires who 'donated' their parts to you. Perhaps they find the attentions of a giant rabbit to be less offensive than the amorous advances of your husband when he's in his normal, human-seeming form."

"See? Whadda I tell ya, Maureen?" Jules said from inside the coffin. "Once you've had a taste of hare—"

"Oh, be *quiet*, Jules!" Maureen hissed, beating the top of the coffin with her pudgy fists. Then the irritation faded from her face, to be replaced by a look of pained desperation as she turned back to her father-in-law. "There's so much for me to try to figure out," she said plaintively. "You've given me so much to think about..."

"Well, there's no need for us to try to figure everything out tonight," Doc Landrieu said kindly. "I just wanted to check on you and Jules. I'd best get back to my work in my modest little lab. I wish I had better news to share, Maureen. But the best thing I can council right now is patience."

Two nights later...

"You might as well just go ahead and let me loose, Maureen. You know I'm gonna bust outta this coffin sooner or later. If you let me loose, things'll go easier on ya."

"Oh, Jules, must you *torment* me so? Can't we talk about something *else*?"

"I been working these ropes, Maureen. I been maneuverin' my big feet out from under me. I gotta tell ya, in all fairness, babe — once I get my feet propped up against the lid of this box, it's game over. It wouldn't matter none if you were a *thousand* pounds. These rabbit legs of mine are like a pair of atomic-powered pile drivers. I'm bustin' outta here. It's just a matter of time."

"And to what *purpose*, Jules?" Maureen snapped back. "Let's say you *do* manage to 'bust loose' — what *then*? You'll make a mess of *me*, I suppose. And then you'll just get beaten up by Shogo again and end up back in this coffin. And next time, assuming you've put me in the hospital or the grave, I won't be here to keep you company, you big doofus!"

"Oh, you think Shogo'll get the drop on me again, do ya?"

"I do!"

"Is that skinny Jap your hero now?"

"I didn't *say* that! Stop twisting my words around!"

"The only reason Shogo put me down for the count was a crummy, weasely sneak attack, the same kinda sneak attack the Jap navy pulled on the Pacific Fleet at Pearl Harbor. Next time, I'll be ready for him. One good kick — *pow!* To the *moon!*"

"Jules, your evil bravado is getting as boring as a marathon weekend of *Gilligan's Island* reruns..."

"So now I'm *boring* you? Was I put on this earth to keep my wifey entertained? Maybe you'll find my plans for you once I manage to kick my way out of this fuckin' coffin a little less *boring*, Maureen."

"Oh, do *tell*, you big, scary bunny," Maureen shot back, doing her best to sound far more nonchalant than she felt.

"When I break outta this box, it's no more Mr. Nice Bunny, un-nerstand? I'm gonna be a cave rabbit — I'm gonna drag you by your hair all the way out to the Bunny Bread factory in New Orleans East. They just reopened it, got their assembly lines rollin' again. I know you got a weakness for them Bunny Banana Muffin Snack Bites they bake out there. We're gonna go out there at night, just the two of us, after all the workers have left. I'm gonna tie you to a post. And then I'm gonna feed you, Maureen. I'm gonna stuff you full of them Bunny Banana Muffin Snack Bites until you feel like you're about to burst. And then I'm gonna stuff you some more. And the whole while I'm stuffin' you, I'm gonna be drivin' you *wild*, babe."

"That's so wicked, Jules, so *perverse* and *depraved...*" She felt her pulse accelerate. "Ohh, tell me more..."

"I'm gonna set up that assembly line so that it feeds Bunny Banana Muffin Snack Bites directly into your mouth. Free up my hands that way. 'Cause the whole time you're munchin' down, I'm gonna be munchin' down, too. On *you*. I'm gonna be drivin' you crazy, Maureen, in all the hundreds of ways a rabbit can drive a woman crazy. And the whole time, you're gonna be gettin' bigger and bigger. And I'm gonna be watchin' you, babe. And watchin' you's gonna drive *me* crazy..."

Maureen trembled. Her heart beat triple speed. "Don't stop talking, Jules!" she whispered desperately. She reached her hand beneath the voluminous folds of her purple mu-mu. It wasn't so easy to find her happy spot, not since her transformation. Her fingers had to work a whole lot harder. But if it held true that pleasure achieved was in proportion to effort expended, then she had a lot to look forward to...

A knock on the door from the kitchen upstairs broke her concentration. "*Go away!*" she shrieked. Then she realized what she'd been on the verge of doing. A few more minutes of this, and she might've taken leave of her senses and let Jules out! "No, I mean, *come back!*" she shouted to whomever was waiting at the top of the stairs. "It's *fine* to come down! I'd *love* some company!"

The door creaked open. Kenji descended the steps, followed by his sister and Shogo. "I hope we are not interrupting anything, Maureen-*san*," he said.

"Oh, no, not anything important," Maureen gasped, quickly rearranging her mu-mu. Looking down at her voluptuous bosom, barely covered by the thin purple fabric, she realized she'd flushed as red as a summer tomato (if tomatoes grew as big as watermelons). "Nothing important at all!" She sat up straighter and attempted to cross her legs. "So, what brings you kids down here to visit with us old folks?"

"We wish again to aporrogize for awrr the trubburr we have caused you and your husband," Kenji said.

"Oh, Kenji, you've apologized a dozen times already!" Maureen said. "It wasn't your fault. Jules and I experimented, like naughty teenagers. We got burned. End of story. Shit happens, you know?"

"Well, *I* don't accept your apology," Jules said from inside the coffin. "When I get outta here, Shogo, I'm gonna give you some payback for playin' the piano with my face, buddy. I'm gonna tear that pinhead of yours off your shoulders and piss a load of steaming bunny whiz down your neck. And Kenji, old pal, you don't wanna hear what I'm gonna do to your sister…"

"Shut *up*, Jules!" Maureen burst out, beating the coffin with her fists.

Kenji stared down at the floor. Emiko giggled nervously and covered her mouth with her hand. Shogo narrowed his eyes and stared belligerently at the coffin, his hands clenching tightly.

"We will not stay rong," Kenji said after clearing his throat. "I have no wish to upset Jures-*san* any more than we have. But I wish you to know that I have sent a message to my contact man in the Japan Self Defense Force, to ask if he wirr share with your Dr. Randrieu the studies which have been done on my sister, my cousin, and myserruf. I hope this will herrp Dr. Randrieu to find a cure for you and for Jures-*san*."

"Thank you very much, Kenji," Maureen said. "That's very thought-ful of you. I really appreciate it. Jules does, too, although he's unable to admit it right now…"

A wave of dizziness washed over her. She clutched the edges of the coffin to maintain her balance. The basement shimmered before her eyes. The entire surface of her skin buzzed with a tingling sensation, as though the inhabitants of a dozen ant colonies scurried over the doughy white wilderness of her body. She smelled a strong aroma of lime, mixed with pungent ozone.

"Maureen-*san*," Kenji said, concerned, "are you okay? You rook sick—"

Maureen clutched the folds of her massive stomach. "I — I feel so *strange* all of a sudden—"

She saw the dimly illuminated basement light up with a bright green flash, so blinding that her companions all covered their eyes. She realized the flash had emitted from her own body. Gallon after gallon of water flowed out of her, drenching her mu-mu and the coffin and pud-dling on the concrete floor. She felt like a sponge being rung out over a sink. She found that she was now sitting on a pile of plastic sheeting, the formerly missing components of her waterbed. Her lap was covered in wads of cotton, remnants of the bedcovers and pillows which had disap-peared at the instant of her transformation four nights earlier.

She pushed the tangled mass of cotton aside. Her lap — it wasn't the size of three large pizza boxes anymore! It was down to the size of just one medium pizza box! She was back to normal!

"I'm ME again!" she shrieked happily. "But what about—"

Just then, pencils of green light shot forth from the seam between the coffin and its lid. Maureen was thrown off balance by a forceful dis-charge against the inside of the lid, which lifted the whole coffin half an inch off the floor.

"*Jules!*" Maureen shouted. "Jules, what *happened*? Did you change? Are you all right in there?" She heard groaning from inside the huge box. "We've got to get this thing *open!*" she yelled, pulling at the chains.

"Uuuhhh... get me outta this coffin..." Jules moaned.

"He may be faking," Shogo suggested.

"Shogo is right," Kenji said. "Your husband may stirr be a maniac rabbit. We must be carefurr." He glanced around the basement. "Do you have toowurrs down here? A spinning drirr? We cood make a ho-whirr in the coffin and rook inside."

"A drill? Is that what you want?" Maureen asked.

Kenji nodded.

"I'm pretty sure Jules keeps a rechargeable drill down here some-where," Maureen said. She walked the basement's perimeter, searching high and low for an electric outlet which had a cord stuck into it. "Oh, here it is! Right next to the rechargeable flashlight I made him get at GoodiesMart." She unplugged both tools and brought them to Kenji. "Here you go."

"Thank you," he said. He quickly drilled a hole in the side of the coffin.

"Hey, watch where you're stickin' that thing!" Jules shouted from inside as the drill's bit punched through the wood. "I already got all the holes in me I need!"

Maureen grabbed the flashlight back from Kenji and knelt down to shine its light through the hole. "He's his old, fat self again!" she yelled joyfully. "No more white fur and pink nose! Hallelujah!"

Within moments, she had retrieved the keys to the locks holding the ends of the chains together and had pulled the lid off the coffin. Kenji used a utility knife to sever the ropes which had kept Rabbit Jules hog-tied, and then he and Shogo helped the hobbled vampire out of his coffin prison.

"Ohh, my knees and ankles, they're *killin'* me!" Jules complained as he stepped awkwardly out of the box. "Y'all want a word of advice? Never let yourself be hog-tied inside a coffin for three days and nights with your legs stuck beneath ya. Least as a rabbit, I was a lot more limber — probably the only thing that kept me from poppin' my knees outta their sockets. Anyway, it sure as hell is damn good to be outta there!"

"I am very preased, Jures-*san*, that you are back to normurr," Kenji said.

"You and me both, pal," Jules said. He turned to Maureen and held out his arms. "Hey? How about a big hug from my best gal? You may not be as big an armful as you were five minutes ago, babe, but you're still a sight for these sore eyes!"

Maureen rushed toward his embrace. But three feet away, her legs stopped her short. "Oh, *no!*" she wailed, staring down at her uncooperative limbs. "It's happening *again!* Oh, body, why can't you give me a *break*, just this once?"

Jules stepped closer so she could lean over and give him a quick peck on the cheek. "Aww, don't worry none, we'll get it straightened out, somehow," he said with a tinge of sadness in his voice. "Look on the bright side, Mo. At least I ain't no killer rabbit no more. So Jimmy Carter can sleep easy."

Although he made certain to show no sign of it, Shogo found himself disappointed, even angry, that Jules had managed to cast off his monstrous form and return to his usual, amiable self. He had been looking forward to more tests of his strength and valor against the rabbit creature. For a few moments on Bourbon Street, he had felt fully, gloriously alive. Now, the thought of returning to his old existence of performing for polite crowds at the opening celebrations of shopping malls and office buildings in Kure made him contemplate committing *seppuku*.

Jules held out his hand in a sign of conciliation. Knowing his cousin Kenji was watching, Shogo forced himself to shake it. "No hard feelings, huh, Shogo?" Jules said. "I'm sorry for them lousy things I said about ya. Y'know, pissing down your neck hole and all. I was under the influence;

your blood's got one evil kick, bud! Still, I'd be lyin' if I said I didn't have at least a *little* fun hoppin' around and committin' mayhem on Bourbon Street. Kickin' that Lucky Dog cart into the daiquiri shop, that was a hoot! Fightin' you, Shogo? Less of a hoot. You got in some good licks, pal. Least my face healed up fast — the guy I feel sorry for is the poor bass player who came to work at Fritzel's the next night and found his over-grown violin smashed to matchsticks."

"Thank you for being so forgiving, Jures-*san*," Kenji said when Shogo remained obstinately silent.

"Hey, no real harm done, right?" Jules said. "Far as I'm concerned, the worst that happened was I lost a few nights' worth of blood collections from tours. I'll make up for it, though. And I'll be able to work the 'giant killer rabbit' bit into my tour spiel. I'll figure some way to connect him to Napoleon. The French like eatin' rabbits, don't they?"

"I bereave so," Kenji said. "I aporrogize for your ross of brudd dona-tions. I myself wirr donate extra brudd to make up for your ross."

"That'll be just fine, Kenji. Mo and me can get into the habit of a little after-dinner toot of the silly stuff. Hey, y'know, that reminds me. When we go upstairs, make sure I give you guys back all the blood that Shogo and Emiko donated. I'd hate to make a mistake, suck down the wrong blood pack, and end up a rampagin' rabbit all over again. Although havin' Mo back as a queen-size hottie... nawww, too dangerous, don't wanna go there."

Shogo noticed Maureen's face grow livid. "Jules Duchon! Are you telling me, after everything we've just been through, that you no longer find me *attractive?*"

"Mo, that's not what I said! You're *gorgeous*, hon! I mean, you're beautiful at *any* size. Even sorta skinny. But you can't fault a man fer havin' his *preferences*, y'know? A man likes what a man likes, and nothin' can change that."

"Well, I know there are *some* men around here who appreciate a well-proportioned gal!" She strode boldly to Shogo's side. "Shogo, I never did thank you properly for saving my husband's mangy hide. Better late than never!" She put her arms around his shoulders gave him a big, wet kiss on his cheek.

He felt her begin to pull away. But then her limbs thought differently. Her arms pulled him in more tightly. Her fingers hungrily massaged the toned muscles of his shoulders and upper back. Her thighs rubbed seductively against his, her smooth white flesh jutting out from within the wispy folds of the mu-mu.

"Hey, Shogo, hands off the merchandise!" Jules growled. "I gave you a pass fer playin' the piano with my face, but some stuff crosses the line!"

"It's not *him*, Jules!" Maureen cried, distraught. "It — it's *me*! I mean, it's these arms and legs and torso of mine! They like Shogo!"

"Well, tell 'em to *unlike* him!"

"I — I *can't*! They won't *listen*!"

"Shogo!" Kenji barked. "Remove yourserrf!"

Hearing his superior's command, Shogo snapped to attention. He had been absorbed in the emotional turmoil which had erupted between Maureen and Jules, contemplating how best to turn it to his advantage. But Kenji had to be obeyed, at least in public. So Shogo disentangled himself from Maureen's grasping limbs and withdrew to a corner of the basement.

A heavy, awkward silence descended upon the room. Emiko ended up being the one to break it. "Might I prease wewrcome Jures-*san* back?" she said, hiding her smile behind her hand. "I know his rabbit form was very *kawaii*, but I rike his sumo wrest-rur form much better!"

Maureen was the first one to laugh. Then Jules joined in, and then Kenji. Emiko, pleased with the laughter, danced to Jules' side and stood on her tip-toes to give him a girlish kiss on his "sumo wrest-rur" cheek.

"Let's head upstairs, folks," Jules said. "It's been a long night, and sun-up's almost here. Mo told me Doc Landrieu sent my mom out to buy us a replacement waterbed the other night, and I'm lookin' forward to tryin' it out. *Anything'll* be better than bein' hog-tied inside that coffin."

Shogo followed the others up the stairs, taking care to stay far away from Maureen.

"Tomorrow night, before I head out on my tour, I'll look up my pal Porkchop for y'all," Jules said when they had entered the kitchen. "He's got to know about some charity jazz concerts comin' up. Probably helpin' to organize some. I'll make sure he puts you guys in the line-up, okay?"

"Thank you, Jures-*san*," Kenji said. "Praying jazz music to raise money to herrp New Orrins, it will be a preasure for us."

Jules walked to his freezer, then motioned for Shogo to come over. He opened the freezer and began searching its shelves. "Ahh, here they are," Jules said. He pulled out six bags of blood marked with Shogo's or Emiko's name and handed them to Shogo. "Much as I hate to give away any blood, this is stuff I don't dare mess with. I can't bear to toss it down the sink, though. Sorta a vampire superstition thing. You'll get rid of it for me, won't you, pal? It belongs to you, kinda."

Shogo stared down at the bags of blood he held in the crook of his arm. He glanced furtively at the dozens of blood bags which remained on the freezer's shelves. The beginnings of a plan began congealing in his mind. His eyes darted to the kitchen's windows. Their latches were old and fragile. Easy to dislodge.

"Of course, Jures-*san*," he said, nodding solemnly. "I am happy to take care of this brudd for you. No probrem."

Fifteen

JULES and Maureen stood on the sidewalk outside Snug Harbor Jazz Club, waiting for their Japanese friends to arrive. The night air was heavy with humidity; the two vampires, with their lower body temperatures, were the only patrons milling about who weren't sweating. The Frenchman Street jazz hotspot was the site of a benefit concert to raise money to bring storm-displaced musicians back to their homes. Kenji, Emiko, and Shogo were scheduled to perform a short set with the house band.

A taxi pulled up to the front of the club. Kenji and Shogo got out on the side closest to the sidewalk, while Emiko exited through the opposite door. "White dinner jackets, huh?" Jules glanced approvingly at Kenji's and Shogo's outfits. "Pretty spiffy. I take it you two are big Bing Crosby fans?"

"No, Louis Armstrong," Kenji said, fiddling with his black bow tie. "Did not Louis Armstrong wear a white dinner jacket like these ones we wear, whenever he want to pray at his concerts?"

"Uh, I don't know about that. I think he usually wore a *black* dinner jacket. I've seen the guy in person, remember." Jules noticed once more the special effort Kenji had taken to properly pronounce the "L" in his hero's first name. It was kind of endearing.

"Jures-*san*, not to argue with your great knowredge of jazz music, but at the wax museum we have in Kure, Louis Armstrong wears a *white* dinner jacket."

"Oh, well, it's settled, then. Not likely the curator of a wax museum in Kure would make a goof like stickin' the wrong jacket on Louis Armstrong."

Emiko stepped around the cab and onto the sidewalk, avoiding a big palmetto bug which scurried across the cracked concrete, its damp exoskeleton shining indigo beneath the club's neon sign. "And what about me, Jures-*san*?" she asked. "Do I rook 'spiffy,' too?"

She twirled so that Jules could admire all angles of her white, strapless evening gown. A silver brooch clasped together dainty elements of lace décolletage which concealed her small but appealingly shaped breasts. She wore a pair of red camellia blossoms with bright yellow stamens, one behind each ear. She smiled openly at Jules, not bothering to cover her mouth, as she so often did. *Nothin' at all wrong with them teeth*, Jules noted.

"You look like a million bucks, Emiko," Jules said. "'Spiffy?' That's not the word. You make them two guys you're with look like corner bums. Gimme one of them thesaurus thingies, I'll come up with a better word."

Emiko giggled. "Thank you, Jures-*san*. You are my garrant sumo!"

Maureen growled beneath her breath.

Jules noticed that growl and shuddered inwardly. Theirs had not been a happy marriage bed, these past couple of weeks. Maureen, leaping upon Doc Landrieu's speculation that her purloined parts' willfulness was actually a withdrawal symptom resulting from her abstaining from drinking Kenji's blood, had started chugging down the intoxicating blood with a vengeance. At first, her return to a diet of Kenji's ichor seemed to do the trick; she'd gotten silly and loopy (usually in concert with Jules, who needed some R&R after running his nightly tours), but her limbs no longer exhibited "minds" of their own. Yet as the days had stretched on, she'd discovered she needed to drink larger and larger quantities of the special blood to tamp down her body parts' awakened consciousness. Also, in conjunction with her blood binges, she'd consumed increasing quantities of fattening snack foods. This invariably made her grouchy the following day when she would tabulate the calories she'd consumed, based both on the bloating she sensed in her tummy and the empty wrappers and bags she irritably picked up around her bedroom.

Finally, one night she'd gotten so smashed that her inebriation had lasted from one evening to the next, and she'd gone in to do her show pretty much shitfaced, stumbling through her monologues and becoming an even more embarrassing spectacle than the abysmal horror movie she was supposed to be lampooning (which, since the film was *I Eat Your Flesh, I Drink Your Blood*, was really saying something).

After that debacle, she'd sworn off Kenji's blood. So now she and Jules found themselves back where they'd started. Lying on opposite edges of the super-king-sized waterbed, facing away from each other, both thinking dark thoughts.

Jules reminded himself that he'd come out tonight to support his friends and enjoy some swell jazz, not to bemoan the state of his marriage. "Okay, everybody," he said, "from the look of things inside, the show's about to get started. Kenji, Emiko, Shogo, I know you guys are gonna knock 'em dead. No need to knock me and Mo dead, though; we're already dead. That's a little vampire joke, guys. Anyway, break a trumpet, break a vocal cord, and break a drum stick, okay?"

* * * * *

Shogo settled himself in behind the unfamiliar drum kit. He felt painfully nervous, far more edgy and uncertain than he'd been that night on Bourbon Street when he'd battled Jules Duchon. Then, changing himself into a killer cat and leaping upon the giant rabbit's back, he had performed actions which had felt completely natural, in harmony with his essential being. He had not needed to think; he had needed only to *do*.

Tonight, however…? He feared he would prove far less handy with these drum sticks he held than the claws he had wielded a few weeks ago. The drums and cymbals he sat behind seemed to stare up at him like hostile strangers. He'd promised Kenji before they had left Japan that he would do his best at this new group endeavor. Although he would never admit it to anyone, he knew in his heart that of the three of them, he was the weakest musician. Yet, he had never backed down from a challenge. If his two cousins were convinced of the wisdom of turning away from being superhero *tarento* in favor of being jazz music *tarento*, he knew he must follow that path, too. For he was a part of their family, their group, their team. Their *uchi*. As a member of the *uchi*, he was duty-bound to support them.

Those ties of duty, inculcated in him since childhood, had been all that had kept him thus far from breaking into the Duchons' house during daylight hours and adulterating their stored blood with traces of his and Emiko's blood. Many days he had awakened with a strong desire to do that thing, to ensure the emergence of savage monsters with whom he would engage in shining, glorious battle. His blood had pleaded with him to do this thing; both his blood which was stored in plastic bags in his hotel's freezer and the blood circulating within his veins. He thirsted for the glory of battle. But time and time again, he had warded off his urges and forcibly reminded himself of his duty to his *uchi*. He would devote his best effort to becoming a jazz music *tarento* in New Orleans. Only in the event of failure would he consider giving rein to his most insistent desire.

The master of ceremonies, Jules Duchon's friend Porkchop Chambonne, an elderly black gentleman dressed in a checkered sport coat, checkered slacks, and a brown derby hat, stepped to the microphone on stage. "Before our next act introduces themselves," he said, "I need to announce a change in personnel. Buddy Johnson, the piano player originally scheduled to play this next set, has taken ill. Our old friend Brad Hammersmith, whom most of you know very well, will sit in in Buddy's place. Now, please give a warm Snug Harbor welcome to our new friends come all the way from Japan, the Acme *Tarento* Jazz Ensemble!"

A different piano player? Shogo stared in dull shock as a complete stranger sat behind the piano, a man with whom Shogo had never rehearsed. Shock gave way to trepidation. Shogo, along with the piano player and bass player, formed the ensemble's rhythm section. They needed to play as a unit. He knew a veteran jazz drummer could sit in with any jazz piano player and not miss a beat. But he wasn't a veteran player; he'd only returned to playing the drums a little more than two years ago, after having learned basic drumming as a teenager. He'd rehearsed with pianist Buddy Johnson, had gotten used to his style and use of chords and improvisation. He'd almost gotten comfortable keeping time to Buddy Johnson's playing. This new man, however? He might as well be from Mars, a sentient cephalopod playing the piano with his tentacles.

Kenji bowed deeply to Porkchop Chambonne, turned and bowed to his fellow musicians on stage, and then bowed to the audience. "It is a great honor for us to come and pray for you tonight," he said. "We are the Acme *Tarento* Jazz Ensemble, come from Kure, Japan. That is close to Hiroshima, a city you may know. I am Kenji Tezuka, and this is my sister, Emiko-*chan*, and this is my cousin, Shogo Fukuda-*san*. Brad Hammersmith-*san* joins us on piano, and Rusty Winter-*san* prays bass. New Orrins is a spe-shur prace for us, and we are happy, very happy to herrp raise money to bring the musicians back to their homes." The crowd politely applauded. "Tonight, we pray some good, ord-time jazz for you. With some spe-shur surprises added."

He picked up one of his two trumpets, the slightly oversized one made of plastic. His hands began emitting the greenish glow with which Shogo was so familiar. The plastic trumpet quickly shrunk down to toy trumpet size, about six inches long. Kenji's hands glowed more brightly with the energy they had absorbed from the plastic instrument.

Several members of the audience murmured and *oooh*ed. One man whispered to his date, "Is this supposed to be a magic show?"

Kenji set the now toylike trumpet on the stand next to his brass trumpet. Then he walked behind his sister and placed his glowing hands lightly on her bare shoulders. As though it were a living thing, the energy flowed smoothly from his hands into her shoulders, then up her neck and across her cheeks, to finally settle within her full lips.

Kenji returned to his place. On cue, the house lights dimmed. Pin light spots illuminated each of the male musicians. Emiko's face, however, was lit from below by the green glow coming from her lips.

"Now we begin," Kenji said. He tapped his foot three times, then played the opening bars of "Hello, Dolly" on his brass trumpet, holding a white handkerchief between his fingers and the instrument, just as Louis Armstrong had once done. Emiko began singing:

"I said harrow, Dah-ree,

Werr, harrow, Dah-ree,

It's so nice to have you back where you berong..."

Shogo made it through the first two stanzas of "Hello, Dolly" without mishap; Brad Hammersmith and Kenji both stuck to the melody, with only minor flourishes, so Shogo didn't find himself getting lost or distracted.

But then came the instrumental break. Kenji went first. That wasn't too bad; Shogo was used to playing behind his cousin, and Kenji, aping the style of the early New Orleans jazz masters, hewed closely to the melody throughout his solo, making it more rococo with quick adornments.

Brad Hammersmith was a musical cat of a different color, however. Shogo quivered inwardly when he realized that Hammersmith was a disciple of modernists like McCoy Tyner rather than traditionalists like Jelly Roll Morton or Fats Waller. Hammersmith immediately grabbed hold of the relatively simple, straightforward song and began taking it places its composers had never intended for it to go. Shogo tried keeping up with the dizzying chord changes, but he became lost almost immediately. *Steady, steady, hold the rhythm...* he told himself. But it was no use. He saw the bassist glance in his direction, a perturbed look on his face. The volume of the bass's strumming grew louder, more insistent, as

Winter attempted to cover up Shogo's faltering rhythm with his own steady beat.

This was a nightmare. Shogo was disgracing his *uchi* in front of a crowd of *gaijin* — most humiliatingly, his antagonist, Jules Duchon. The only saving grace was that the pin light spot directed at him shone only on his hands, not his face.

The bassist performed his four-bar solo. Shogo refrained from playing behind him. He noticed his hands were trembling. Then it was his turn for a four-bar solo on drums. Somehow, he managed to get through it. But even to his own ears, it sounded amateurish, off-kilter, the performance of a timid, clumsy novice.

At last, the instrumental break was over. The song returned to its standard melody for the final stanzas. Emiko stepped back to the microphone, the glow from her lips casting an emerald light over the front of the bandstand and the uplifted faces of the closest audience members, and she began singing again:

"So gah-ree, gee, ferras,

Find her an empty knee, ferras,

Dah-ree wirr never go away,

I said she never go away,

Dah-ree wirr never go away again..."

Emiko finished the song by grabbing the miniature plastic trumpet from Kenji's instrument stand and playing a few squeaky, toylike end notes. The energy in her lips shone through the translucent plastic, making the tiny, tootling trumpet look a glass sculpture injected with glowing green neon gas.

The audience, thrilled with this closing flourish, applauded enthusiastically. Shogo dared to hope that Emiko had sucked up all the attention in the room, so that no one but the bassist had noticed the faults in his playing.

But then he felt a hand on his shoulder. He turned his head. Standing next to him was a wiry young black man, dressed in a sharkskin suit, a pair of drum sticks protruding from his jacket pocket. The club's house drummer.

"Buddy, I think maybe you bellied up to the bar a few times too many tonight, huh?" the man said. "Take five, brother. Let me sit in. You been throwin' everybody else off. Tonight's not your night, man."

Shogo slowly rose from his seat. He had lost face, most grievously. He did not bother to collect his drum sticks. His jacket brushed the side of the snare drum, and his sticks fell to the floor. He left them there. He retreated to a far corner of the bandstand and hid in the shadows. He wished he could plunge off the edge of the world.

"Thank you for your very kind apprause," Kenji said, not noticing the change of drummers. "For our second number, we will pray the jazz crassic, 'Ain't Misbehavin',' written by the great Fats Wah-rer. This will feature my sister, Emiko-*chan*, who wirr perform for you in a new way not seen in New Orrins before."

Shogo crouched down in the darkness. What Emiko was about to do was not new to him; he had seen her do it many times. For a person witnessing it for the very first time, however, he knew it would seem magical, unforgettable, completely enchanting.

Good. His cousin's performance should efface any memories of his own failure from the minds of the audience. There was that to be thankful for, at least.

But his fellow musicians... they would not forget his bumbling, he knew.

The instrumentalists played the opening bars. Emiko turned away from the audience. She glanced seductively back at them over her shoulder and gave a wink, then strode to the wall which stood behind the bandstand. She placed her glowing lips against the wall, as if kissing it. Shogo shielded his eyes, knowing what was coming. The bandstand suddenly brightened in a flash of green light. When normal vision returned to the audience's retinas, they saw that Emiko no longer stood facing the back wall. She had *entered* the wall. She had transformed into a two-dimensional cartoon of herself, a wide-eyed anime maiden in a flowing white evening gown, twin camellia blossoms behind her ears.

The instrumentalists vamped to allow the audience to recover from their astonishment. Then, after Kenji stamped his foot three times, Emiko began to sing:

"No one to tawrk with,

Awrr by myserrf,

No one to wawrk with,

But I'm happy on the shewrf,

Ain't misbehavin',

I'm savin' my ruvv for you..."

Her cartoon image danced effortlessly across the rear wall; to Shogo, she appeared, as she always did when in this form, like a lyrical vignette from a Studio Ghibli animated fantasy. Emiko laughed between her lyrics as she flowed around a corner from the rear wall to an adjacent wall, causing the audience to suffer whiplash as they uniformly turned their faces to stare, open-mouthed and astounded.

"Ain't misbehavin',

I'm savin' my ruvv for you..."

The instrumentalists took their turns at brief solos, but no one was paying them any attention. Emiko giggled like a delighted little girl as she flowed from wall to ceiling and stared down at the concertgoers; then she performed a stylized version of traditional Japanese *geisha* dance, mixing this with moves from older American styles, the Charleston and the boogie-woogie, performing flips on the ceiling. The audience, lost in wonder and excitement, some puzzling furiously over how she had pulled this trick, but many not caring about the mechanics of the stage magic, cheered again and again, making the music almost impossible to hear.

Emiko pirouetted across the ceiling to the wall closest to the concert hall's front doors, then glided down the wall into the frosted mirrors behind the bar. She blew kisses to the shocked bartender from the mirrors, then launched into the closing stanza of her song:

"Ain't misbehavin',

I'm savin' my ruvv for you..."

She dropped to the bottom of the mirrors, hidden from the audience's sight behind the bar. Then the mirrors, along with the massed bottles of brand-name liquor arrayed on shelves above the bar, reflected a dazzling green flash. A second later, Emiko, returned to three-dimensional flesh, strode from behind the bar to saucily conclude her number:

"And onrry *you*!"

Her eyes alight, no longer with borrowed energy but with euphoria that her performance had gone so well, she blew playful kisses to the audience as long as they continued cheering... which to Shogo seemed to drag on for half the night.

How he envied her.

Over a hundred people surged towards Emiko, surrounding her, congratulating her, fawning over her, competing madly to catch her attention and ask her a question. Shogo noticed that Jules Duchon had joined his friend Porkchop Chambonne away from the crowd, next to a corner of the bandstand. He crept closer to hear what they were saying.

"Where did you come up with these foreign musicians, Jules?" the elderly musician asked. "Are they, y'know, night folk, like you and your wife? They sure got their tricks, don't they?"

Shogo saw Jules smile. "Naww, they ain't 'night folk' like me, Chop. They're what ya'd call superheroes. Like Green Lantern and the Sub-Mariner from the funny books. But even with all them crazy super-powers they've got, their big dream is to play jazz in New Orleans."

"Well, you can tell your friend Kenji, the trumpet player, he's got him some chops. Nice tone, real nice. Sweet-like. Reminds me of some of the old guys I used to play with. And that little Emiko gal? What can I *say*, man? She's got a nice voice, but when you combine that with, y'know, *whatever* it is she does, turnin' herself into a cartoon or whatever — that's some hot stuff, man. That's dynamite. The only dud in the bunch? That guy who played the drums... if you can call that playin'. He sort of stunk up the joint. Had me feelin' sorry for him. Heck, had me feelin' sorry for the *rest* of them up there on the bandstand, tryin' to play to his messed-up beat..."

"Yeah, well, I can tell you this, Chop — Shogo's musical specialty ain't beatin' them drums with drum sticks. It's beatin' my *face* with an upright bass and piano..."

Shogo had heard enough. His face burning with shame, he crept quietly toward the emergency exit door, then slunk out of the club through an alleyway. He had no idea how he would be able to face Emiko and Kenji. Emiko would try to console him, he knew. Kenji would insist on more rehearsal time for all of them; he might discretely arrange for Shogo to meet with a local percussion teacher on the side. Yet nothing they would or could do would wipe away this night's blot on his honor. Only he was capable of righting his loss of face. But he knew he would need to accomplish a truly heroic feat to efface his shame.

He found himself on the sidewalk in front of the club. He was wandering without purpose; right now, his only desire was to stay away from the crowd who had witnessed his failure. He began walking up Frenchman Street toward the French Quarter, toward the site of his sole triumph in New Orleans, when he heard a familiar voice just behind him.

"Shogo?"

He turned. It was Maureen. Jules Duchon's wife.

Sixteen

SHOGO stared with blank confusion at Maureen, the strange woman whose limbs seemingly had a will of their own, and which had expressed their desire for him in a very tactile fashion. Why had she followed him? Would her limbs pursue him for as long as he remained in New Orleans? He didn't want her company. He didn't want anyone's company.

"I thought I might find you out here, Shogo," she said. "What happened up on the bandstand... that must've been painful for you. I'm sorry."

"I have no wish to speak of it, prease," he said.

"I hear you. I won't press. I just thought... well, I thought you might need a friend about now, someone who's not one of your cousins."

Shogo grunted. He wanted very much to be alone. But he saw no way to refuse Maureen's companionship without being rude in an egregious fashion.

"Would you mind buying a girl a cup of coffee? There are a few places around that are still open. Places we could walk to."

"What about your husband?"

"Jules? He'll want to hang out with his musician buddies. That's not for me. I can't follow all that jazz talk. I mean, Chop is extremely nice, and he's been a good friend to Jules for years and years, but I feel like a fifth wheel whenever I'm around the two of them, y'know? Besides, when a couple's been together as long as Jules and I have been, some nights, you just want some time apart. And we've been going through a bumpy few weeks, Jules and me..."

"Oh? To me, you seem very happy. Always raughing and joking."

Maureen sighed. "Oh, sure, that's what we show people. But when we're by ourselves, the knives come out... So how about that cup of coffee?"

"Do you rike the coffee at the Crover Reaf Grirr?"

"The Clover Leaf? Sure, that's all right. The waiters there are a bunch of flirty swishes, but if that doesn't bother you, it doesn't bother me. Me, they'll completely ignore, unless one of them's been watching my show on public access cable. Sure, the Clover Leaf'll be fine. Let's go."

They began walking toward Bourbon Street.

"Did you like any of the other acts?" Maureen asked. "I thought Johnny Savoy and His Wailin' Banshees were pretty good..."

"I did not pay much attention," Shogo said.

"I understand. You know, I'm a performer, myself. I've got my own show on public access cable. I know *all* about *pressure*. It's a live show. No room for screw-ups. No do-overs. I'll admit something to you, Shogo. This past week? I *bombed*. I mean fell on my *face*, hit the concrete nose-first after flopping over the balcony of a fifteen-story building. *Boom! Splat!* You think *you* found yourself in hot water up there on that bandstand tonight? What you went through was a nice soak in a hot tub compared with the broiling *I* went through."

Shogo grunted. He wasn't really listening, but he pretended to.

"And it was all because of *Jules*. Nothing he did *directly*, mind you. But I bombed so badly because I was trying so darned hard to fix things with him. You see, Doc Landrieu figures this problem I've been having — y'know, this business with my limbs all having minds of their own? He says it's a kind of withdrawal symptom that I got when I stopped drinking your cousin Kenji's blood. So I've been trying to get over it by going back to drinking his blood. *Lots* of it. Otherwise, my body won't let me get anywhere near my husband, and that's been pissing Jules off worse and worse. It worked okay, at first. But then I found I had to drink more and more of Kenji's blood to get my body to shut the hell up. One night this past week, I went on such a binge, I was still slobberknockered the *next* night when I rolled out of bed. Jules saw what was going on. He *says* he told me I shouldn't go into the studio. I guess I must've insisted. Even so, a *decent* husband would've made *sure* I didn't leave the house that night. But I ended up over at the studio, in front of that live camera. In front of my thousands and thousands of TV fans. Absolutely slobber-knockered.

"I couldn't remember any of my lines. I just made crap up, whatever came into my drunken head. I stumbled around and knocked over pieces of the set. I missed all my cues. And then Jules showed up with his tour group, like he always does. And you know what that sewer rat had the *nerve* to do? He *poked fun at me*! Yes, my own husband! He made jokes at my expense, in front of my TV audience! There I was, drunk as a skunk due to my best efforts to fix things so *he* could get some loving, and what did he say to my audience? 'That film you're watchin' is so *bad*—' he was talking about *I Eat Your Flesh, I Drink Your Blood*, an American International Pictures drive-in abomination from the late 'Sixties; '—this film you're watchin' is so *bad*, my wife had to get *shitfaced* just to sit through it!'

"Can you believe the *nerve* of that man? *Can* you? I mean, it's one thing to have some fun at my expense when it's just the two of us. But it's another thing *entirely* to slam me in front of a tour group and my TV audience! Oh, he thought he could get away with it because I was too drunk to remember anything. But what he *forgot* is that the tech crew gives me a DVD of each episode to take with me. So I've been able to replay his smart-ass remarks again and again. Oh, *that man*! Doesn't he realize the stress I've been under? He only thinks about himself and his own problems! He wants a piece of ass? Well, he should ask his father-in-law, then — Amos used to work in the morgue! The next time Jules wants a piece of ass, they can take a trip to the morgue, and Amos can pull it out of the ice box for him!"

Oh, these Americans, Shogo thought, trudging dutifully toward the Clover Leaf Grill and what he hoped would be a quick cup of coffee. *Always so eager to share their most personal embarrassments with whomever will listen. The most elevated among them lacks the dignity of even the most humble Japanese rice farmer.*

"I'm sorry to burden you with all this, Shogo," Maureen said. "It's just that, ever since I stopped working at Jezebel's Joy Room, I don't really have anybody to talk with anymore, apart from Jules. And I can't very well complain *about* Jules *to* Jules, can I? I mean, I love him, Shogo, I do; but sometimes, he makes me want to just *strangle* him…"

"I understand what you are fee-ring," Shogo said. He also wanted to strangle Jules Duchon, in front of a large, cheering crowd. Perhaps not strangle him to death, no; but conclusively defeat him once again. And why settle for just once more? Why not overcome him again and again, gain glory after glory by grinding him into the mud repeatedly? He was beginning to see a way he could make that happen.

"Thank you, Shogo! That's so *kind* of you to say. You're a very kind and understanding gentleman."

"A man rike Jules Duchon must be taught a stern resson. He must be taught a resson again and again."

Maureen grinned and nodded her head. They reached the Clover Leaf Grill; she waited for him to open the door for her. "You know, Shogo, I couldn't agree more! Why, you almost sound like you've known Jules as long as *I* have. It takes *forever* to pound anything *new* into that thick head of his…"

* * * * *

Ah, such smells! How wonderful it is!

The Bunny Bread Bakery, newly refurbished in the months following Hurricane Antonia, was a mesmerizing place, with its automated ovens, conveyor belts carrying loaves of bread from one corner of the facility to another, and its slicing machines and packaging machines, all working tirelessly throughout the small, dark hours of the night. Shogo had never been inside a bread bakery and snack cake factory before (he certainly had never snuck into one in the middle of the night before). He decided he would like to come back here during normal business hours and take a tour of the facility, if they offered one. The pervasive aroma of freshly baked bread was delightful enough all on its own to bring him back; the smell was so strong, Shogo could close his eyes and imagine this entire facility was made of bread and cake, like the witch's hut in the fairy tale.

His favorite machine of the many automated machines in the bakery (and the key to his plan) was the giant mixer. It stirred the batter which would be baked into the moist, icing-covered cubes of Bunny Banana Muffin Snack Cakes, those packaged snack cakes which Shogo had found to be ubiquitous throughout the French Quarter, sold next to the cash register in nearly every tee-shirt shop, souvenir store, and take-out food joint.

He watched the giant spindle blades, each bigger than the oar of a life boat, stir the thick batter, which fell down a chute into a tremendous stainless steel vat, until the batter attained a uniform, dull yellow consistency. The blades each rotated, and as they rotated they followed four of their fellows in a circular path, and each group of five circling, rotating blades proscribed the circumference of a larger circle. Circles inside circles inside circles, all endless.

Two days ago, the day after his humiliating failure at Snug Harbor Jazz Club, he had broken into the house of the Duchons through the kitchen window which they left unlatched. He had mixed small quantities of his and Emiko's blood into about half of the bags of blood which the vampires had stored in their freezer. He knew of no way to ensure that Jules Duchon would be the only one to drink the mutagenic blood; it was equally as likely that Maureen would drink it and be changed into a vicious, destructive creature. But he reasoned that even if it should be Maureen who became a rampaging monster, still he would be able to use this situation to his advantage. He would not deploy the brutal methods he had used with Jules Duchon to subdue Maureen; he would be more considerate of her well-being. But still, he would capture her in a suitably spectacular and public fashion, showing up Jules Duchon, who would undoubtedly try to rescue his wife in his bumbling, clumsy fashion and fail miserably before Shogo showed him how it was done properly. That, too, would be a triumph for Shogo.

He watched the mixer spindle blades turn their endless circles. Circles. The Americans had invented the idea of the superhero, in their illustrated stories published on newsprint back in the decade leading up to the Great Pacific War. During that war, some Americans, such as Jules Duchon himself, had taken to wearing masks and had thought of themselves as real superheroes. But the era of truly real superheroes had not arrived until the Americans had dropped their atomic bombs on Hiroshima and Nagasaki, triggering changes in hundreds of Japanese women's wombs and affecting the maturation of dozens of special Japanese adolescents whose glands had just begun their years of greatest activity. The glory years of Japanese superheroes had been the 1960s and early 1970s, when the heroes had driven out demons, monsters, and gangs of science criminals from the home islands and ushered in an era of social harmony.

And now, as if to complete a circle, Shogo had come from Japan to America, to teach one of the original American superheroes how the job should be done. Just as Japanese corporations such as Toyota and Honda had taken the management principles invented at Ford Motor Company and General Motors and perfected them, then returned those perfected principles to America in the form of their own factories in Alabama and Kentucky, which out-produced and outshined their American predecessors in every way.

Circles...

Even at the very moment he had been adulterating the Duchons' stored blood with his own blood and Emiko's, Shogo had known that this action would not be sufficient. After either Jules Duchon or Maureen had been transformed, had rampaged, been captured by Shogo, and then reverted to normal after a three-day span, the Duchons would surely have

Dr. Landrieu inspect their blood supply, to ascertain whether any other bags had been mistakenly mislabeled and not returned to the Japanese trio when they should have been. So this stratagem of Shogo's would only net him one more night of martial glory; two, at most.

A sense of disappointment had shriveled his spirit. Yet in the very midst of this disappointment, as he had been stoically mixing small quantities of his and Emiko's blood into the Duchons' blood bags, he had latched onto an idea which promised many more nights of martial glory to come. A long time ago, when he had been a teenager desperately seeking any sources of wisdom concerning his blossoming superpowers, he had found a translation of an American book, a novel called *Superfolks* by an author named Robert Mayer. The book had told the story of a superhero, called Indigo by some, whose superpowers had gradually faded and who had gone into an ignominious retirement. Indigo (that had not been his actual superhero name, but a code name applied to him by his enemies in the U.S. government) had come from the planet Cronk, and his sole weakness was meteorite fragments from his destroyed planet, fragments called Cronkite. Unable to defeat him in direct combat, Indigo's enemies had conspired on a long-term plan to take his invincible superpowers away from him. They had purchased construction and utility companies in the city where Indigo resided, and they had introduced tiny quantities of Cronkite into the concrete with which all new buildings were built and into the water supply, so that long-term exposure to small doses of Cronkite radiation would depower the hero.

In a flash of insight, Shogo had realized he could work the inverse of the plan formulated by the enemies of Indigo. They had sought to take Indigo's superpowers away from him. He sought to give Jules Duchon, or other vampires in New Orleans (and there must be others, he reasoned), monstrous forms and evil personalities. Both plans could work by introducing the transformative element (Cronkite in Indigo's case; his blood and Emiko's in Jules Duchon's) into the environment and making it ubiquitous, so the intended target could not avoid its effects.

Shogo had seen Bunny Banana Muffin Snack Cakes everywhere in the French Quarter. He recalled that many of the tourists who had taken Jules Duchon's vampire tours and donated blood had stashed such snack cakes in their purses or backpacks and nibbled on them throughout the evening. In fact, the Duchon family served those very same snack cakes to their blood donors, along with cups of orange juice. They seemed to be a standard part of the diet of tourists exploring New Orleans. If he could introduce his and Emiko's blood into those snack cakes, their blood's mutagenic properties would enter the tourists' digestive tracts and eventually into the tourists' blood streams. Any vampire who fed upon the blood of tourists would eventually be exposed.

The Americans had invented the idea of the superhero, and when they had dropped their bombs on Hiroshima and Nagasaki, they had unwittingly made superheroes real. The Japanese superheroes had enjoyed their decade of glory in the 1960s. Then their very success, their elimination of their foes, had caused that glory to fade. The sun rises, and the sun sets. Yet the setting sun eventually rises once more. Shogo, whose parents had been exposed in their mothers' wombs to the radiation of American bombs, who himself had been exposed as a teenager to the writings of the American author Robert Mayer, would renew the faded glory of the Japanese superheroes. He would establish a new era, a second era of Japanese super-glory, and he would do so on American soil.

Circles...The rising sun was a circle, too. The rising sun on the flag of Japan. Yes, in gaining glory for himself, he would accrue glory to that flag, as well.

Shogo opened the backpack he had carried with him. He removed the remaining bags of Emiko's blood and the many bags of his own blood (he had broken into Dr. Landrieu's house during daylight hours, when the doctor and his wife had been asleep, and used the doctor's blood extraction equipment to draw more blood from himself). He leaned over the railing above the great vat which held the batter which would eventually be baked into thousands upon thousands of Bunny Banana Muffin Snack

Cakes. He emptied the bags of blood into the batter, one by one. He had brought many bags. It took him several moments to empty them all.

He watched the automated spindle blades mix and mix and mix, stirring the blood into the batter. Mixing it and mixing it until the red liquid disappeared entirely into the hundreds of gallons of dull yellow batter. Circles within circles within circles...

Seventeen

JULES shivered. The emotional temperature prevalent in his bedroom was equivalent to the frozen atmosphere at Neptune's poles.

"Maureen," he pleaded, "c'mon, hon, don't *be* like this. You ain't hardly said a word to me since we went to Snug Harbor three nights ago and you skipped out on me after the concert. Can't you at least let me know *why* I'm in the doghouse? Huh? Is this still about that night you were blasted on Kenji's blood and I made a joke or two about it on the set of your show? I told you, I was just havin' a little *fun* with you, babe. You and me, we're supposed to be *entertainers*, ain't that right? All the TV technician guys thought I was funny! I got a good laugh from my tour group! But I was just joshin' around... I didn't mean to hurt your feelings, really, I didn't..."

Maureen sat on the edge of the waterbed with her back turned resolutely away from her husband. She silently stared out the window.

"Oh, come *on*, Mo! I said I'm sorry — how many times and how many ways do I hafta say it? Be forgivin', fer once! You act like I drowned your puppy, or somethin'! And you don't even *have* a puppy!"

Maureen did not utter a sound, nor turn her head so much as a centimeter.

Jules' patience had stretched as far as the elastic waistband of his pants had been stretched when he'd pulled them on that evening — in other words, well beyond its design limit and to the verge of its snapping point. "All right — *be* that way! It's not enough fer a man to go out and slave himself on the streets of the French Quarter every night so his wife can drink her fill — he's gotta be *perfect*, too? Enough's *enough*, Maureen! I'm not stickin' around this house so's you can ignore me some more. I'm *outta* here! I'm gonna go catch me a movie or hear some good music. Stew all you want, babe. I'll be back when I'm good and ready..."

He stormed out of the house, making sure to slam the front door as noisily as possible (but without busting it; he knew if he broke it, he'd face a world of nagging until he fixed it). "Women..." he muttered under his breath as he stomped down the front stoop steps to the sidewalk. "Can't live with 'em, can't be dead with 'em, either..."

He wasn't in the mood to see a late-night movie or catch a set of jazz by himself. He knew he'd just mope; he might even get to feeling low enough that he'd be tempted to fang a wayward tourist or a homeless person, and he'd been striving to drop that habit. In the old days, before he'd revealed his secret to Erato, he would've tracked his cab driving pal down and rode around in his Town Car with him, taking in the endlessly intriguing sights of nighttime New Orleans. That wasn't an option any longer. Chop had a gig tonight, so he was out. If Doodlebug were in town, he'd be a good friend to talk with about this Maureen situation; but Doodlebug was in California. His old buddies from his morgue nights had married and had kids; some of them even had grandkids by now. Preston was still in St. Louis with the other black vampires; Jules had noticed construction crews heading into the subterranean spaces beneath the downtown casino, so maybe Preston's bunch were getting their old home dried out and cleaned up while they were on extended vacation. Dragging Straussman out of the High Krewe's palace didn't seem likely, not after Straussman had warned him to stay away; besides, the only music the butler seemed to like was opera, and the only movies he'd deign to watch were highfalutin foreign films with subtitles. *Bleech* on that.

So the only person left who might possibly want to hang out with Jules was Kenji. Jules had no idea whether his Japanese friend was even still awake; it was nearly one in the morning. But he figured he had nothing to lose by checking. He squeezed himself into his Cadillac and drove to the downtown Residence Inn.

He had the desk receptionist ring Kenji's room for him. Emiko answered. "Hello, Jures-*san*," she said. "Oh, I am afraid my brother is asreep. He was practicing trumpet awrr day and became very tired. Is this something very important you need to tawrk with him about?"

"Naww, Emiko, it's nothin' urgent. It's just... well, I kinda had to get outta my house for a while, and I'm lookin' for somebody to spend a couple hours with, maybe see a late movie or somethin'..."

"Oh, but I wudd *ruvv* to spend a few hours with you! Wudd that be okay? I read in a free newspaper that a ho-terr on Poydras Street is showing an outdoor movie at midnight. An *Ewr-vis* movie! I wudd very much rike to see an outdoor Ewr-vis movie! Wudd you take me, Jures-*san*?"

An outdoor Elvis movie on Poydras Street? Not exactly what Jules'd had in mind. But it seemed as good a way as any to kill some time. Besides, they'd already missed half the movie, so even though Elvis the Pelvis wasn't Jules' cup of chicory coffee, he wouldn't have to sit through that much of it. And maybe afterward he'd take his "date" over to the Trolley Stop, show her off to those knuckle-dragging cabby hacks and cops he used to hang with, and watch their chins fall into their gravy. Who said that just because a guy was married, he couldn't have a knockout gal-pal or two? Let Maureen stick *that* in her pipe and smoke it!

When they arrived at the W Hotel on Poydras Street, Jules and Emiko found about thirty audience members sitting in the side courtyard, watching a nicely restored print of *King Creole* being projected onto a side wall of the hotel, a smooth, white surface mostly without windows. Hotel staff had set up about a hundred and fifty chairs, obviously hoping for a larger crowd, so Jules and Emiko had plenty of seats to choose from. Traffic was almost non-existent downtown this time of night on a weeknight; very few errant headlight beams penetrated the courtyard to disrupt the film, parts of which could be seen from blocks away.

"I watched this movie many times on DVD when riving in Kure," Emiko whispered to him. "This is Ewr-vis in New Orrins. He prays a teenager singer who sings in a crub owned by criminaws. I watched it to find out more about New Orrins before I come here with my brother."

Jules glanced at a promotional leaflet which had been left on his seat. The W Hotel, trying to market itself as a hip destination in the post-Antonia environment, was showing a whole series of outdoor movies, all of them films which had been made in New Orleans. Jules was bummed out to see that he'd missed *Angel Heart*. He was a big Mickey Rourke fan, and watching Mickey as a down-at-the-heels private dick slouching around the French Quarter was always a treat. But the movie's biggest draw, Jules thought, was Robert DeNiro's over-the-top turn as "Lou Cipher." That name had to be one of the *dopiest* puns in the long history of devil movies. Jules always chuckled whenever he thought about it. He had a weakness for puns.

"Oh, there is a very good musicawr number coming soon!" Emiko whispered with great excitement. "I want to *dance*, Jures-*san*!"

"Sorry, Emiko — dancin', well, that's not my thing..."

"Oh, but you *must*, Jures-*san*! We wirr dance in *my* way! I did not terr you this before, but I have saved some super-energy from three nights ago. Enough to dance in my way, and for me to herrp you to dance in my way, too. Come!"

She dragged him out of his seat, her tug surprisingly powerful. *Me dance her way? What the hell's she talkin' about?* "I don't know about this, Emiko," he complained. "I don't think this is such a great idea..."

"Ret yourserrf have some *fun*, Jures-*san*!" she said, pulling him toward the wall upon which the movie was being projected. "But remember, you must continue to horrd my hand. Do not ret go. If you ret go, you might get rost in the anime worrwd, and I might not be a-buh to find you. So do not ret go."

Anime world? He didn't want to go into any "anime world." Dealing with *this* world was tough enough. And he didn't want to dance, either.

His knees scoffed at the very thought of dancing. He hadn't danced to pop music since he'd seen the south side of three hundred pounds — and that had been a long, long time ago.

But before he could pull away, she leaned forward on her tiptoes and kissed him on his lips. At the same time, she touched the wall with her free hand. Jules shivered as a portion of the super-energy Kenji had granted her at Snug Harbor leaped into his lips and spread at electric speed throughout his body. *Oh, please*, he thought, *not a* rabbit *again, anything but that*! But before he had time to finish thinking this panicky plea, Emiko had pulled him with her into the wall.

It was a new universe. *A two-dimensional universe, it's gotta be*, he told himself. So why did everything he see around him still look *three-*dimensional? Elvis and Walter Matthau, playing the villainous owner of the King Creole Club, looked normal to Jules, apart from both being in black and white, and each being fifty feet tall. The King Creole Club itself, which he now stood inside while Elvis sung the song "Trouble" on its stage, looked to him like a normal interior space with depth, width, and height (although it, like Elvis and Walter Matthau, could only be seen in tones of white, gray, and black; and it, like them, was *huge*, with chairs and tables that dwarfed him and Emiko).

But when Jules looked *beyond* the King Creole Club, beyond the boundary of the wall into which Emiko had pulled him — out there, out in the courtyard of the W Hotel, things and people looked *strange*. Everything and everyone had multiple, strobing ghost images attached. It hurt his eyes to look at them.

Instead, he glanced at his partner, who had already begun dancing to Elvis' rendition of "Trouble" while holding tightly to Jules' hand. She was still dressed in the pink miniskirt, pink calfskin midi-boots, and white bowling league shirt embroidered with her name that she'd been wearing before, but now the colors were brighter, more vivid. All her features were simplified, with all their human imperfections erased. Her eyes had turned nearly three times their former size, but to Jules, this looked perfectly normal. She had become a beautiful cartoon of herself.

"Dance, Jures-*san*! Dance!"

He looked down at himself, curious as to what a simplified, perfected Jules Duchon cartoon would look like. What he saw pushed the needle of his Surprise-O-Meter sharply all the way to the right.

She had turned him into a cartoon *sumo wrestler*! He was nearly naked! His only covering was one of those weird adult-diaper kind of things the fat Jap wrestlers wore — a strip of cloth wound around his hips and between his legs!

His scalp felt weird, as though it were being stretched, pulled back from his face. He felt the top of his head with his free hand. His hair had been gathered and tied into a massive round knot atop his scalp.

"*Emiko*!" he yelled at her over the wailing of Elvis' warbling. "What did you do to me? This is *nuts*!"

Emiko beamed at him, her smile outshining everything else on the makeshift screen. "I have cawrred you before my garrant sumo, and now you rearry *are* my garrant sumo! I give you a taste of Japan, Jures-*san*! Have fun!"

Dancing, she pulled him all around the King Creole Club. They darted straight up the sides of forty-foot-tall barstools, leaped onto the bar, and twirled across its top. They joined Elvis on stage, Emiko singing along to "Trouble" and staring longingly up at his pelvis as she scurried like a mouse between Elvis' giant legs, compelling Jules to scurry along with her. They treated a scowling Walter Matthau like Mount Fuji, scaling his mountainous form until they reached the summit, where his black hair was slicked down with Vitalis. Then Emiko jumped off, nearly frightening Jules out of a hundred years of undead life — she still held fast to his hand, and so dragged Jules off Matthau's head along with her! But rather than plunging downward, they gently descended like flower petals falling through a light but steady breeze, twirling languorously as they glided to the floor.

The song ended. Suddenly bored with the King Creole Club, Emiko dashed out of the W Hotel's courtyard wall, flowing into the sidewalk and pulling Jules after her. They scampered beneath the shoes of the thirty startled audience members. For Jules, looking up at the outside world from this angle was even more disorienting and vertigo-inducing than staring out from the King Creole Club had been — the strobing crotches above him and towering pillars of skyscrapers above those asses and bellies, littering the sky with their blinking ghost images, made him sick to his stomach. He tried concentrating his full attention on Emiko. Where was she taking him? How long would this last? The thought that she had complete control over him — and she did: he was both literally and figuratively in her hands — suddenly terrified him.

She pulled him across the sidewalk and through the curb and out into the street, the wide blacktop lanes of Poydras Street, sandwiched between the facing glass walls of lofty office buildings and hotels. "Emiko! Where are we going? Where are you takin' me? What are we *doing?*"

"We're having *fun*, Jures-*san!* Emiko-fun! Let yourserrf enjoy!"

"Enjoyment" of this deranged experience was the farthest thing from his addled mind. A delivery truck overtook them. Jules nearly screamed as its clattering steel mass passed over them, its axles and driveshaft spinning madly, overpowering his retinas with after-images of industrial-strength death, whirling and grinding and pulverizing annihilation-machines.

"Emiko! For Varney's sake, let's get *off the street!* I can't take this!"

"Okay! I am your fairy princess — your wish is my command! We go!"

She yanked him back toward the comparatively safe harbor of the sidewalk. Jules tried reminding himself that this wasn't his first trip to the rodeo — every time he'd changed his form into that of a bat or a wolf and then changed back, he'd plunged portions of himself through a terrifying dark dimension of absolute cold and silence. But at least he was pretty well used to that dreadful experience. More importantly, going through it was an ordeal he subjected *himself* to — he maintained complete control.

Now, however, nothing was in his control. Nothing.

"Emiko! Aren't you gettin' tired? Does your super-energy ever run *out*?"

"Don't worry about that, Jures-*san*! I am fine! I wirr know when to reave the anime world. Untirr then, we have fun!"

They flowed from the sidewalk into the base of One Shell Square, the tallest skyscraper in the city's Central Business District. Running with the lightning speed of Golden Age Flash Jay Garrick, Emiko zoomed up the white slate side of the office tower like a miniskirt-wearing rocket, dragging Jules as though he were a sumo-shaped purse. The skyscraper shrunk in size — or were he and Emiko getting larger? Jules couldn't tell the difference. He just wished this E-ticket ride would end.

"I want to *see* you, Jures-*san*!" she giggled. She reached over and undid his wrapper. The diaper-thing which had encompassed his hips unwound and fell between his legs, leaving him completely bare.

"Oh, my garrant sumo! You are very *garrant*, indeed!"

Even in this cartoon form, Jules was still unable to see his own willy; whether vampire or sumo, the voluminous folds of his belly blocked his line of sight. But whatever Emiko saw clearly pleased her. She reached out and grasped him. The touch of her perfect cartoon hand on his cartoon genitals sent shivers of mind-bending pleasure shooting through every photon of his round form. That pleasure went from mind-bending to mind-*obliterating* as she began stroking him.

Jules lost track of what came next. Later that night, he would be able to vaguely remember Emiko turning her backside to him, then leaning over and flipping her miniskirt onto her back, revealing polka-dotted panties, which magically disappeared in a puff of orange smoke.

Had any of the handful of late-night pedestrians walking from downtown clubs to their cars bothered to glance up at the top of the One Shell Square building, they would have been astonished to witness an eighty-foot-tall cartoon sumo wrestler *shtupping* an equally gargantuan anime maiden on the skyscraper's wall, their flailing limbs flowing around the building's corners, animated fireworks exploding silently above their heads.

Jules was enormously relieved to find Maureen already asleep when he arrived home an hour before dawn. Irregular snores stuttered from the back of her throat. He hadn't known what he would've said to her if he'd found her awake. Would he have blurted out a full confession? Was there truly any confession for him to blurt?

He kicked off his shoes and plopped himself into the bed, not bothering to take off his clothes. They weren't dirty. They didn't smell of sex. *He* didn't smell of sex — after Emiko had finally returned him to normal, he'd discovered himself to be as clean as if he'd been thoroughly soaked and rubbed down in a Japanese bath. His armpits even smelled like cherry blossoms.

Had it really happened? Had he been unfaithful? Or had it all happened only inside his head?

Even if it *had* happened the way he kind of remembered it, did having sex with a cartoon while he'd been a cartoon himself actually *count* as infidelity? Or had it been *virtual* sex, on the same level as him wanking off to Internet porn? *I mean, Maureen wouldn't get ticked off at me if she caught me strokin' off to online photos from* Big Girls Pictorial, *would she? It's not like that's never happened before. Besides, when a wife won't put out, doesn't that give her husband a perfect right to satisfy his carnal needs with a little porn?*

He forced himself to close his eyes. But as soon as his eyes were shut, his overwhelmed brain flashed images on his inner eyelids, those horrible, nausea-inducing strobed versions of the three-dimensional world as seen through two-dimensional cartoon eyes. Then, when his eyes snapped open again, his body remembered the sensation of fucking anime Emiko from behind, that pleasure so exquisite it had verged on a sensation utterly unbearable — like getting a blow-job from the heavenly mouth and tongue of the Archangel Gabriel while he simultaneously jammed his celestial staff up your ass.

He shivered and pulled his pillow over his head. *Ohhh, is this gonna be a looooong day...*

One thing he knew for certain. He didn't want to get within kissing distance of Emiko's lips ever again. He'd found out what it was like to be an *otaku*. And he hadn't appreciated the experience.

Eighteen

"**S**HOGO, thank you *so* much for coming over," Maureen said. "I'm so terribly sorry I needed to bother you like this. But something I heard — it's tearing me up, ripping my heart out. I just had to talk with you about it."

Maureen sat on the edge of her bed and stared down at her hands. She needed to touch up her nails, she really did; but now wasn't the time. Not after what she'd heard from her old friend, Chloe.

"You have been very kind to me and my cousins since we have come to New Orrins," Shogo said, fidgeting in the chair she'd provided for him. "I am... happy to be of assistance."

Maureen took this as a green light to launch into her tale. "Chloe and I used to work together as performers at Jezebel's Joy Room. She left me a message on my answering machine earlier today. About something she'd seen. She was out late last night, working an extra shift as a hostess at the Tropic Topic Club downtown; she's trying to scrape together enough extra cash to get the transmission of her little Suzuki car fixed. Anyway, she was walking along Poydras Street, heading for her bus stop, when she happened to look up at the top of the One Shell Square building. She saw something completely *bizarre*. Two cartoons fucking — please excuse my language, Shogo, but I'm under a terrible stress. One of them was a Chinese or Japanese girl in a pink miniskirt. The other... the other was some kind of sumo wrestler, big and fat. But here's the thing, Shogo — Chloe insisted to me the cartoon sumo wrestler had *Jules'* *face.*

"She didn't know what to make of it. She thought it must be a prank some hackers were playing. Or maybe the Chinese military trying to infiltrate our energy infrastructure. Or space aliens. But to me... well, I want to be as delicate as I can, Shogo. I hope I don't hurt your feelings. But to me, it sounds an *awful* lot like something your cousin Emiko may have had a hand in. I'm not accusing her. Not yet. But I've got an awful lot of questions I need to ask. I cancelled my show tonight. I — I'm too broken up to pay any mind to bad horror movies. You're the only one I can turn to, Shogo. The only one I can pose these questions to. Kenji, he's too, well, you know, too *innocent*. He's like a Japanese Boy Scout. And she's his *sister*. I simply *couldn't* pose these questions to him. But you're a more worldly man than your cousin is. And after our time spent together at the Clover Leaf the other evening, I feel like we're friends."

Shogo leaned forward. "What do you need to ask, Maureen-*san*? I wirr do my best to answer."

"Okay. First off — does Emiko have the ability to turn other people into cartoons, like she can do to herself?"

Shogo nodded. "*Hai.* That is one of her powers."

Maureen bit her lip. She felt like she might cry. But she held it inside. "Second question. Have you noticed, or have you heard, any... *indication* that Emiko might be attracted to my husband? Does Emiko like fat men? I mean, *really* fat men?"

Shogo pursed his lips, then nodded again. "She rikes to attend sumo matches. She rikes rooking at the wrestrurs. There have been American sumo, very, very big men. Even much bigger than biggest Japanese sumo. She rikes those sumo the best."

"Ah-*ha*!" Maureen cried, slamming her fist into her palm. "I *knew* it! That little *minx*! Has she ever said anything to you about Jules? About wanting to get her hands on him?"

Shogo furrowed his brow. He set his chin on his fist, looking much like a Japanese version of Rodin's sculpture, *The Thinker* (or was it *Rodan's* sculpture?). "I will try to remember... *hai*, she has made some mention..."

"Of *what?*"

"Of finding your husband... *kawaii*."

"And *what* does '*kawaii*' mean?"

"It means, in Engrish, 'cute,' I bereave."

Maureen sprang off the bed. "That cartoon *bitch*! I'll tear her teeny-tiny *tits* off! When I'm through with her, she won't look like Sailor Moon anymore — she'll look like the evil queen from *Snow White* after she transformed into a syphilitic old *crone*! And when I'm through with Jules — when I'm through with *Jules... Aaaaaahhhhhhh!!!*"

Now the tears came. All her frustrations, all her anger, all the bitter, conflicting emotions that had been building inside her over the past weeks came rushing out, a torrent bursting through a broken dam. "Oh, Shogo, I don't know what to *do*! My whole life has turned to *shit*! I can't — I can't be a wife to Jules, and now he's — he's looking for love in all the wrong places! And my body... this body, Shogo, it barely *listens* to me anymore. It has a mind of its own — no, make that *three* minds of its own. They're driving me *crazy*, Shogo. They're making *demands...*"

Her left leg jutted forward, pulling her toward Shogo. Then her right leg followed suit.

"Demands that... that I just can't *fight* anymore. I'm so *tired* of fighting them, Shogo. You have no idea how *exhausting* it's been. They pummel me and pummel with their demands, never letting up, yowling at me like cats in *heat* until they wear me down..."

Her legs, pushing aside her mental objections like a hurricane wind scattering used tissues, continued walking her toward Shogo. Her arms, no longer under her direction, beckoned to him.

"I'm — *sorry*, Shogo." She straddled his lap, facing him. "I just don't have the strength to fight them anymore..."

Her arms — Alexandra's arms, really — reached around his neck and pulled his face close. But it was Maureen's own lips she kissed him with, her lonely, confused lips alone.

* * * * *

Edna Landrieu was sick and tired of being a "good girl." As far as blood was concerned, Amos had been keeping her on a starvation diet, just a little sip here, a little sip there. Oh, sure, she was still perfectly capable of eating regular food, unlike her big hulk of a son, Jules, who had to turn wolfish to wolf down anything solid. But *blood*... blood was what she *dreamed* about. What she *wanted*.

So... the *hell* with it! Wasn't she an adult? Wasn't she free, white, and twenty-one? Okay, a little past twenty-one, maybe. But really, had she been on this Earth (and under it) all these years, only to have some man tell her what she could and couldn't put in her own mouth? (A darned good man, best she'd ever met; but still...?)

So, here she was. Using her key to skulk into her son's house when nobody was home and sneak some blood out of his freezer. Well, considering how large Jules had been when he'd come into the world (eleven and a half pounds! Popping him out of her had nearly torn her in *half*!) and how much trouble he'd give her since, that boy *owed* her a few bags of blood.

She opened the door and tip-toed inside. She reminded herself again not to feel guilty. *After all, don't I help* earn *that blood? Don't I make all the souvenirs to sell to them tourists? What right do they have to hold out on me?* The *real* reason she had come here on the sly, while Jules was leading a tour and Maureen was at her TV studio, wasn't that she felt sheepish about asking them for some blood; she didn't want to risk one of them blabbing about it to Amos.

Heading for the kitchen, she heard noises coming from the upstairs bedroom. *Somebody's home? How's that?* Maybe one of them had been feeling under the weather and had skipped out on their job? Well, she hadn't told Amos a white lie about going shopping and taken a bus all

the way over here for *nothing*. She was going to drink her fill, come hell
or high water!

Once she'd crept into the kitchen and closed its door behind her, she
debated which would be a quieter way to boil water — in the microwave
or on the stove top? She didn't want to wait around for the blood to defrost on its own. She was *thirsty*. And there was no way, practically, that
she'd be able to sneak that blood back into her own house, not with that
snoopy husband of hers eagle-eying her. The microwave would hum, and
its bell would ring when it was done. That was no good. So, stove top it
was, even though it would take a bit longer.

She searched Maureen's cabinets for a sauce pan of the proper size.
Then, after she'd filled it with water from the sink, she went to the
freezer. *Boy, oh boy, does that blood look good,* she told herself as she
stared at the stacked bags of frozen ichor. How many should she defrost?
One? Two? She decided three would be best. After all, who knew when
she'd have another chance to get over here on her own? Best to top off
her tank while she had the chance.

She picked out the three bags which looked the most full. *In for a
penny, in for a pound.* She waited for the water to come to a boil, then
turned down the setting so it wouldn't boil over. She plopped the bags in
one at a time, rubbing her hands with glee at the thought of the satisfac-
tion which awaited her. The only thing that had ever felt like this had
been Christmas Eve when she'd been a little girl, waiting at the top of
the stairs just before midnight for Santa to slide his fat ass down the
chimney.

Right now, the only thing that would make her life better would be
if stubborn ol' Amos would loosen his grip on his wallet and let her buy
that new vacuum cleaner she'd been wanting so badly. Yeah, maybe her
old machine still had a few months of life left in it. But that new vacuum
cleaner she'd been eying on the Home Shopping Network — that great,
big, gorgeous hunk of metal and plastic was a cleaning *monster*. She had
to have it! Those attachments! All those different speeds and settings!
Watching those infomercials had made her want to pick up the phone

and punch in Amos's credit card number so *bad*, they got her hands to shaking, flustering her so that she'd been momentarily unable to concentrate on knitting her vampire tea cozies.

Life was too short to put up with a wimpy vacuum cleaner, wasn't it?

Okay, maybe not a *vampire's* life. Still, the same principle applied, she figured.

* * * * *

Jules arrived home almost in a panic. He'd been shocked to discover, when he and his tour group had reached the TV studio, that Maureen had cancelled her show for the evening. She *loved* doing that show. The only reason she would've absented herself would've been if she'd been feeling deathly sick. But why hadn't she called him? He would've ended the tour early and come home to take care of her — she knew that. Heck, even without her calling him, he'd ended the tour forty minutes early, promising either a partial refund or a free tour on another night to any disappointed customers.

Looking up from the front stoop, he saw that her bed side lamp was on. She had to be up there, lying on her waterbed. He tried not to let himself think the worst. No, it wasn't that she hadn't called him because her withdrawal symptoms malady had suddenly lurched from annoying to malignant, and she'd found herself too weak — or too unconscious — to pick up the phone. The explanation was much less dire, he told himself; she'd lost her voice, maybe, and she hadn't wanted to bother him with a phone call while he'd been leading a tour. Sure... that must be it. He'd find her upstairs, taking a nap or reading a home decorating magazine or painting her toenails. Everything would be fine. She'd laugh at him for getting his tighty-whities in a bunch with all his worrying.

He closed the front door quietly behind him. If she were taking a nap, he didn't want to disturb her. He'd just tip-toe up the stairs and take a peek in the bedroom to make sure she was all right. If she was asleep, he'd go back downstairs and fix himself a nightcap, defrost himself a nice mug of blood. He had a package waiting for him on the dining room table, a really swell hardbound compilation of *Marvel Mystery Comics* from the 1940s that he'd ordered. That had been his treat to himself for getting the new business rolling. So he'd settle himself into the big easy chair by the window, his mug of blood on the side table, and lose himself in the adventures of Captain America and Bucky, the Human Torch and Toro, and the Sub-Mariner and all his undersea weirdos for a few hours. He'd have to show the book to Kenji, too. Kenji would appreciate all those old superhero stories from Jules' own era of superheroic doings.

He reached the top of the stairs. He heard some noises coming from inside the bedroom. She was still up; good. Maybe she'd want to talk a little before he went back downstairs.

He quietly opened the door. "Hi, hon. I knocked off early 'cause I heard you were sick—"

"*Jules!* What are *you* doing here?"

For Jules, it was like one of those moments in a suspense movie when time slowed to a crawl. There was his wife, yanking the sheets up around her neck and staring at him bug-eyed, as though he were a prowler. She hadn't been painting her toenails. Unless Shogo had been painting her toenails for her. And seeing as how they were both naked, and Jules didn't smell any nail polish, and Shogo didn't seem the type who would take pleasure from painting a woman's toenails, anyway, he rather doubted a pedicure had been the evening's main event.

He slapped his hand over his eyes, not wanting to believe what he'd just seen. But then he forced himself to look. Time sped up again, but not so fast that he didn't note every horrible detail — the way Shogo's muscles flexed as he grabbed for his pants; the animal-like fright in Maureen's eyes; the stain on the sheets. "What the *fuck's* been going on here?"

Maureen flushed as red as a she-devil. "Jules, darling, it's not what you're thinking—"

"So what am I *supposed* to be thinkin'? That you two have been playin' *doctor*? Is this an episode of *Marcus Welby, M.D.*?"

"They wore me *down*, Jules! These — these *limbs* of mine, they wanted Shogo, and they wore me down!"

"Yeah? Really? When I walked in just now, I didn't see your *head* puttin' up much of an argument! It looked to me like your lips were joinin' in on the action, too!"

Maureen tossed her head so that her blonde hair dislodged from her face. Her formerly aghast expression lost its blush and turned hard and vindictive. "Oh, *you're* really one to be hurling accusations, Jules Duchon! You want to tell me what you did last night? Did it involve the top of the One Shell Square building and a certain cartoon *hussy*?"

Jules' jaw dropped open. "How did you hear about—"

"Oh, a little *birdie* told me, Jules! It just happened to be flying around the top of the One Shell Square building while a cartoon sumo wrestler with *your face* was doing Emiko doggy-style, you son of a bitch!"

"But, but — she *made* me do it!"

"She *made* you do it? Do you realize how *pathetic* that sounds, Jules? Are you a *child*? Did your little playmate on the playground convince you to eat mud pies that you'd made together?"

"You weren't *there*, Maureen! You didn't see what went on! She — she turned me into a cartoon sumo wrassler without even *askin'* me! And then she dragged me all over downtown, after warnin' me that if I let go of her hand, I'd get lost forever in the anime world! It wasn't my idea to go to the top of the One Shell Square building! She *dragged* me up there!"

"Oh? And what were you doing out on the town with Emiko in the *first* place?"

"I wanted some company! You weren't talkin' to me! I went to see if Kenji would hang out with me for a couple of hours, and he was asleep, so Emiko said she'd go out with me instead—"

"Oh, how *convenient*!"

"Yeah? And how 'convenient' is it that the same night you should call in sick to your show, Mr. Cutie-Scary Man here ends up in your *bed*? You gonna blame *that* on a coincidence? Or are you gonna keep blamin' it on Flora Ann's bossy *pussy* yankin' you around like a marionette?"

Maureen's eyes narrowed dangerously. "Don't you go talking about my *body* that way, not even my *borrowed* parts... not if you want to touch this body ever again..."

Shogo finished his frantic pulling on of clothes. "I bereave I shall be reaving now—"

"YOU SHUT UP!" Jules and Maureen said in unison.

"I'm not *done* with you yet, pal," Jules said to Shogo. "Stick around a minute; we got us some business to hash out, get me?" He turned back to Maureen. "Look — maybe that last crack of mine stepped over the line. Sorry. But if you've got an out, Maureen, then *I* do, too. I mean, Emiko, she used her superpowers to *seduce* me! She turned me 'cute' or '*kawaii*' or whatever she calls it, and she twisted my emotions all around! You *know* me, Maureen! Better than anybody does! Do you honestly think it's *my style* to drop my drawers at the top of the tallest building in the Central Business District? It wasn't my *idea*! She had me under her *thumb*! I *swear* that's how it happened, Mo! I swear on my *mother's grave*—"

Jules' *cri de coeur* was cut off by a different variety of cry — a cry of terror and agony that started out frenzied and grew weaker with each passing instant. It came from the street below.

Jules and Shogo both rushed to the window. They saw a frail old man lying on the sidewalk on the far side of the street, incongruously dressed in frayed jean shorts, high top canvass sneakers, and a torn Johnny Rotten T-shirt, and sporting a green-died mohawk and multiple facial piercings.

Standing over the octogenarian punk, partially obscured by shadows, was one of the oddest-looking creatures Jules had ever seen — a cross between a purple-haired old biddy in a pink house dress and a Buck Rogers-style vacuum cleaner, with suction nozzles for hands and what looked like twin storage tanks on her back, the storage tanks melding into the exaggerated curvature of her bent backbone. Flexible tubes ran from her elbows to the storage tanks, which were decorated with stream-lined fins of bright chrome.

"That'll teach you to run your *filthy* mouth at your elders," the crea-ture shrieked at the cowering old codger in the punk regalia. "Not feeling so spry and cocky now, are you? You better apply for your AARP card, and fast, while you've still got time left on your clock to enjoy it, you piece of *trash*! I hope you get the arthritis even worse than what I've got! See how *you* like it! I'm sick and *tired* of the *filth* that blows around this city! As of tonight, I'm *cleaning it all up!*"

Jules couldn't believe his ears. He *knew* that voice — knew it as well as he did any sound on Earth.

"*Mother!*" he screamed out the window. "What are you *doing?*"

Nineteen

JULES ran down the stairs of his house three times as fast as a quarter-ton vampire had any business running. He burst onto the street, followed shortly thereafter by Shogo. They found the elderly punk rocker still lying on the opposite sidewalk, moaning to himself, "What're all these brown spots on my hands? What did I have for dinner? Where'd I leave my keys...?"

Jules spotted the creature his mother had become stalking toward the far corner. "Mother! *Wait*! What the heck *happened* to you?"

She paused and turned back toward him. She still had Edna Landrieu's face, still wore her familiar cats-eye bifocals, but those suction hands of hers whirred ominously. "I finally got what I *wanted*, son. That cheapskate Amos wouldn't buy me a new deluxe vacuum cleaner from the Home Shopping Network. So I made my own." She held up her suction hands. "What d'you think, boy? Nifty, huh? Works great, even better than what they showed on cable TV!"

"She must have drunk the brudd..." Shogo said in a low voice, as if talking to himself.

The blood...? Thoughts ping-ponged off the askew walls of Jules' mind. Had his mother been drinking blood out of his freezer? Was there any possibility he hadn't cleared out all of Emiko's and Shogo's blood from his stash?

"Mother," Jules said, crossing the street and cautiously approaching her, "have you been sneakin' blood from Maureen's and my freezer?"

"Well, *yeah*," Edna said defiantly, waving her suction hands at him. "What *of* it? Don't your dear old mother *deserve* a toot of the good stuff once in a while? How come everybody in this whole darned *town* seems to wanna keep me from havin' anything that even *resembles* a good time? I'm *sick* of it! *Sick of it*, I tell ya!"

"Mother, you ain't well," Jules said slowly, as though he were speaking to a particularly backward child. "You better come inside with me and Maureen. Get off the street. We, uh, we need to take care of you, Mom. Come inside with me, and lemme give Amos a call—"

"I don't like your *tone*, boy. Don't you be speakin' down to your own mother. I'm the woman who shoved your eleven-and-a-half-pound bulk out her unmentionables! Darn near cracked me in *half*, you did, like I was a turkey wish bone. I don't need Amos fussin' with me. I got things to do — this town's been *needin'* a good sweepin'-out, and I'm just the woman to do it. So I'll be on my way, thank-you-very-much."

"Mom, I — I *can't* let you go! Not when you're like *this*! Now come inside with me, or—"

"Or *what*? Or you'll *drag* me inside? You just *try* it, Jules Augustine Duchon!"

She aimed her suction hands at him. Jules braced himself, having no idea what to expect. But rather than sucking something out of him, Edna reversed the spinning of the blades contained within her appliance hands, expelling what she'd stored in her tanks — her nozzles shot out a gray, sooty cloud of whatever she'd recently sucked out of the man lying on the sidewalk.

The cloud smelled *awful*, a combination of the stenches of untreated sewage, rotting mangoes, Bourbon Street gutters at the end of Mardi Gras, and sick mule flatulence. The cloud stung Jules' eyes like a bucketful of acid rain, blinding him. It gagged him and choked him, making him double over with revulsion.

By the time he managed to regain his breath and open his eyes, the cloud had dissipated, and the creature his mother had become was gone. Behind Jules, the man in punk regalia weakly lifted himself off his knees. He hadn't regained all of his stolen youth, Jules saw, but Edna's expulsion of the filthy life essence she'd sucked out of him had regressed the man's age from an advanced eighties to around his early fifties; young enough for him to flee into the Quarter, wailing like a middle-aged banshee.

"Your mother is too dangerous to roam free, Jures-*san*," Shogo insisted. "Allow me to retrieve an *otaku* from my ho-terr room. Then I wirr become a creature strong enough to stop her from doing harm."

"That's *crazy talk*, Shogo," Jules shot back. "What do ya think you're gonna do — smash a piano over my mother's head? You think I'd even let you *try* that? This is my *mother* we're talkin' about!"

A firm knock on the door interrupted the debate. Maureen opened the door for Kenji and Emiko. "Thank you both for getting over here so quickly," she told them. "There's been a terrible mishap — somehow, when Jules thought he'd handed back all of the blood Shogo and Emiko gave us, he must've accidentally left some in the freezer. Edna came over earlier without us knowing she was here, and she drank three bags of our stored blood. Now Jules and Shogo say she's turned into some sort of crazy vampire vacuum cleaner creature that can suck life essence out of people. Amos hasn't gotten here yet. I think the news devastated him — I babbled out over the phone what I just told you, and he just seemed to fall apart..."

Kenji looked grim. "I am so sorry this has happened," he said to Jules and Maureen. "We rike your mother very much. We wish no harm to come to her. We wirr do awrr in our power to restore her to her rightfur serrf."

Jules heard a screeching of brakes from the street outside his window. He glanced out in time to see Amos Landrieu's vintage Mercedes Benz leap the curb and knock over an A-frame sign advertising the reopening of the Kit-Kat Klub on Iberville Street. "Doc's here," Jules said.

"Thank Varney — if there's ever been a time we need a big brain around, it's *now*."

Jules headed out the door and trotted down the steps to greet his father-in-law. He almost didn't recognize the man who exited the Mercedes — Amos looked as though he'd aged thirty human years or five hundred vampire years since Jules had last seen him, just a few hours earlier. Jules momentarily suspected that Edna had managed to get to him and had sucked out his life essence, too. But then he saw his friend's deterioration had been due to shock.

"Why didn't you *follow* her, Jules?" Amos cried when he saw his son-in-law. "Why did you let her get away on her own? She can't be left on her own! She *can't*!"

Jules grabbed him before Amos could trip over the sign his car's fender had knocked over. "It couldn't be helped, Doc — I'm *sorry*. She blinded me with some kinda smoke or gas that she blew out of her hands. C'mon upstairs. We'll all put our heads together and figure out what to do next, okay?"

Jules helped him up the steps and through the front door. "Maureen, get Doc a glass of cold water. Or do you want a shot of whiskey, Doc? I think we got a bottle stashed away somewheres..."

"Don't bother with me!" Amos insisted, waving them all away and stumbling into a sofa. "It's *Edna* we must be concerned with! Only *Edna*!" He collapsed onto the sofa and hid his face in his hands. "It's my fault... all my fault... I wanted to trust her, wanted her to be independent again, like she had been before the storm... so I let her go out on her own... and the first thing she does is come here and drink dangerous blood... I should've gone out with her..."

"Doc, listen," Jules said, "if it's *anybody's* fault what happened, it's *mine*. *I'm* the guy who fucked up and didn't double check that I'd cleared all of Shogo's and Emiko's blood out of my freezer. That was like a *bomb* waitin' to go off. I mean, it could've been Maureen who got turned into a monster. It could've been me, again. But thanks to my slip-up, I turned my own mother into a vampire vacuum cleaner..."

"She's my *wife*," Amos groaned, still covering his face. "I'm *responsible* for her. I *failed* her. I may have *doomed* her..."

Jules laid a fleshy hand on Amos' shoulder. "Doc, man, you gotta pull yourself together. You *gotta*. Goin' to pieces won't help my mother none. We need that big brain of yours workin' at full capacity..."

Maureen brought Amos a glass of water. He waved her away. "You all don't understand," he moaned. "You think I'm capable of being her *savior*? It's beyond my powers. I told you as much when I was searching for a cure for Maureen's problem — my equipment might as well be a child's first chemistry set, for all the good it does me. Worse than that — *I'm* not good enough. I'm no research scientist! I'm a *dabbler*, an *amateur*! I was a fairly average pathologist who got himself elected city coroner three times — *that* was the sum total of my accomplishments. I'm not the man my Edna needs right now..."

Jules kept his hand on his father-in-law's shoulder. "Doc, you're *way* underestimatin' yourself—"

"Jules, don't try to make me feel better. Just... *don't*."

Jules realized with a sinking sensation that the main responsibility for solving his mother's conundrum had fallen on his own pudgy shoulders. Doc wasn't going to step up to the plate. Kenji, Shogo, Emiko...? Edna's welfare wasn't their responsibility. Maureen? She had her own problems to deal with. Jules found himself wishing wistfully that Doodlebug still lived in town. Rory, when he wasn't preoccupied with shopping for the perfect cocktail dress, had a knack for seeing all the angles and finding solutions. But he was in California, and by the time he could manage to get out here, Jules' mother might be beyond redemption.

No, the responsibility was on *his* shoulders. He couldn't slough it off on anybody else. This was his *mother*. He tried recalling the deductive methods he'd used when the High Krewe had forced him to serve as their private detective. "All right," he said slowly. "Let's review the stuff we already know. Maureen and I already went through this sorta thing, so we know a little bit about how this weirdness works. Our transformations wore off three nights after the initial change happened. I guess that'll happen to my mom, too — but that won't help us none, 'cause she's outta her mind, and she probably don't have enough sense to stay out of the sunlight when dawn comes. So whatever we figure out, we gotta put it in practice and make it work *tonight*, before the sun comes up. We gotta find a way to subdue her and jam her into a coffin, then keep her there for the next three days, same as what y'all did for me. Doc, you think that animal tranquilizer you used on me when I was a big bunny would work on my mother?"

"It... it might..." Amos groaned from behind his hands.

"The problem would be gettin' close enough to her to use it," Jules said. "She's got that weird power of suckin' people's youth outta them, leavin' 'em old codgers. We don't know if her power only works on regular humans, or if it works on vampires and superheroes, too." He hated shooting down his own ideas. But as the "mastermind" of this operation, that was one of his jobs, he realized — poking holes in dumb notions before those dumb notions could get anybody hurt or killed. Normally, this sort of thing was Doodlebug's line of work. But Doodlebug wasn't here.

"Lemme think this through," Jules said. "Maybe one of you could distract her while I stick the needle in her? Kenji, maybe you could shrink some stuff and then shoot off those fireworks of yours? Or Shogo, you could turn into some kinda big, hairy monster and jump around in front of her?"

"I have torrd you, I am wirring to fight your mother," Shogo said.

But then Jules saw the flaws in his plan. "Naww, forget it," he said. "Too risky. Too much chance she'd zap all three of us before I could get that tranquilizer into her bloodstream. We'd all end up ready for the Old Superheroes' Home, and Mom would still be a homicidal maniac, runnin' wild until she gets fried by the sun..."

"Awrrow me to suggest an idea," Kenji said. "Wudd it be possiburr to shoot the tranquirrizer from a gun?"

"Kenji, you've *got it*!" Jules said triumphantly. "Sure, just like on that old show, *Mutual of Omaha's Wild Kingdom*! The guys on safari would hide behind a tree or a bush and shoot elephants and rhinos with tranq darts from special tranquilizer guns. Doc, you think that could work?"

Amos looked up at him, his eyes bleary and unfocused. "I... I suppose it could. If we had a tranquilizer dart rifle. Which we don't. It's a very specialized item, Jules. You won't find it in the sporting goods department at the local twenty-four hour GoodiesMart, I'm afraid..."

"Would they have a rifle like that at the Audubon Zoo? Could we go and borrow it, maybe? Or steal it, if we have to?"

"They might have such a gun at the zoo, Jules. Or they might not. You might be able to steal it in time. Or you might waste what is left of the night in a futile search for an object which may or may not exist. If the queen had testicles, she'd be king... If I'd never left Edna alone in the house that night the prowler broke in, we wouldn't be facing this terrible dilemma now..."

Jules sensed himself growing panicky. "Doc, c'mon, get your game face on! We *need* you! We need that big brain! Thinkin' stuff through, it's not my forte. We need a *big brain*..."

And then an image popped into his head. A memory of an old comic book he'd once owned, one of his favorites before Malice X had burned down his old house on Montegut Street and Jules had lost every old comic book, pulp magazine, and jazz record in his collection. It had been an issue of *Action Comics* or *Superman* from the nineteen-fifties or nineteen-sixties, one of many, many Superman comics from those years whose covers had featured the otherwise invincible hero being turned into something bizarre-o by the rays from a chunk of Red Kryptonite.

The story he remembered? Superman had been transformed by Red Kryptonite into the Superman of the far, distant future... a super-being with a gigantic head housing a colossal brain. He'd been turned into Super-Brain Superman.

"Guys and gals," Jules said, "I think I may have me an idea that could solve our problems. But it'll take some blood from Emiko, and a whole lotta *luck*..."

* * * * *

Trash! Trash! Must-clean-it-all-up!

Dorothy Edna Landrieu remembered a time when this stretch of Oretha Castle Hailey Boulevard had been a decent place to shop. Decades ago, when it had still been called Dryades Street; back when Franklin Roosevelt had been president. Back then, the storefronts lining the avenue hadn't been boarded-up, derelict spaces defaced with graffiti and garbage — they'd been quaint little shoe stores, furniture stores, and clothing shops owned by nice, friendly little Jewish men wearing their odd little skullcaps. The prices on Dryades Street had been much, much cheaper than at the big stores on Canal Street, and if many of her fellow customers had been Negroes, oh, well... they had needed to shop for their shoes and clothes *somewhere*, hadn't they? Just as she had.

Now this whole street was a garbage heap. The storm hadn't done this. This part of the city hadn't flooded or been smashed up by hurricane winds. This had all been *people's* doing. Trashy people — alcoholics and drug addicts and criminals — had turned this once nice place into a dump.

It was time somebody swept up the trash. And, by golly, she had been granted the power to do just that.

Where to start, though? The sidewalks were littered with broken bottles and yellowed newspapers. Every alcove smelled of pee. Needles and other nasty things sat in broken display cases which had once held children's school shoes and book satchels. She found herself wishing that strange blood she'd drank had turned her into a *bulldozer*, not a vacuum cleaner.

She spotted a cluster of men loafing on a corner a block away, drinking quarts of malt liquor. Two of the four didn't have the decency to wear a shirt, she sniffed. The other two had let their raggedy pants hang so low, she could see their disgusting underwear.

One of the men tossed an empty malt liquor can onto the sidewalk. Edna saw red...

Trash! Trash! Must-clean-it-all-up!

She dialed her speed setting to Maximum and speed-shuffled up the block to where the four men stood, startling them. "Young man!" she barked at the figure who had discarded the can. "You pick up that garbage *right now*!"

"Yo, dudes, check this *out*..." one of the others said to his companions, marveling at Edna's appearance.

"Halloween come early this year?" another man drawled.

"Cracker lady, you on the *wrong side* of St. Charles Avenue," a third man warned. "Who let you out of the nursin' home, anyway?"

Edna kept her attention focused on the litterer, who seemed flabbergasted that she had dared confront him. "I said, you pick up that garbage right *now*," she repeated, "and all the rest of the filth you've scattered about! And put it where it belongs!"

The litterer fingered a knife that hung from his belt. "'Put it where it belongs!'" he said, imitating her voice. "And where would *dat* be, Grammaw? Up yo' old, nasty, dried-up *snatch*?"

Patience had never been one of Dorothy Edna Landrieu's virtues — not when she'd been raising Jules; not when she'd spent four decades trapped in her grave; and never since. Her potent dose of Shogo's blood had winnowed down her already limited pool of patience to a barely existent puddle.

She switched on the suction, not even bothering to chide the litterer for his filthy potty mouth.

Half a minute later, the gaseous essence of the four men's youth swirled within her storage tanks. Two of them tried to run when they saw what initially happened to the man who'd tossed the liquor can. But they quickly discovered that atrophied muscles and arthritic joints weren't conducive to fleeing. One of them tripped on the raggedy hems of his low-riding trousers. His newly bald head, pocked with liver spots, smacked into the filthy asphalt with a sickening crunch.

What a heady *rush* this was! Topping off her storage tanks gave her a buzz even more powerful than her first experience with alcohol, that evening over a century ago when she'd gulped down half a bottle of communion wine, huddling with her giggling parochial school girlfriends behind the gym building at St. Alphonse's.

Hoarding a big load of stolen life essence gave her a taste for more. Much, much more. *This* was the stuff. Cleaning up her beloved hometown wasn't only virtuous — it made her feel like the queen of the world!

Get out the grime! Toss away the trash! Clear away the clutter! Grind up the garbage! Go, go, GO!

There was so much for her to clean up. An entire city, choking on filth and nastiness, awaiting her cleansing touch…

Twenty

"**Y**OU'RE all lookin' at me like I'm *nuts*," Jules said to his five companions. "Yeah, I've had me some nutty ideas over the years, I'll admit it. But I'm tellin' ya, this *ain't* one of them. It can work. It might be the only thing that *will* work! We need us a big brain, even bigger than Doc's. *This* is how we get it!"

"But Jules," Maureen said, "what if you turn into a giant rabbit again? Or something *worse*? What will we do then? We could end up with *two* out-of-control monsters to deal with!"

"That's where you're wrong, Mo. See, I'm only gonna drink Emiko's blood this time — not a mix of Emiko's and Shogo's. I'll still have my own mind, my own personality. You didn't go all Mr. Hyde evil when you got turned into a big fattie, did ya? That's 'cause you only drank Emiko's blood. And we got us a pretty good idea now of how Emiko's blood affects us vampires. It's just like Red Kryptonite, see, just with the big difference that the vampire who drinks it gets turned into some version of whatever it was that was thick in his head just before he drank it. Think about it — right before we drank it last, you were remembering those nightmares you'd been havin' where you'd gained back all your old weight, and I was tellin' you about that damned kid who'd been hecklin' me, the one wearin' the *Alice in Wonderland* White Rabbit shirt. We gotta figure that right before Mom drank the blood, she was grumblin' to herself about that new vacuum cleaner she wanted that Doc wouldn't get for her.

"But what we've never tried is *steerin' the change ourselves*, by thinkin' really, really *hard* about what we *want* to change into. That Superman comic I'm talkin' about? I musta read it at least half a dozen times over the years, before Malice X burned up my collection. I know exactly what the Superman of the future looks like, Super-Genius Superman with his big, tall, bald head shaped like a flesh-colored watermelon. The artist made him look like one of them big-brain spacemen from that sci-fi flick *This Island Earth*. If I had that comic right here in front of me, I could stare at it while I drink a glass of Emiko's blood. I could picture myself as Super-Genius Jules. I could *steer* the change — I *know* I could!"

"But you don't *have* that comic book in front of you," Maureen said. "Malice burned it up. It's *gone*."

"Oh, but nothing is ever *gone* now," Emiko said, "not in these days of the Internet! The Internet remembers *everything*! Do you not have a computer over there, on that taburr in the corner?"

"That's *right*!" Jules said. "You can look up any shit you *want* on the Internet! Thanks, Emiko! Hey, you got any problem givin' another blood donation? We can pull Doc's phlebotomy equipment outta the closet."

"No probrem," Emiko said.

"Maureen, you go sit at the computer—"

"Jules," Amos said from the sofa, "shouldn't *I* be the one to take this risk? Aren't I the most appropriate candidate to transform into a super-being with augmented brain power, since I possess at least some scientific background to start with?"

"I couldn't let ya do that, Doc," Jules said. "I mean, thanks. But that's too big a sacrifice. You're the only vampire I know personally who's had the willpower to stay completely off blood. This would screw that. Besides, we need you as a backup. In case my experiment with Emiko's blood goes hinky, we're still gonna need somebody with a big brain to pick up the pieces and figure out how to save Mom. I'm countin' on you to be that big brain. You up for it, Doc?"

Following an uncertain pause, Amos nodded.

Maureen sat at the corner table and turned on the computer. "What do you want me to search for, Jules?"

"Well, type in 'Superman.' And 'Red Kryptonite.' Add 'big brain,' 'Super-Genius,' and 'Superman of the future'—"

"Not so *fast*, Jules! I can't type that quickly! And how do you spell 'Kryptonite,' anyway?"

After a few minutes of pulling up various search results, they found what they were looking for — a scan of the cover from *Action Comics* number 256, dated September 1959, featuring the great Kurt Swan as cover artist. Better still, the fan who had scanned and uploaded the cover and provided a plot synopsis ("The Superman of the Future! He comes from the year 100,000 — or *does* he?") had also scanned some of the key interior pages, so Jules was able to refresh his memories of that classic Silver Age story.

While Jules was flipping through screens of page scans (contrary to his remembrances, it wasn't a Red Kryptonite story at all, but a story about time travel, and *phony* time travel, at that), Amos drew a pint of blood from Emiko. He emptied the blood into a tall ceramic mug and handed it to Jules. "You're a good son, Jules, to take a risk like this for your mother. I'll be sure to tell her, once she's back to her normal self."

"Thanks, Doc. I can always use some extra 'good son' points." He stared around the room at his friends — well, he couldn't count *Shogo* as a friend, not after what had happened; but he reminded himself to put aside his anger and resentment at the man who'd cuckolded him. Any distractions right now would be disastrous. He had to concentrate on one thing, and one thing only. *Super-Genius Jules.* He raised the mug in a toast. "Bottoms up, y'all. Get ready to say hi to Super-Genius Jules!"

Staring determinedly at the computer screen, he drank every last drop of the supercharged blood. He felt it burn his throat and esophagus as it headed for his stomach. *Gotta think about growin' my brain. Makin' my brain the biggest organ in my body. All that fat around my middle? All that spare mass goes into my brain. I'm gonna become a vampire computer — a super-vampire-computer. A thinkin' machine made outta meat instead of silicon. I'll make Mr. Spock and Einstein look like morons. Big brain, bigger brain, biggest brain... c'mon, already, CHANGE...*

He felt the change coming on. He steadied himself against the side of the computer table. His stomach twisted. The coils of his guts ground against one another. He felt like he was riding one of those loop-the-loop roller coasters without a seat belt, hanging on with sheer animal terror to avoid going *splat* all over the midway.

Then the room lit up with a flash of greenish light. He smelled an intense odor of lime-scented ozone.

Maureen was the first to react. "Oh, sweet Varney... he did it! He actually *did* it..."

Jules looked around him. It was as though he were seeing his companions for the first time. Three of them were mutated humans, genetic products of ancestral exposure to gamma radiation produced by a primitive nuclear fission device. Two of them were former humans, persons who had been dragged through death's curtain by an infection/infusion of extradimensional energy not originally native to planet Earth, energy which apparently had been deposited here by a cosmic accident, or possibly brought here by alien intelligences. Jules made a mental note to investigate this phenomenon later, when he had time.

"Jules, honey," Maureen said haltingly, "how, uh, how do you *feel?*"

Her question clearly illustrates her limited powers of intellect and her skewed sense of priorities. "Let us not waste our limited time with inquiries as to my sensory status," Jules said. "I require immediate access to Dr. Landrieu's equipment and his notes concerning the unique biology of our Japanese guests."

Super-Genius Jules placed the stack of notebooks and print-outs back on the table. It had taken him three minutes to absorb and analyze materials it had taken Amos three weeks to compile. "Dr. Landrieu, I must compliment you on the quality of your written observations concerning the three Japanese mutants. Your notes, such as they are, are most thorough. Your analyses of those observations and the tentative conclusions you postulated, however, reveal your intellectual limitations. Still, for a vampire possessing merely above-average human intelligence, with an I.Q. falling within the ninety-eighth percentile for normal homo sapiens, your work is laudable. I commend your efforts."

"Thank you... I think," Amos Landrieu replied. "So, did my work give you any leads to start with? My wife is out there somewhere, roaming through the city, not in her right mind. And we only have another seven hours before sunrise."

"I am already formulating a possible solution," Super-Genius Jules said. "While we have been speaking, I have been electro-mentally absorbing the digital data housed within your computer's memory drives, adding this to the analog data I captured from your notebooks and other printed materials. It may be necessary for me to obtain and analyze additional tissue samples from the two mutants in question. Or I may be able to proceed using the data we currently have on hand. I will inform you in another few moments."

Maureen and Kenji flipped through news channels on the Landrieus' TV, while Emiko used Amos' laptop to search online news sites for any relevant stories; they all sought clues as to Edna's current whereabouts, or what her possible destination might be. Shogo stood off by himself, warily eying the transformed Jules.

"I think I found something," Emiko said, looking up from the screen. "A story posted onry five minutes ago, about four men taken to Touro Hospitaww. Very *orrd* men, many years orrd, who craimed to be *young*."

"What part of the city are they from?" Maureen asked. "Does it say?"

"No, the story does not say."

"Everyone, here is something," Kenji said, motioning for them all to pay attention to the TV set. "A news story about a strange attack in the Uptown neighborhood."

Super-Genius Jules shifted a portion of his attention from internal computations of several million bits of data to the TV. A bystander had taken phone video footage of an encounter between Edna Landrieu and a pack of young men near the intersection of Claiborne and Louisiana Avenues. Super-Genius Jules recognized the pink house dress Edna wore; he noted how patches of rouge on her cheeks and the purple dye in her hair could be captured by the phone camera, but the rest of her face, head, and arms could not. He watched with interest her assault on the feral pack of young men; the onlooker with the phone camera had not captured the precipitating incident or any earlier, nonviolent interaction between Edna and the youths. He noted the impressive speed with which she was able to withdraw and absorb life essence (more accurately, cellular energy) from the five men, sucking this essence from them as a mandrill might suck the juice from an orange. She swiftly and efficiently reduced them to withered shadows of their formerly vital and youthful selves, leaving them with barely enough residual cellular energy to continue basic life-sustaining functions. Most interesting.

She had become a far more efficient predator than she had been previously; such an efficient predator, in fact, that she was capable, all by herself, of upsetting the delicate ecological balance between predators and prey in New Orleans. That, combined with her obvious lack of self-control (which, he noted, had exhibited itself even before her recent transformation), dictated that Super-Genius Jules reassess his priorities.

Performing a thorough internal review of his own bio-emotional responses and motivations, he realized that his actions up until this instant had been guided by residual feelings of awe for the maternal figure, a complex mix of obligation, loyalty, affection, and guilt, with much of the latter stemming from buried memories involving the voiding of bodily wastes in early childhood. The portion of his super-brain which had been involved in computations of data taken from Dr. Landrieu's computer and notebooks had formulated a way to reverse Edna's transformation. However, Super-Genius Jules realized that, given Edna Landrieu's psychological makeup and clear lack of self-discipline, combined with other factors for which he lacked data (had the substitution of Japanese mu-tant blood for ordinary human blood been truly accidental?), this adverse transformation would not be the last. The welfare of the entire New Or-leans ecosystem outweighed the fate of any single individual. (He con-templated the source of this insight. Had he not once seen this truism played out in dramatic form during the climax of a fictional film set in the future, in interstellar space? Yes: *Star Trek II — The Wrath of Khan*.)

"I have formulated a technical solution to the current, short-term problem," he announced.

"You *have*?" Amos said. "So *quickly*? Well, let's have it, man! Every second counts!"

"I have decided, however," Super-Genius Jules continued, "not to share this technical solution with you."

"*Whaaa-at*?" Amos and Maureen blurted out in unison.

"Dorothy Edna Landrieu, formerly Dorothy Edna Duchon, exhibits a habitual inability to control bio-emotional impulses. She exhibits far less self-control of such impulses than any of the other top-of-the-pyra-mid predators, colloquially termed 'vampires,' who currently reside in the New Orleans metropolitan region. I have calculated the likelihood that this evening's rampage on her part will be only the first of many such rampages to be a 93.87521% probability. Furthermore, I have de-termined that the ecological health of the New Orleans biosphere, taking into account the balance between the predator population and the popu-lation of prey, would benefit from the expulsion of Dorothy Edna Land-rieu from the ranks of peak predators. Logic dictates that she should be allowed to expire as of the next occurrence of daylight. 'The needs of the many outweigh the needs of the one.' That is a quote."

Maureen nearly fell off her chair with astonishment. "*Jules*! What are you *saying*? Do you mean — can you actually *mean* you want your mother to *fry in the sunlight* tomorrow morning?"

"Yes. That is the only possible conclusion, all factors considered. The best course of action is for us to take no further action tonight and to allow, as you might put it, 'nature to take its course.'"

"That — that's *inhuman!*" Amos Landrieu cried.

"Jules, that's completely *heartless!*" Maureen added.

"You are allowing the primitive, reptilian portions of your limited brains to lead you to such mistaken judgments," Super-Genius Jules said. "A dispassionate examination of the course of human history reveals that applications of inappropriate compassion have led to at least as much civilizational ruin and large-scale suffering as applications of such presumably negative emotions as hatred and fear have. However, my time is limited. I do not wish to waste any more of it in non-productive debates on this subject with persons of insignificant intellect. My own self-preservation is paramount."

"Your own 'self-preservation?'" Maureen said. "What are you talking about, you melon-headed *geek?*"

"I choose to ignore your childish, *ad hominem* insult," Super-Genius Jules said. "Unless I take decisive action, in three evenings' time, I shall revert to my former, immeasurably inferior form. That is not an acceptable outcome. Therefore, I shall utilize the mass-manipulation abilities inherent in the vampiric genome to significantly raise the probability of my own long-term survival as a separate, independent entity."

Before anyone in the room could react, a cloud of grayish smoke surrounded Super-Genius Jules, a cloud that stank of underarm sweat, foot odor, and morning breath. When the cloud congealed, reverting to its original state as pale vampire flesh, two bodies were revealed to be standing in the middle of the living room — normal-headed Jules, about a hundred and eighty pounds less obese than formerly; and Super-Genius Jules, whose watermelon-shaped head, unreduced in size, now rested on a considerably shorter, more compact, more muscular, and far thinner body than it had before.

"That's much better," Super-Genius Jules said. "I will now take my leave of you. I advise that none of you attempt to follow me. I am perfectly capable of disabling automotive vehicles from a distance. To illustrate that I am not bluffing, I will now demonstrate my mentally-generated electromagnetic pulse."

He folded his newly muscular arms across his chest and blinked like Barbara Eden on *I Dream of Jeannie*.

Every electrical appliance in the Landrieus' house went instantly dark, allowing Super-Genius Jules to make good his escape.

Twenty-One

FOLLOWING a moment's worth of stunned confusion on the behalf of everyone left in the house, Amos managed to locate a flashlight. He shined its beam on the remaining Jules, who swayed unsteadily in the center of the living room.

Maureen steadied him. "Jules! Is it really *you*? Are you back, honey?"

"Muh-mostly," Jules said. He prodded his midsection, his fingers gauging the shrunken number of folds of excess adipose remaining. "I seem to be a little less gargantuan than before. But personality-wise, mentality-wise... yeah, hon, I'm back."

"Do you have any memory of what just happened? Do you remember what you said and did as Super-Genius Jules?"

"Actually — yeah, I *do*. More than that — I can remember his *thoughts*. His intentions. The results of his calculations, his theories, his conclusions..." He turned suddenly to Amos. "Doc! Don't you have a generator in your basement? Didn't you once tell me it's a model whose motor is shielded from electromagnetic pulse, the kind that could result from a solar flare?"

"I do have a generator," Amos said. "And yes, anticipating a possible recurrence of a solar flare on the scale of the Carrington Event, I did invest in the high-spec model, the one with the shielding. It should still be in good working order."

"You've got to get me a working computer as fast as possible," Jules said. "If neither of yours will power up, have Maureen drive back to our place and grab our machine. I — I've still got a lot of his solution in my head, but it's beginning to fade. I don't know how long I'll be able to hang onto it; this normal-capacity brain of mine doesn't have the long-term capability to store and process those memories. If nothing else, get me a pad and pen and working lights. And Doc, do everything you can to get your lab equipment in working order. I'm going to need it.

"Oh, another thing — I know what he's got planned for the immediate future. His number-one priority is to prevent reverting to what we'd call 'normal Jules' in three nights time."

"He'd still change back, even though he separated his body from yours?" Maureen said.

"It's not 'his body' — it's still *my body*, and it will revert to a smaller, hundred-and-eighty-pound version of *me* after three nights have passed. At which point, having the same personality makeup and desires as I do, that second Jules will return to me to be reabsorbed. Despite Super-Genius Jules' superior intellect, I'm still the base model, just like I was when I changed myself into three obese dwarfs when I fought Malice X. The base template — *me* — emanates electro-mental-magnetic impulses which would compel the same biochemical changes to occur in both bodies simultaneously. When the mutagenic properties of Emiko's blood reach their time limit in *this* body, they will also reach their time limit in *that* one, and our bio-chemical states will remain synchronized... unless he can manage to put enough shielding between his form and mine."

"Shielding?" Doc Landrieu said. "What sort of shielding are you talking about?"

"Salt water, mostly. That, and distance. He's calculated that if he places himself at a depth of at least eight hundred feet of salt water and remains, at minimum, three hundred miles distant from me during the time period when Emiko's mutagenic blood goes inert in my body, he will evade the electro-mental-magnetic signals which my body broadcasts, just as you could evade being dosed with gamma radiation from a nuclear event if you sheltered behind enough lead shielding. Vampires don't need to breathe, and our bodies are enormously resistant to high-pressure. He's heading for the Gulf of Mexico. He intends to steal a boat or stow away on one. He'll go out a couple of hundred miles, hiding in a storage hatch below decks during the daylight. Then, when he's far enough away from me, he'll attach weights around his legs and jump over the side. Once he's several hundred feet beneath the surface, he won't have to worry about sun exposure, either."

"But even so," Emiko said, "won't the effects of my brudd in him *stirr* wear off after three more nights?"

Jules shook his head. "We can't count on that, Emiko. He's gambling that his highly evolved mental powers, combined with his vampiric abilities to control and manipulate his own physical form, will allow him to synthesize for himself the mutagenic properties of your blood — he intends to mentally, biochemically replicate those properties in his own system prior to his hitting the time limit. Don't forget, he's already performed a thorough analysis on samples of your blood. He's dedicating the efforts of every brain cell in that massive cranium of his to ensuring the continuation of his own independent existence. But right now, his plans and the impact those plans may have on me are of a distinctly secondary concern. Saving my mother is what I need to concentrate on. That lousy, big-brained *bastard*, cold-bloodedly consigning my mother to such a horrible end…"

"I'll see to that generator," Amos said. "And then I'll check the status of the computers and my equipment downstairs."

"My famirry and I," Kenji said, "we shudd try to rocate your mother. Try to keep her from hurting more peopurr, if we can."

"I have an idea of how I cudd herrp find her," Emiko said.

"Actually," Jules said, "I need you all to divide your efforts. Doc'll have to stay here with me to help run the lab equipment. A couple of you should try to locate my mother. The other pair need to track down Super-Genius Jules before he boards a boat. I can't promise I'll be able to replicate the serum he devised for my mother. Great chunks of his scientific formulae are fading away from my mind with each passing moment. In case I fail, we need to catch him within the next several hours and force him to divulge what he knows. He'll be heading for a marina with access to the Gulf."

"I can search for both your mother and Big-Brain Jures-*san* at the same time," Emiko said. "As Anime Girr, I can rook out from TV screens and computer screens awr over the city, even from the navigation screens in cars."

"I did not know you cudd do that," Kenji said, a hint of reproach in his voice. "You did not terr me."

"Back in Kure, I practiced," Emiko said, staring abashedly at the floor. "I was bored there. I found new things to do. I am sorry I did not mention this."

The electric lights in the room came back on. "Doc's got the generator running," Jules said. "I need to head downstairs to his lab. I'll leave it up to you to split up into two teams and coordinate your searches. Let's keep in touch by cell phone."

He had a pretty good idea why Emiko had never mentioned this new use of her super-abilities to her brother. Jules had gotten to experience the frisky minx side of her personality up close and personal. He could just imagine what sorts of intimate activities she'd chosen to spy on through the screens of thousands of TV sets and computers in Japan.

Still, he didn't let himself focus on this titillating notion for more than an instant. He had more important things to think about. And not much time.

The phone on the wall of Amos Landrieu's basement lab rang just as Jules was in the middle of measuring out precise quantities of a dozen potent chemical compounds in separate glass vials. "Get that, will ya, Doc?" he said.

"Of course."

A moment later, after a brief conversation in a muted voice, Amos told his companion, "It's Emiko. She's located Super-Genius Jules. He's in a BMW sedan equipped with iDrive. She has the longitude and latitude of the car's recent position, thanks to the satellite connection the iDrive is tied into. I've written the coordinates down. She wasn't able to see anything through the car's windows. Complete darkness; not even any street lamps. But she can describe his heading and general position from glancing at the navigation maps on his iDrive screen. He's in the eastern part of the city, on State Road 90, heading east."

"He's going for the Rigolets," Jules said. "I'll bet he's hoping one of the marinas out there's been repaired since the storm. Hitchin' a boat there'll allow him his fastest escape out into the Gulf. If he can't find any working boats in a marina at the Rigolets, he'll keep going east, towards Slidell in St. Tammany Parish. Plug them coordinates Emiko gave you into Google Maps on the laptop. Then call Maureen and Kenji with my 'twin brother's' most recent position. I already sent them out towards the marinas in the east. With any luck, they might even be ahead of him, able to cut him off."

"I'll do it right away, Jules. How's it coming with the serum?"

"I *think* it's coming along okay..."

"You don't sound too certain."

"Five minutes ago, I was sure of what I was doin'. I *understood* what I was doin'. Now, it's like following the steps for bakin' a cake when you ain't never baked anything before. You just follow the recipe and hope for the best."

"I pray the recipe is a good one..." Amos said.

He returned five minutes later. "I looked up the coordinates. You were right about his heading for the Rigolets. Those coordinates put him close to the Fort Macomb Marina. That's where I told Maureen and Kenji to go. Do you need any help with the equipment?"

"One of the last things I can remember from Big Brain's instructions is linin' up those test tubes in the order I was supposed to mix 'em, addin' one to the next to the next. I think... I think the serum won't turn out right if you switch around the order the different chemicals get added.

But, y'know, I can't be sure. Not anymore. Doc, you ever read a story called 'Flowers for Algernon'?"

Amos raised an eyebrow. "By Daniel Keyes? Yes. A long time ago. But it's stuck with me."

"I never read it. Didn't even know there was a story by that name, not till tonight. Just a little something I picked up from Big Brain. He gets bored easily, so while he was doin' all them millions of calculations, he was also tyin' into lots of side readin' material through your computer. But even though I never read that story myself, I saw the movie version. It was called *Charley*. Starred a guy named Cliff Robertson. Damn sad story. It's about this retarded guy who gets an experimental operation that turns him into a genius. Only problem is, the operation wears off. He goes back to bein' retarded. And on his way back down, he realizes how all his old coworkers at the donut shop where he pushed a mop, other guys he thought were his friends, had all been makin' fun of him behind his back, when he didn't know any better. And the whole time while he's losin' his smarts, he knows that's the kinda treatment he has to look forward to again."

Amos put a hand on his shoulder. "I'm sorry, Jules. I truly am. It can't be easy, going through what you've been experiencing tonight."

"Actually, Doc, ain't no reason to feel sorry for me. Least I'm not retarded — despite what *some* people may think. Besides, I got a chance to meet a Super-Genius egghead from the inside... and boy, was he an *asshole*. I'm *glad* to have him outta my head. Wasn't it William F. Buckley who said he'd rather be governed by the first two hundred names listed in the Boston phone book than by the faculty of Harvard University?"

"Buckley, you say? I didn't think political commentary was on your list of preferred reading, Jules."

"Never picked up a copy of Buckley's mag. I prefer *Big Cheeks Pictorial* when it comes to leisure-time readin' from the newsstand. Naww, that was somethin' Super-Genius Jules absorbed from the Internet during his 'spare time' — the entire online archives of *The National Review*. Least I got one good quote out of it."

"Do you need me to help mix together those chemicals?"

Jules shook his head. He picked up the first of the glass vials and emptied it into a flask. "The way I got 'em lined up here like a set of alphabet blocks in a row? Doc, even a dummy like me couldn't screw this up."

* * * * *

"There's the BMW he must've come here in, parked over there," Maureen whispered to Kenji as they both quietly exited Jules' Cadillac. "But I don't see Super-Genius Jules anywhere..."

Kenji did his best to scan the dark marina. Only a sliver of moon was out tonight. None of the street lamps which had once surrounded the rural marina, tucked away in the eastern corner of Orleans Parish on a narrow spit of land separating Lake Pontchartrain from the marshes which led to the Gulf of Mexico, had been repaired since the hurricane. He could barely make out the dark mound of Fort Macomb, a masonry fort built in the years following the War of 1812. It was gradually subsiding into the encroaching muck, its massive brick walls cracking and crumbling, their slow-motion death throes hastened by the fury of the recent storm.

"I think he is hiding," Kenji whispered back. "I think he saw the approach of our headlights."

"Are there any boats here that he can *use*? I can't see very well, but the boats I *can* see look pretty... sunken."

Kenji had to agree. The paths leading from the small parking lot to the marina's docks were obstructed by the wrecks of several cabin cruisers, pleasure craft which had been tossed out of the water by Antonia's winds. The radar and radio mast of a large fishing vessel protruded from the black water, which obscured all but a foot of the boat's hull.

"We wirr see," Kenji whispered back. He motioned for her to follow him. "We wirr go to the docks and rook at the boats more crosery. I wirr shrink any boats that rook seaworthy. My power's green grow wirr herrp us to see."

They walked around the wrecks of the beached pleasure boats. Kenji hoped the chorus of frogs croaking — there must be thousands of them surrounding the marina, infesting the old fort — would cover the sounds of their footsteps through the mud, the *squish-squish* their shoes made. When they reached the docks and stepped out of the mud onto weathered wood, he glanced down into the water. He thought about those glowing fish Jules had told him a false story about, that first night they had met; he felt sad that such fish were not real, after all. How pleased he would be to look down from these forlorn docks and see luminescent fish brightening the dark waters with their graceful passage, a happy reminder that there was more to life than struggle and strife.

Near the end of one of the docks, a forty-foot-long fishing vessel, intact and seaworthy, floated atop the water. Kenji approached it. "I wirr shrink this one so he cannot use it," he whispered to Maureen.

"What if he's aboard it?" Maureen whispered back. "Will he shrink, too?"

Kenji shook his head. "My power wirr not affect him. I cudd not shrink Jures-*san* when he was a big rabbit. If Super-Genius Jures-*san* is inside this boat, we wirr know soon. The boat wirr shrink around him. He wirr burst out of it and fawrr into the water."

Kenji knelt next to the fishing boat. He placed both hands on its hull and concentrated on the mental symbol which allowed him to best focus his power, an origami dove which he folded smaller and smaller, which collapsed in on itself but never lost its shape. His hands began glowing green. The glow spread from his fingers and palms through the vessel's wooden planking and steel fittings. The boat glowed more and more brightly as it grew smaller, its light illuminating the surrounding docks and the nearest of the low-lying islands of marsh grass which dotted the waters leading to the Gulf.

He did not shrink it all the way down to the size of a child's bath toy. Such an effort was not necessary; he only needed to make it small enough that Super-Genius Jules could not take it out to sea. He removed his hands once the boat had been reduced to the size of a canoe.

He looked around him. The next closest dock had been crushed by the storm-driven pincer-squeeze of two large fishing craft docked on its opposite sides. The twin craft were both partially capsized now, their masts and rigging lines tangled in each other like two sets of knitting needles tossed heedlessly into a basket full of unruly yarn. The dock next over, however, had remained in serviceable shape. Two undamaged fishing craft were moored to it, rocking in the waves caused when water rushed into the vacuum Kenji had created by shrinking the first boat.

He walked swiftly out onto the undamaged dock and approached the nearer of the two fishing vessels. He felt a twinge of guilt that he was possibly depriving fishermen of their livelihoods; they had obviously suffered losses during the storm and had perhaps only recently been able to resume their occupations. Living his whole life in Kure, close by the shore of the Inland Sea, he had known many fishermen and witnessed many destructive typhoons.

He vowed to himself to return here once this crisis had passed and restore the shrunken fishing boats to their original sizes. Maintaining the energy he had borrowed from the boats inside himself for more than a brief time would be painful, perhaps; normally, he either released it into the air or passed it along to Emiko. And making things grow, restoring the borrowed power to them by reconverting it to mass, was far more taxing than making things shrink. But he felt a sense of responsibility to the men who owned and sailed these vessels.

He knelt by the first of the two boats and placed his hands upon its hull, concentrating once again upon his collapsing origami dove. *Forgive me, worthy fishing vessel*, he thought as his hands glowed green again. *I promise I will return you to your original stature and seaworthiness, perhaps as soon as tomorrow morning...*

He felt a fresh surge of borrowed energy flow into him from the rapidly shrinking craft. Normally, he would not attempt to hang onto such a great quantity of energy; it temporarily increased his strength, but it also dizzied his senses, and keeping it from leaking out through his skin wearied him. He eagerly anticipated reaching the point when the boat would have shrunken to the size of a rowboat. He wondered whether he could safely contain the energies still to be borrowed from the other fishing craft in the marina, on top of what he had already absorbed. Possibly a new strategy was called for; perhaps, regarding the other seaworthy craft, rather than seeking to shrink the entire vessel, he should focus his shrinking power on their engines only...?

"Kenji, look *out!*"

Maureen's shouted warned reached him too late. A booted foot smashed into the side of his head, spinning him around and knocking him face down onto the splintered planks of the dock. The force of the unexpected blow made him lose control of the vast store of borrowed energy he'd absorbed. Bolts of green energy burst forth from his hands. One blast shattered the fishing vessel which had been in the process of shrinking, scattering diminished nets, cranes, davits, pilothouse, and broken planking across the harbor. A second bolt disintegrated a floating warning buoy.

But the third out-of-control blast caused the most damage — it tore through the metal shell of the marina's large storage tank of diesel fuel, igniting the fuel oil. The resulting blaze, spreading along with the rapidly spilling fuel, threatened to reduce the entirety of the partially rebuilt marina to cinders.

Kenji pulled himself to his feet. "No! What have I done?" he shouted in Japanese. Not pausing to react to the sneak attack which had laid him low, unmindful of the peril the flames posed to him, thinking only of the fishermen who would again find themselves without a living should their marina and fishing fleet go up in smoke, Kenji ran toward the blazing fuel tank.

A wave of blistering heat forced him to retreat. He circled the damaged storage tank until he found a section not yet on fire. Leaping over rivulets of escaping fuel, knowing all too well how soon those rivulets would become serpentine rivers of fire if he failed to act, he pressed his palms against the tank. It was *hot* — so hot he nearly cried out. But he forced himself to maintain contact with the metal and ignore the pain until he could focus his thoughts on his key symbol and press his power into service.

The blazing fuel tank shrank rapidly. Knowing his painfully blistered palms and fingers would swiftly heal, Kenji maintained contact with the fire-hot metal, absorbing as much mass as he could stand. Finally, after what seemed like an endless struggle between his superhuman power of concentration and the psyche-shattering impact of physical pain, he had reduced the storage tank with its remaining fuel oil to the size of a mop bucket. It still burned, but the formerly uncontainable inferno had been shrunken down to the dimensions of a dying campfire. Kenji stomped it out with his boots.

"Kenji!" Maureen shouted again. "Look over there! On the water!"

A patrol boat emblazoned with the markings of the Louisiana Department of Wildlife and Fisheries pulled away from the westernmost dock and through the harbor toward open waters. "I salute your public-spiritedness, Kenji!" Super-Genius Jules announced through an electronic bullhorn. "I counted on it to allow my escape. Am I correct in assuming you were able to track me here because of residual memory traces I left behind in my idiot brother's brain? I judged the probability of such memory traces leading to an interruption of my escape to be 42.74261% — worrisome, but not dire enough to make me cancel my plans."

Kenji pointed his glowing arms in the direction of the fleeing patrol boat. "Turn around," he shouted over the noise of the vessel's throbbing motor. "Return to the dock, or I wirr sink your boat."

"I don't believe you will attempt such a rash action," Super-Genius Jules answered. "The extent of your control over discharges of your purloined energy is extremely limited. In all likelihood, any attempt by you to disable or sink this craft would also result in my death — and I know you do not want to risk that, because you are uncertain that my dying will not also result in the death of your friend. Apart from this, you are no killer; unlike your cousin Shogo, perhaps. And you have no reason to desire me dead — you want the knowledge in my brain."

"*Jules!*" Maureen screamed after the departing boat. "If there's any shred of decency left in that overgrown skull of yours, *help us!*"

"By allowing my mother to expire, I *am* helping you," Super-Genius Jules insisted. "You simply lack the intellect to appreciate this."

"You're a *heartless monster!*"

"You think I am bereft of all sentiment? That isn't accurate. I love you, Maureen, even though that love will not ever be reciprocated to my person. I love you enough that I wish you to be happy with my idiot counterpart. I formulated the contents of a serum which will cleanse your body of all lingering byproducts of your ingestion of Kenji's blood, allowing you to resume physical relations with your husband once more. How good is your memory?"

"Good enough!"

"Then make every effort to remember this — mix together fifteen parts standard human blood, six parts lemon juice, point two parts powdered, dried aloe plant, point zero seven parts venom of *Hapalochlaena lunulata*, the Greater Blue-Ringed Octopus, and point zero five parts venom from *Hydrophis caerulescens*, the Dwarf Sea Snake. The venom from the octopus and sea snake must be *fresh*, understand? Ingest one quarter liter of this mixture by mouth every twelve hours for one week. For best results, add a daily colonic of the same, alternating with the twice-daily oral ingestions. If I can locate a wireless computer aboard this vessel, I will email the formula to Dr. Landrieu, in case you should forget.

"Farewell, Maureen! I wish you nothing but happiness in all the years of your undead existence!"

Maureen and Kenji watched the running lights of the patrol boat grow smaller and fainter as the boat headed for the Gulf. They had no way to pursue him; Kenji had shrunken or sunk all the other seaworthy craft in the harbor.

They didn't have long to berate themselves for the failure of their mission, however. For soon after the lights of Super-Genius Jules' boat disappeared behind a distant island of saw grass, they received a call from Emiko, alerting them that she had located the whereabouts of Edna Landrieu.

Twenty-Two

"**T**HAT was another call from Emiko," Amos Landrieu told Jules. "She's spotted your mother. Edna has been attacking college students along Tulane University's fraternity row."

Jules grunted. "Yeah, Mom's always had a thing about college kids, ever since watchin' the CBS Nightly News durin' the Vietnam War years, right before she passed on. Beatniks and hippies used to drive her *nuts*. Not their demonstrations and political slogans — their *dirtiness*. Call Shogo. He's somewhere Uptown, lookin' for Mom on that scooter he rented. Tell him to meet us at the corner of Broadway Avenue and Frerret Street. Tell the same to Maureen and Kenji. While you're doin' that, I'll pack up the serum."

Amos placed his calls. Meanwhile, Jules stared at the flask filled with the precious antidote serum with increasing bafflement. "Uhh, Doc," he said, "I think we got us a problem."

"What is the difficulty, Jules?"

"You remember the genius mouse, Algernon, from that 'Flowers for Algernon' story? How when he died, Charlie knew his own smarts would soon be kaput, too?"

"Yes. Why?"

"Well, my mouse just died. I can't remember shit about none of this technical stuff anymore."

"But you've already mixed the formula. Your job is done—"

"No, Doc, it's *not*. Yeah, I got the serum sittin' there in a flask, all nice and pretty. But I can't remember if we're supposed to *inject* it, get her to *drink* it, or atomize it and get her to *breathe* it."

"We'll just have to bring along enough equipment that we can try all three methods," Amos said. He looked intently at his companion. "Jules, let me ask you something. Despite your vampirism, you've always tried to be a good Catholic, like your mother. I've never drunk a drop of blood from a human being... do you think the heavenly powers would be offended if I prayed?"

Jules shrugged his shoulders. "You're askin' me that question too late, Doc. Maybe I woulda been smart enough to answer you twenty minutes ago. Eh, wouldn't hurt to try, I guess. Unless your lips catch fire — that might hurt."

Amos sighed. "Let's go — we've got just a little over three hours before sunrise."

When they arrived on Fraternity Row, Jules quickly spotted a pretty convincing clue that his mother had recently been in the vicinity. A group of elderly men sat in beach chairs arranged around a big-screen TV on the porch of one of the frat houses. All of the old codgers wore matching fraternity jerseys, red shirts embroidered with a trio of bright blue Greek letters.

"Doc, pull over here," Jules said. "Looks like Mom's been up to no good."

Jules exited the car. "Good evening, gentlemen," he said to the men. One of them was using a remote to aimlessly click through dozens of channels. "Any chance that one of you has seen an old lady with purple hair and vacuum cleaner hoses for arms?"

"Is she *single*?" the least desiccated of the men said.

"'Fraid not," Jules said. "Uhh, this woulda been the same lady who just pulled a big presto-change-o on you guys. Can any of you tell me what direction she went in?"

"'Presto-change-o?'" another of the men said, scratching his bald pate. "Was there a magic show? Did I *miss* it?"

"How come we got two hundred channels of cable TV," the man with the remote muttered irritably, "and you can never find a rerun of *The Lawrence Welk Show* when you want one?"

"Jules, are you finding out anything?" Amos shouted from the car.

"No luck," Jules shouted back. "If I stick around here any longer, they're gonna start askin' if I've clipped any coupons for Metamucil—"

Just then, Jules saw Emiko heading toward him, flowing along the sidewalk's surface in her two-dimensional anime form. "Jures-*san*! Come with me! She is a few brocks away, in a prace with many correge bars and many students. Come quickry!"

Jules spotted Shogo heading up Broadway Avenue, the throttle on his rented Vespa scooter wide open, the little vehicle wailing and puttering with all the gusto its tiny engine could muster. "Here comes Shogo," Jules said. "Good deal — we're gonna need him." He pulled open the passenger door of Amos' Mercedes. The force of Jules' yank dislodged the passenger seat from its worn-out stays, and it lurched forward. "Doc, follow Emiko. Sounds like we'll find Mom on Maple Street. She's hittin' the college bars there."

"Should we wait for Maureen and Kenji?"

"No time," Jules said. He stuffed himself into the front passenger seat, taking care not to trample the padded lunch container sitting in the foot well which held the precious flask of antidote serum. He had to contort himself, as though he were attempting to sleep in a midget's coffin. He fumbled for the seat adjuster on the side of his chair. "Doc, where's the gizmo that'll let me push this seat back?"

"Jules, wait until I can rearrange some things behind you—"

"Oh, here's the lever — never mind, I found it—"

"Careful!"

Jules slid backward much more quickly than he'd intended. He heard a stomach-churning *crunch* as his seat back compressed a bag sitting on the floor behind him. "Oooh, that didn't sound good..." he said.

"My *equipment...*"

The night was not going well.

"Just go, Doc," Jules said, a sinking feeling in his guts. "We'll figure out *somethin'...*"

* * * * *

There had been a time, long ago, when Edna Landrieu had *liked* bars. Not *all* bars — even back in the more genteel days of her youth, there had been many drinking establishments where a lady was not welcome or where it was not wise for her to venture, dank haunts whose patrons were of dubious moral stature: Italian immigrants and longshoremen and sailors and whatnot. Still, even some of the seedier places in her neighborhood had managed to set aside a place of honor and comfort for her and others of her sex, a separate room where she could be treated with dignity and enjoy a beer or two... or three.

But then those horrible beatniks and hippies had *ruined* the bars, just as they had ruined the parks and the French Quarter and almost everything which had once been nice and enjoyable and proper in New Orleans. They disrespected their elders and the police and the military and the clergy. They shoved their Free Love in everyone's faces, as though decent people had any desire to see their filthy, naked body parts! Yes, that was the worst thing — they were so *filthy*! They *stank*! Stray dogs groomed themselves better! When she was a young lady, college men had been *gentlemen.* The college men of her day would have been *ashamed* to be seen out of doors without a jacket and tie and a nice hat. But the college "men" of today... beasts! Savages! Louts with the gutter morals of Greek sailors, and the disgusting tattoos to match!

Filth, that's what they were. *Garbage.* Acres and acres of *trash* strewn about, blowing through all the neighborhoods of the city she loved. Someone needed to clean it all up. And she was just the woman to do it.

The intersection of Maple Street and Hillary Street, an island of raucous commerce in an otherwise quiet, tree-lined residential neighborhood of Victorian homes, looked to be as auspicious a locale as any in which to ramp up her "Clean Up New Orleans" crusade. Each corner of the intersection held a bar — Bruno's Tavern, T. J. Quill's, the Doors Pub, and Rocco's Tavern — and from each bar came the sounds of drunken laughter, billiards playing, and degraded music (even some of that horrifying "rap" Jules had warned her about, worse than the Beatles, hard as that was to imagine). Undoubtedly, each of those houses of sin was stuffed to overflowing with vile beatniks and hippies, pawing each other's private parts and plotting to overthrow America, Jesus, and Walter Cronkite, Edna's Big Three.

She marched herself up the steps to the front entrance of Bruno's Tavern. A brawny bald man with tattooed arms, an earring, and a strange little square beard on his chin (a sailor?) blocked her way. "Ma'am?" he said. "I'll have to ask to see a photo ID, please."

Edna felt for her purse. Then she realized she had left her pocketbook at home. "I don't have it with me," she said. "But I'm over twenty-one," she added with a girlish giggle.

"Sorry. I have to see a photo ID, or I can't let you in. Those are the rules."

Edna narrowed her eyes. "Sonny, I been drinkin' in bars since the year of the Spanish American War—"

"I don't care if you've been drinking in bars since the Punic Wars, Granny. No photo ID, no drinking in *this* bar."

"'Pubic warts'? What's this about 'pubic warts,' young man?" *Now, isn't it just like this younger generation to pop off with somethin' vile when conversin' with their elders?*

He needed his mouth washed out, that was for sure. That nasty mouth needed the dirt sucked out right of it.

Edna revved up her motors.

* * * * *

From a block away, Jules saw a crowd of panicked college kids pouring forth from every exit door in Bruno's Tavern, fleeing for their young lives. The ruckus prompted curious onlookers at T. J. Quill's, the Doors Pub, and Rocco's Tavern to peer outside; a moment later, crowds spilled out of those establishments, too. Maple Street and Hillary Street, both narrow, formerly residential corridors, quickly filled with students, most of them in varying stages of inebriation. Upperclassmen trampled weaker, smaller freshmen in their frenzied rush to get away.

Then Jules saw the cause of the stampede. His mother burst through the front door of Bruno's, her pink house dress whipping around her varicose vein-striated ankles like a battle flag. "You nasty, filthy *hippies!*" she screamed after them, waving her suction tube arms about her head. "You and your Free Love! You forced that nice man from Texas, President Johnson, to quit his office!"

Students stumbled over each other running down the steps to the street. Several of them tripped and fell. Edna straddled one of them, a young, slender blonde woman whose pale limbs were entirely covered with interlocking tattoos. She aimed her suction arms at the young woman's body. Jules witnessed the student's youthfulness melt away — her smooth arms, decorated with dozens of brightly colored butterflies, dragons, and unicorns, became wrinkled, haggard, and dotted with age spots; her shapely, toned legs, equally tattooed, acquired sagging masses of cottage cheese-like cellulite and bulging purple veins.

Momentarily transfixed by this sight, Jules watched the menagerie of fantasy creatures inked on the woman's body turn into a mass of puckered grotesqueries worthy of the cover of *Mad Magazine. Yeech,* he thought; *so this is what America has to look forward to once today's nutty kids reach their Dentu-Creme years...*

He shook himself out of his horrified reverie as Shogo pulled up alongside him on his motor scooter. "Shogo," he shouted through the Mercedes's window, "power up! Turn into the most intimidatin' monster you can manage! I'm gonna need ya to grab my mother from behind, pin those vacuum cleaner arms behind her, and hold her while I get the antidote down her gullet somehow. You up to it?"

"*Hai*! I wirr not fai-urr!" Shogo opened a leather pouch on his belt and removed a wriggling *otaku*, a Japanese superhero fanboy who had spent the past six weeks in the form of a miniaturized Hello Kitty. Seconds later, following a flash of green brightness, Shogo transformed himself into a man-sized Hello Kitty, feline features flat and cartoonish. He then assumed his pose of most intense concentration, which resulted in an even more dazzling green light-burst. The resulting creature, Jules thought, appeared to be a cross between Hello Kitty and the entire *kaiju* cast of *Destroy All Monsters*.

"Doc, wish me luck," Jules said as he pushed open his door. "If I end up senile and toothless, make sure to mix my blood ration with Motts cinnamon apple sauce, okay? Not the greatest, but it beats yogurt."

Wishing he hadn't broken the syringe in half earlier when he'd slid his seat backward — the only syringe Doc had brought along — Jules grabbed the flask of antidote serum from its insulated bag. How he was going to get his mother to say "AHHH" and open up long enough for him to get her medicine down her throat, he had no idea. He had no choice but to assume he'd figure something out as he went along, somehow (the story of his long existence).

The hideously transformed Shogo rushed ahead, leaping over fallen students in his obvious eagerness to confront Edna. *Can't deny the guy's a natural-born scrapper*, Jules thought with grudging admiration. "Hey, Shogo!" he shouted after him, struggling to keep pace. "Don't forget, she's a whole lot stronger than she looks!"

His mother, glancing up from sucking the youth out of a bearded, long-haired student, did a double-take when she saw Shogo charging in her direction. "What are you supposed to be — the Creature from the Black Lagoon?" she said.

Shogo tried grabbing her. She ducked underneath his lunge and jabbed him in the solar plexus with her suction arms. "Gotta warn ya, you big ugly," she said, "suckin' the youthfulness outta them hippies has got me feelin' *spry!*"

Jules wouldn't describe the transformed Shogo as "spry" — muscle-bound, ungainly, and lumbering was more like it. Edna, darting with the swiftness of a hummingbird, scurried beneath him and popped up out of her crouch behind him. She hoisted her leg, aimed her foot at Shogo's scaly rear end, and kicked him with enough force to drive a three-hun-dred-yard field goal.

The clumsy, top-heavy Shogo went sprawling — straight towards Jules and his precious antidote.

"Shogo, look *OUT!*"

Too late! In a collision of meaty monstrosity with voluminous vam-pire, Jules felt the glass flask shatter against his chest. The irreplaceable serum splashed all over his shirt and pants while he was in the process of getting knocked on his ass.

He felt the serum soak through to his skin. The sensation chilled him in ways far beyond the physical. *So that's it*, he told himself, falling into a chasm of despair. *Game over. There's no stopping Mom now...*

Shogo leaped up from where he had fallen. "I wirr *not* be *humir-riated* by an *orrd woman!*" he bellowed. He charged toward Edna, his scaly arms held wide to sweep her into a monstrous bear hug. Jules watched as his mother, steely eyed, held her ground. She raised her suc-tion arms and revved her motors to their highest velocity. Her vitality-sapping extraction stopped Shogo's charge cold, as though he'd slammed into an invisible barrier; ten feet away from her, he sagged, then dropped to his knees and fell upon his face, his claws only inches from her skinny ankles.

Jules watched Shogo's black fur turn gray and his once-shiny green scales fade to a dull, cloudy yellow. Edna was turning him into a candidate for a *kaiju* assisted living facility. *She's takin' my revenge for me,* he thought, the notion rattling around his brain like a tarnished penny tossed into the bottom of a dry, dust-choked fountain. *All I gotta do is stand here, and the lousy bum who screwed my wife gets what's comin' to him. She's gonna leave him a dried-out husk. And all I gotta do is just do nothin' at all...*

But he couldn't "just do nothin' at all." It wasn't right. Despite what Shogo had done to him, Shogo didn't deserve to die. And Jules was the only person on the planet with even a snowball's odds in a New Orleans summer of convincing his mother to cease and desist.

He picked himself up from the street. "Mom, cut it out! Leave him be!"

She ignored him. Given her state of mind, he figured she would. He started running. Getting his bulk moving any faster than a walk was always a strain.

This would be bad. As bad as his final fight with Malice X. As bad as that long walk down to Courane L'Enfant's vampire torture cellar. As bad as trying to keep Maureen alive after the storm.

Aww, hell, it sucks, havin' a conscience...

"Ready or not, Mom, here I come..."

He shoved his way between his mother and the prone, withering Shogo. Immediately, whatever new sprightliness he'd achieved by losing a hundred and eighty pounds earlier that night vanished. Less than a second after hurling himself into the enervating field created by his mother's suction arms, Jules felt all his former age-and-weight-related symptoms return — the shrill arthritis in his knees, ankles, and hips; his chronic shortness of breath; the sense that his heart was a rusty lawnmower engine wheezily pulling a loaded Cadillac hearse.

"Jules Augustine Duchon!" his mother thundered. She switched off her suction. "What are you *doin'*, gettin' between me and that pug-ugly ruffian?"

Jules tottered on his weakened joints. "Mom, you gotta cut this out... you *gotta*. You ain't no homicidal lunatic... you're a sweet old lady who loves MGM musicals and Christmas displays on Canal Street..."

"Who're you callin' a 'homicidal lunatic,' young man? I'll let you know, I'm here to clean up this town! And boy oh boy, does it *need* a good cleanin'! Now, you get out of my way, and I mean right now, or you're gonna get some of the same what I gave to those hippies and that Black Lagoon Creature there!"

"No can do, Mom. You wanna suck the youth outta these folks? You do it to me, your only son, first. Got me?"

Mother and son locked eyes. Two generations of Duchon stubbornness butted heads. Irresistible force met immovable object. Age met... well, not "beauty," certainly, but something approximating a rough-hewn (*very* rough-hewn) nobility.

"Well, if *that's* the way you want it," Edna said at last, "I guess you're never too old for me to tan that fat behind and learn you a lesson..."

She switched back on her suction.

Jules' accelerated aging resumed full force. He felt his arteries hardening like the fossil trees of the Petrified Forest. His skin grew slack and frail. His teeth came loose in their gums. His muscles (such as they were) atrophied. He fell to his knees. The impact with the street nearly shattered his now brittle kneecaps. He hollered with pain, noticing the newly tremulous timber of his voice.

"Mother... don't *do* this... Try to remember... remember the sweet, lovin' woman inside that vacuum cleaner..."

She merely upped the speed of the motors driving her suction blades. Now his shirt, still soaked with the spilled antidote, pulled away from his sunken-in chest, drawn to her suction nozzle hands.

His mind began growing fuzzy. How could he reach her heart, turned so savage and hateful by Shogo's blood? They'd shared so many happy, warm decades together in their little house on Montegut Street... the nights of long ago seemed so much closer than memories of the past week... he remembered singing Jeanette MacDonald and Nelson Eddy duets with her as they'd watched old musicals on their little twelve-inch black-and-white TV... those had been the good times...

Could he remember the lyrics to "Indian Love Call"? His throat was scratchy and clogged, but he started singing. "When I'm calling you, ooo-ooo-ooo, ooo-ooo-ooo..."

His mother looked confused. Her rotors sputtered to a stop. Then she replied, with uncertain lips: "Will you answer too, ooo-ooo-ooo, ooo-ooo-ooo?"

Jules carried the tune forward: "That means I offer my love to you, ooo-ooo-ooo, ooo-ooo-ooo..."

And Edna, transfixed, replied: "If you refuse me, what shall I do, ooo-ooo-ooo, ooo-ooo-ooo?" Her eyes grew moist, then clouded over entirely with tears. She shook her head as though she were trying to unscramble loose pieces inside her skull; as if she were waking from a bad dream. She stared at her son as though she were seeing him for the first time that night. "Baby boy, what are *you* doin' here? And what am *I* doin' here? And how come you gone so *bald*? And... and..." She stared at her suction arms with dawning horror. "Oh my *gosh*... what've I been *doin'*? I — I been a *bad girl*, haven't I?"

Amos rushed over from the car, followed close behind by Emiko, as well as Maureen and Shogo, who had arrived only a moment earlier. "Edna, dearest!" Amos cried. "Are you yourself again? Are you back with us?"

Edna stared down at her suction tube arms, then glanced over her shoulder at the storage tanks nestled between her shoulder blades. "Myself again...? Not hardly, Amos. I look like the Presidents' Day Special at Sears Brand Central..."

"But your thoughts — you don't want to clean up the whole city anymore? You don't want to suck the youth out of every unkempt college student between here and Houston?"

"You mean the hippies and beatniks? Heck, *no*. I don't wanna be anywhere *near* 'em. Live and let live, that's *my* motto... but if they can all live someplace far away from me, I'm good with that."

Jules spat a tooth onto the street. "Anybody got some cinnamon apple sauce?" he said through a haze of befuddlement.

"Edna," Amos said gently, taking her elbow, "would it be possible for you to reverse your suction rotors and expel some of that life essence you borrowed onto Jules, Shogo, and the others?"

"You mean, I can *do* that?"

"Jules said you did it once already, back in the Quarter, across from his house."

"Well... okay, then, I'll try. Just gimme a minute here to figure out these switches... Uhh, okay, think I got it figured. Fountain of Youth, here we go..."

She switched on her rotors in reverse mode, expelling a cloud over Jules and Shogo that smelled of underarm sweat, hair tonic, morning breath, and partially digested sushi. Jules began feeling less achy. Hazy black and white memories of Jeanette MacDonald crooning in a hoop shirt were replaced with more focused and timely thoughts. Grunting, he rose to his feet, happy to discover that his knees didn't protest like they would've twenty seconds earlier. He glanced over at Shogo. The Japanese superhero's fur had returned to its black color, and his scales and spiny plates were again a lustrous, shiny green. Jules helped him to his feet.

Maureen rushed over to him. "Oh, Jules, I saw *everything*! You were *marvelous*! You saved Shogo! And now you're good as new, darling!"

Amos guided Edna from one fallen septuagenarian to another, directing her to spray puffs of her youth-restoring cloud onto them. Jules heard police sirens approaching from the direction of Carrollton Avenue, several blocks distant. He signaled for Amos to take her back to the car, and to hurry.

"Save some youth gas for the Lawrence Welk Fan Club at that frat house over on Broadway," he told his mother. "Then we gotta get the hell outta here, pronto!"

Twenty-Three

"**S**o what you're sayin', Doc, is that it was a *good thing* that Shogo spilled the antidote all over my shirt?"

Amos nodded from one of the leather side chairs in his parlor, his eyes warm with gratitude and relief. "Most definitely, yes. That accident was extremely fortuitous. Having Edna ingest the antidote as fumes through her suction nozzles was perhaps the quickest way for the serum to be metabolized by her body."

"It wasn't my singin' that turned her from evil back to lovable?"

"I'm sure your singing 'Indian Love Call' to her helped. With a voice like yours, how could it *not?*"

Jules glanced over at his mother. She was taking advantage of the break in all the evening's frantic activity to get some house cleaning done before sun-up. She hummed the tune to "Singin' in the Rain" to herself while vacuuming the shelves that held her collection of Franklin Mint Film Classics collectable gold-trimmed china dinner plates (Amos had started a subscription for her as a present for her most recent birthday). "So, if the antidote worked, Doc, how come she's still in Hoovermatic mode?"

Amos shrugged his shoulders. "I can only suppose that Super-Genius Jules, realizing his time constraints, opted to formulate a serum which would only counteract the effects of Shogo's blood, not of both Shogo's *and* Emiko's blood. Perhaps counteracting Emiko's blood was a far more complicated effort. He must've realized that once her mind was no longer addled, we would be able to convince Edna to stop her rampage and come with us. I assume, and I suppose *he* assumed, that she will physically revert to normal in three nights' time, just as you and Maureen did."

"In the meantime, your house'll be spotless."

"After this, I'm afraid I'll simply have to give in and buy her that new vacuum cleaner from the Home Shopping Network she wants so much."

Jules grunted. "At least she wasn't pinin' for no A1 Abrams battle tank just before she drank Emiko's and Shogo's blood — just think how much trouble she woulda given us then."

He peered over at Shogo. Their visitor looked a lot younger than he had at the beginning of that evening; Edna had fed him a bit more rejuvenation gas than she'd needed to, perhaps, for he now appeared to be a gangly, pimply-faced teenager. Shogo had not uttered a word to him since Jules had thrown himself between Edna's suction nozzles and the Japanese superhero.

Shogo looked deeply ashamed. He stared at the floor as though wishing it to swallow him up. Jules thought he looked like a teenager whose grandmother had just caught him masturbating to a *manga* comic about schoolgirls and cute little magic ponies.

Three nights later, Edna was in the midst of thoroughly vacuuming the rugs at her son's and daughter-in-law's house (she had run out of things to clean in her own home) when a sudden flash of green light temporarily blinded her, Jules, and Maureen. When their vision cleared, they found that Edna had returned to her normal shape and size. Unfortunately, all of the dust and dirt she had suctioned up from Maureen's floors and deposited in her now-vanished storage tanks cascaded down her back and spread in a gray cloud throughout the living room.

When he'd finished coughing, Jules asked, "Well, Mother, how does it feel havin' fingers again?"

Edna grinned. "It'll sure make eatin' my fried chicken easier!"

Maureen eyed her husband with concern. "Jules, it's been three nights since *your* change, too. Do *you* feel any different?"

Jules prodded his middle to see whether any additional poundage had magically grafted itself to him. "Not a bit, hon," he said. "Although I guess it's too early yet to know whether Super-Genius Jules succeeded in his plan to avoid revertin' to a second Regular-Joe Jules. If a hundred-and-eighty-pound version of dumb ol' me shows up on our doorstep later tonight or sometime tomorrow night, askin' to get reabsorbed into the Original J.D., we'll know Super-Genius J.D. wasn't as smart as he thought he was. Otherwise, we gotta figure he's keepin' the fishes and crabs company, somewhere at the bottom of the Gulf of Mexico, enjoyin' his independence, day-dreamin' about differential equations or what-not."

A knock on the door interrupted them. Jules opened the door for a solemn Kenji, Emiko, and Shogo.

"May we come in?" Kenji asked.

"Sure, guys, c'mon in," Jules said. "What's up? The three of you look like you're headin' to a funeral. Anything the matter?"

The three guests removed their shoes and left them next to the door, then entered. "We are returning to Japan," Kenji said. "We reave New Orrins tomorrow night."

This was a surprise. "Why? The music thing not workin' out? You all gettin' homesick or somethin'?"

Kenji shook his head. "I must terr you some things, Jures-*san*. We are reaving New Orrins because we have caused you and your famirry much trouburr."

"Well, yeah, sure. But that business with my mother and Shogo's and Emiko's blood, that was an accident—"

Kenji shook his head again. "No, Jures-*san*. That was no accident."

"Huh? What do you mean?"

Kenji turned to his younger (now much younger) cousin. "Shogo. Terr Jures-*san* what you torrd me."

Shogo stared down at the floor. When he spoke, his words came out in a barely audible monotone. "I came into your house without your knowing, Jures-*san*. I mixed my brudd and Emiko's brudd into your other brudd in your freezer. I wished for you or Maureen-*san* to become fierce monsters..."

Now it was Maureen's turn to be astonished. "*Whaaat*? You wanted me and Jules to turn into *monsters*, Shogo? Why the hell would you want *that*?"

Shogo kept his gaze leveled at the floor. "I desired the grory of fighting and winning against fierce monsters. I have no such grory in Japan, because awrr our fierce monsters in Japan were banished before my birth. I was very happy to fight Jures-*san* when he turned into a giant rabbit. The peopurr in the French Quarter gave me much honor. I desired to have such fights again, many times."

Jules felt hot blood rushing into his face. "So this — all that happened — it was 'cause of a big *ego trip*?" His hands clenched into fists. "You mean to tell me you endangered my mother, you endangered my wife, you almost got me and you both *killed* — just so you could get some applause from a few tourists and fry cooks?"

"*Hai*," Shogo said, his adolescent voice cracking.

Jules controlled his impulse to grab the Japanese teenager by his skinny throat and shake his head until his few marbles flew out his ears. "You dumb asshole... if *that's* what you wanted, you shoulda become a professional wrassler! Least then, you'd get *paid* for your rough-housin', and you'd be on TV!"

"I am sorry, Jures-*san*," Shogo said.

"Don't apologize to me. Apologize to my mother, dumb-ass!"

"*Hai*," Kenji agreed. "Do so, Shogo."

Shogo shuffled across the room to where Edna stood. He fell to his knees before her, then bowed, prostrating himself so that his forehead touched the newly dusty floor. "Honored, revered Edna-*san*," he said, "I am most humbury sorry for doing wrong to you."

Edna stared sternly down at the prostrate teenager. "I hope you got a grammaw back in Japan who's gonna *tan your hide*, young man," she said. But then, after another few seconds of glaring at him, she grinned, and added, "On the other hand... I ain't had so much *fun* since Fat Tuesday in 1936, that Mardi Gras when the whole Sixth Fleet was in town on shore leave! Goin' berserk is *fun*, 'specially when it ain't your fault! Whoohaa! That was like a *vacation*, boy! And I ain't had me a proper vacation since 1962, when Jules won a big wad in a poker game and treated me to a weekend in a motel by the sea in Biloxi. Bein' a human vacuum cleaner and cleanin' up some hippies, though, that beats that tatty little beach in Biloxi, hands down!"

She leaned over, pulled Shogo up off the floor, and gave him a big Duchon family hug.

To show there weren't any lingering hard feelings, Jules and his whole family went to the Residence Inn the following evening before the start of their nightly vampire tour to see Kenji, Emiko, and Shogo off.

In the lobby of the hotel, Emiko, her face abashed, took a series of small, halting steps toward Maureen. "I, too, must aporrogize, Maureen-*san*," she said, bowing low and staring at the floor. "I dishonored your husband, and so dishonored you and your house. I am most sorry."

Maureen, stony eyed, said nothing. After a few seconds of dreadful silence, Emiko retreated to the shelter of the pile of the trio's luggage.

Kenji broke the silence. "I am responsiburr for my sister and my cousin," he said to Jules and his assembled family. "I brought them here. Awrr harm done to you is on my head. Prease terr me what I can do to make amends. I wirr do anything which you say."

"Look, Kenji," Jules said, "I appreciate the thought, really. But enough with the apologies already, okay? Yeah, your family caused my family some trouble. But the important thing, the *really* important thing is this — Maureen wouldn't have gotten through Hurricane Antonia without you and all your help. That counts more than anything. *Way* more. I mean, Shogo coulda turned me into a monster or a giant hamster a *hundred* times, and I'd *still* owe you, Kenji, 'cause of what you did for Maureen."

"That is — very generous, Jures-*san*."

"Besides... I'm gonna miss you guys. You helped get the word out about our vampire tours. And I even enjoyed your music. I mean, really; I'll never hear 'Hello, Dolly!' again without thinkin' about y'all. In your own, kinda weird way, you helped give this old town a little boost when it was flat on its back, helped distract us from all our problems. That was a good thing, y'know? Even the Big Easy can use a helping hand now and then."

The airport shuttle van pulled up in front of the Residence Inn. Jules helped the Japanese trio load their luggage into the cargo hold. Then the Duchons and the Landrieus bid their visitors a safe journey back to Kure. Amos told Jules that he and Edna would meet him back at Jules' house a half hour before the start of the tour, in time to prep the phlebotomy equipment and set out the souvenirs.

Jules and Maureen watched the airport shuttle van pull away. "So that's that," Maureen said as the van turned the corner and disappeared from sight.

"I guess so," Jules said.

They stared at each other in silence. Then they each tried speaking simultaneously:

"I'm so sorry about Shogo, Jules—"

"I feel awful about what happened with Emiko—"

They both laughed. Then, benefitting from the synchronicity which comes from nine decades spent mostly in one another's company, Jules and Maureen said at the same time:

"Let's just forget about it, okay?"

They walked around the corner. The narrow downtown street, barely wider than an alleyway, was deserted, its few businesses all closed for the night. High above the dark rooftops of the century-old commercial blocks, the illuminated, neoclassical pinnacle of the old Hibernia Bank Building stood out in the sky, like a Greek temple perched atop an angular granite Mount Olympus.

"Your more slender double never showed up," Maureen said. "What do you think that means?"

"Guess it means I got me a much smarter twin hangin' out at the bottom of the ocean," Jules said.

"You want to check to see if your vampiric powers work?"

"Ehh, I guess so..."

Jules concentrated on a bat. Then he concentrated on a wolf. Then, for the hell of it, he concentrated on a big, white rabbit.

Nothing. Not even the tiniest puff of a gray cloud of fleshy smoke.

"No go," Jules said. "I won't even bother tryin' out my vampire hypnotism. I always sucked at that, anyway."

"Looks like we're even, then," Maureen said. "I don't get to be a bat, either. You gonna miss it?"

"I'll miss it some, yeah. But not as much as I been missin' crawlin' in the sack with you, babe."

She looked at him with worried eyes. "You think Doc'll be able to come up with those exotic ingredients that Super-Genius Jules' formula calls for?"

"You talkin' that sea snake venom and what-not? I know he'll give it his best shot. Maybe Doodlebug can help; he's got all kinds of weird connections, thanks to that magical-mystical-mystery institute of his.

And if that doesn't work out? We'll figure out somethin' else. We always do, don't we? Let's head home. We got us a business to tend to."

He grasped his wife's hand. She accepted this with only a tiny ripple of revulsion, and they walked hand in hand, like they used to during those long-ago nights in 1917, right after Maureen had ushered Jules into the twilight-world of vampirism. He glanced up at the shining white top of the former Hibernia Bank Building. So much had changed since the storm. Whole neighborhoods had been wiped out by floods. Businesses that had survived and thrived over a hundred years had been destroyed. Families had been split up, scattered all over the country by the mass evacuation. Half of New Orleans' population might never return to rebuild.

But just like the old Hibernia Bank Building, New Orleans was still here. Hibernia Bank had been bought out and absorbed by a bigger bank, Capital One. So Hibernia Bank was gone; yet the building it had inspired remained, glowing in the night sky, and thus, so did the memory of a worthy but expired enterprise. A memory which whispered that names might vanish, that surface details might change and change again, but the essence of things endured.

So he didn't have his vampiric powers anymore. Would that make much of a difference in his nightly existence? Unless another storm evacuation caused him and Maureen to run out of blood again, probably not. The storm had pushed him out of his comfort zone, forced him to abandon his old, comfortable habits. Now he had an opportunity to make his living and support his family as a legitimate businessman, a worthy part of the community... not a killer. All in all, as tough as the transition had been, he had to count that as a big plus, a real step forward. Doodlebug would be proud of him. Maybe even Erato would come around, now that Jules was no longer fanging victims.

This was a good night. The air felt fresh and invigorating, with just a hint of early fall's coolness. Uplifted by a surge of happiness, he squeezed Maureen's hand.

Now, if he could just shake that nagging feeling that Shogo hadn't been completely forthright with him, that there had been something he hadn't been telling...

Epilogue

ELIVERY time again. First stop? As always, Bunny Bread delivery driver Paul Mandikens' first-thing-in-the-morning destinations were his long list of customers in the French Quarter.

He felt darn lucky. Up until six weeks ago, he hadn't been sure he still had a job. He'd known he didn't have a home to return to; Google Maps had shown him that much, revealing to him, while he'd been living in a FEMA-rented motel in Houston, that Hurricane Antonia's floods had completely inundated his apartment complex in New Orleans East. The storm and its flood waters had done a bad number on the Bunny Bread factory, too.

But the Bunny Bread folks had done a bang-up job of refurbishing their facility. They'd even bought a new fleet of delivery trucks to replace those vehicles, his old truck included, which had died in the flood. His boss, Mr. Galois, had called him and asked him to come back to New Orleans, telling him that Bunny Bread would offer its refurbished offices as temporary living quarters for its homeless workers while the company worked with FEMA to find available apartments. Paul had been going stir-crazy in Houston, sitting in that cramped motel room watching TV all day, wondering what the coming months would bring. So he'd been more than happy to accept Mr. Galois' offer.

He backed his truck to the edge of the loading dock. Then he jumped out of his seat, eager to get his daily duties started. Man, it felt great to be back in his old routine. He grabbed a hand truck and loaded it with cartons stuffed full of boxes of Bunny Banana Muffin Snack Cakes, then unloaded the cartons inside the big box on the back of his truck, stacking them carefully against the walls.

Back in his driver's seat, Paul checked his list of delivery customers. It seemed like each week, his list got a little longer, as more and more souvenir shops and convenience stores and restaurants reopened. He was constantly bumping into old, familiar faces, business owners he'd formerly delivered to and had started delivering to again. His life had turned into a rolling reunion, each little renewed acquaintance a happy occasion, everybody asking him where he'd evacuated to and how he'd made out with the storm. He'd sure been plied with plenty of free cups of coffee; enough to float a boat, it sometimes felt like.

And not only old business had been reopening in the French Quarter. New businesses had been springing up, too. At one of his stops the day before, he'd picked up a flier for something called the *Real* New Orleans Vampire Tour. That was new.

He buckled his seat belt, then drove his truck through the gates of the Bunny Bread Bakery, heading for the I-10 interstate and the French Quarter. A vampire tour, huh? He'd have to try that out some night. It sounded like a real hoot.

About the Author

ANDREW FOX has been a fan of science fiction and horror since he saw *Destroy All Monsters* at a drive-in theater at the age of three. His books include *Fat White Vampire Blues*, winner of the Ruthven Award for Best Vampire Fiction of 2003; *Bride of the Fat White Vampire*; *Fat White Vampire Otaku*; *Fire on Iron*, a Civil War dark fantasy; and *The Good Humor Man, or, Calorie 3501*, selected by Booklist as one of the Ten Best SF/Fantasy Novels of the Year for 2009. In 2006, he won the *Moment* Magazine-Karma Foundation Short Fiction Award. His stories have appeared in *Scifi.com* and *Nightmare.com*, and his essays have been published in *Moment* and *Tablet* Magazine. Companion volumes *Hazardous Imaginings*, a collection of his politically incorrect science fiction, and *Again, Hazardous Imaginings: More Politically Incorrect Science Fiction*, an international anthology which he edited, were published together in 2020. His next novel, *Hunt the Fat White Vampire*, will be published in June 2021. He lives in Northern Virginia with his family, where he works for a federal law enforcement agency. He can be reached at http://www.fantasticalandrewfox.com.

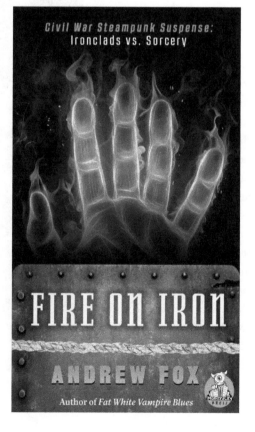

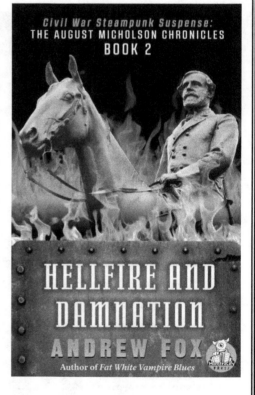

CPSIA information can be obtained
at www.ICGtesting.com
Printed in the USA
LVHW050845290321
682812LV00006B/27